D1872183

Post-Apocalyptic

C J Powell

Copyright © 2022 by C J Powell

All rights reserved.

No portion of this book may be reproduced in any form without written permission from the publisher or author, except as permitted by U.S. copyright law.

New Year, New Macadamia

It's amazing how quickly we forget stories. Though everyone might bang on like rabbits about something for a day or two, if by the time the weekend rolls over a reality star gets engaged or a pop sensation dies, poof, all is forgotten.

Attention spans are so short, and the news so saturated, that if no one mentions something again, you start to question whether or not you saw it in the first place.

Murder Hornets Unleashed: Pfft.

Aliens Found On Venus: Nah.

World's Oldest Man Sprouts Wings And Warns Of Shadowy Elite Controlling Your Every Move: Does he though?

Were Di Blasio ever a company? Had the influencers ever been cool?

Who was Trent Macadamia?

Who cares? Lady Gargantuan has just arrived at the Met Gala in a giant egg made of spam. Extra! Extra! Read all about it!

The Mandela Effect. A theory. A reality. The idea that a percentage of the population think something and the rest think the opposite. Ask them over there and they think Nelson Mandela died in prison in the 80s. Ask them over there and they know he lived until the year 2013.

Go deeper and some believe our world is populated by people from two different dimensions. Dimensions that merged when they turned on the Large Hadron Collider in Switzerland. Dimensions with slightly different timelines.

Though there may be two different species of humanoid sharing the planet, this dimensions theory is not quite right.

Humans are just easy to manipulate. Throw enough film, radio, and tv at them, sprinkle in a few "was that a dream?" moments, and their memories become blurry. Fiction becomes fact. Fact becomes fiction. People become factions. Factions become distractions.

Was the titanic a real ship, or was Leonardo DaVinci just a really good actor? Leonardo DeCapulet? DiCaprio!

Did Kenneth Bailey really grow wings for his birthday, then disappear into obscurity with the rest of the Di Blasio influencers, or was that just an advert for protein shakes? I don't know, but the chocolate peanut flavour is actually delish. And, according to some guy with rigid pecs on YouTube who appears to not know they've invented T-shirts and who also has absolutely no background in any sort of science, it's super nutritious.

But that's besides the point! We were asking questions and doing our own research with an open mind, not getting side tracked with the top ten ways to butter a scone — the tenth of which will blow your freaking mind!!!

Who was Trent Macadamia?

Trent Macadamia was a private investigator.

Trent Macadamia was a martyr.

Trent Macadamia was an actor. He has an IMDB profile.

Wrong.

Post-Apocalyptic

The sun creeps out over cream houses of dry-stone birthing a kaleidoscopic sky of orange through to dazzling blue. As the dawn chorus chirps its merry morning tune, a lone postman freewheels his bike beneath a line of oaks and along the dirt path that runs parallel to the slow, meandering River Wey.

The day is turning out to be another beautiful one. An English country corker.

It's insufferable.

Every infernal tweet is a stab in his aching head. Every bump in the road a kick in the nuts. And every time Trent Macadamia, former PI, current small town postie, glimpses that golden star that sustains all life on earth gleaming through the dappling leaves, he wishes it would go supernova and wipe out everything for a squillion cubed miles if only to stop the ache in his throbbing head.

Screw this job, and the push bike it rode in on.

Once more he's awake and out of the house by 5 a.m., head thumping from his session the night before.

Like always.

He just wants to be in bed. But Mum wouldn't stand for it.

She's already told him with an overenthusiastic wag of the finger that, "if you miss another day of work because you've been drinking, then you're out."

And who else will rent him a room? No one. He's checked.

He blazes out of the forest and on to the main road heading towards the centre of town. The roads are always quiet at this time, so he doesn't bother to look. And besides, a pasting by a car might knock some of the horrid memories from his head.

As he coasts across the village square, the day continues to be hatefully picturesque.

The warm smell of baking bread precedes the cheery, "Good morning, Trent," from the baker hanging out of his shop door as Mac blazes past. He raises a flour covered hand.

Like always.

"Morning Jean," replies Mac, trying to sound about as normal as he can.

No one else is up. Why would they be? It's stupid o'clock in the morning.

Five a.m. hadn't existed in London. Not as morning. It was only ever late night. 5 a.m. in London was a time to be alive. A time to nurse a good black coffee over a pad of notes. Trying to connect the dots while the city slept. A time to crawl home from a night working a case. Brain fried through lack of sleep, but satisfied in a job well done. Feeling fulfilled with dues paid.

Five a.m. here makes him want to throw middle fingers to the world much like an angst-ridden teen at a death metal concert.

A glimmer of hope rounds the corner ahead. The Jogger. She holds his focus. Her hair seems to float behind her. Light and blonde and... buoyant? Tight leggings on slim legs.

There's a slight clumsiness to her gait that suggests she hasn't always been a runner. Mac likes it. Thinks perhaps she grew up hating sport like him. Maybe they have more in common than being the only ones to see this side of the morning.

She's a stunner. One hundred percent his cup of tea.

It must be Wednesday or Friday... Or maybe a Monday. He's kind of lost track of time a bit. But those are the days she runs. He knows that at least. Realises that might sound a little bit stalkery. But there's worse things you can know about people, right? Like where they live, or what colour their underwear is... Which, of course, he doesn't. He just likes to see her in the morning. Chill out with all the accusations.

Next time he has one of those mornings off, he might try running too.

"Hiya," she says as they pass each other. Her brief smile is like quality dish soap cutting through the burnt-on cheese of his depression.

He glances back.

Like always.

Unlike always, the tip of his handlebar connects with the wing mirror of a parked car.

With a "Gah" of surprise, he twists his grip in order to correct his course and steers out towards the centre of the road, sending himself careering across the street, into the side of a parked Porsche, and flipping over the handlebars.

For a moment he just lies there, eyes closed, reclining on the soft convertible top of the car. Snuggles down. Wanting to evaporate. It's quite comfy. He could fall asleep. It wouldn't seem out of character. Everyone already thinks he's totally bonkers.

They all saw him on television last year. And though the wider world has almost forgotten him, small towns remember small town's people when they do big things.

He should get up. It's best not to cause a scene. Despite having him as an offspring, his mum still feels she has some standing in the community. And what kind of son would he be to ruin that for her?

And also the Porsche owner might spot him and it's not like he has any money to pay for damages.

He rolls back off the car and picks up his bike. Looks around. Hopes no one, specifically The Jogger, just witnessed the village postman and local disappointment, smashing into a rather expensive sports car.

He changes to a lower gear as he starts up the hill towards the sorting office.

Now, wouldn't it be nice to have a day without his usual bad luck? Because that's what he's beginning to think he's cursed with.

No normal person has a life filled with so much misfortune. He often fantasises at night, in that half-drunken, room spinning stupor before he passes out, that perhaps in the past his mother, on some sort of voyage to an unnamed jungle or arctic wilderness, had angered a witch doctor who proceeded to dance around an eldritch fire and bring down a terrible curse on her future first-born son. Considering some of the things he witnessed last September, he wouldn't put it past the world to have a few more secrets hidden up its sleeve.

He regularly ticks off his failings while brushing his teeth in the morning. Something he knows is not the best bet for building a solid base of self-esteem. But also something he can't help but do.

Father left him. Tick.

Routinely ostracised and made the butt of jokes at school. Tick.

Left home to seek his fortune only to become poorer and lonely. Tick.

Managed to get embroiled with a conspiracy of murderous, winged shadowy elites who, for a time at least, would have stopped at nothing to drive him insane, then murder him and a rag-tag group of others in Studio One of the BBC. Tick.

Forgotten and left behind by said elites and everyone who he fought them with. Tick.

What brings him down most is that, for whatever reason, he's not even worth pursuing by The Guardians. Why hadn't they come for him yet? Did they feel he wasn't worth it now the entire world, or what felt like it, had moved on? Had they succeeded in their aim after all?

He must be the only person to have ever lived that could find a problem with not being murdered.

And it wasn't like he was hiding. Heck, just last week, two local nobs posted pictures of him all over social media with hashtags linking him with Kenneth, The Guardians, and Di Blasio in an effort to embarrass him when no shadowy elites came a-murdering and thus, proving his story false.

And that's exactly what did happen. Nothing. No one came. No stab-happy shadowy elites.

No Nige.

He hadn't heard from Nige in months. Was that good or bad? He hadn't decided.

Oh, and then, to add to his confidence crushing morning mirror tally, there was the classic – twenty-six and living with his mum, with only one friend to his name – his mum's current boyfriend, Vikram. If that wasn't a fat tick on the checklist of loser failings, he didn't know what was.

And he knows Vikram only hangs out with him because Mum is pulling his strings. Since Kenneth's last birthday show, no one else talks to him unless it's to poke a little fun.

Except maybe the baker with his cheery 'good mornings'.

But, as Mac continues up the hill to the sorting office, his imagination flies into overdrive. The cheery 'good mornings' are a ruse. Big old jolly Jean proceeds into the dark recesses of his delicious smelling kitchen and laughs all day with his wife about how much of an idiot that Trent Macadamia is.

"I said good morning to him this morning," says the imaginary baker, as he pounds out some dough for ice buns, "and he thinks I meant it. What an idiot! Bwahaha!"

Mac pulls his bike up to the office, locks it to the railing just outside, and heads in, fuming.

"Morning Trent," says Vikram, who stands at his desk. He smiles beneath his well-groomed beard. It's grey but still has a hint of black. His wispy comb over is perfectly placed to let everyone know that pattern baldness won't take him alive.

"Yes, I am." Mac slams his satchel down on the desk in front of his would-be step-father and perches on the corner. "Mourning the fact that you left for work without me, amongst other things." He raises his eyebrows and purses his lips in facial accusation.

Vikram removes the stack of letters he'd been sorting from beneath Mac's bag. Doesn't look Mac in the eye for a moment. "Your mum said it'd be good for you to get a bit of fresh air on your way to work. So I thought it best not to give you a lift."

The corners of Mac's mouth twitch into a mimicry of a smile. "Thanks. I appreciate the thought." He does not appreciate the thought.

"Lots to do today."

Vikram is his boss and the only reason he has the job. He'd tried other avenues when he'd escaped London, but most places just laughed him straight out of the door. *"Ha! Aren't you that Di Blasio terrorist actor dude?"*

"Lots to do, hey?" At least that'll occupy him for a bit on his steady and slow slog towards the grave.

But, lots to do for the village isn't that much, really. It's still just traipsing around the same old roads trying to avoid the same old people delivering the same old fast food offer leaflets, bi-monthly village newsletters, and utility bills (because who actually writes letters anymore?).

"Heading to the pub again tonight?" He tries to ask the question in a way that might suggest the last trip had been Vikram's idea.

Vikram's cheeks flush and not just from the cold bite of the winter morning. Mac knows what's coming.

"Your mum doesn't want you going," he says, still not meeting Mac's eye. "She thinks... maybe you're drinking too much. And..." He hesitates.

"What?" Mac folds his arms.

"And so do I. Probably best you don't go out for a little while, hey?" He smiles. Tight-lipped. "It's not affecting your work. You manage your shifts. But it's not healthy for a young lad. Shouldn't you be out making friends? Meeting a nice girl."

The Jogger runs through his mind.

"Where am I supposed to meet a nice girl if not at the pub? There's literally nothing to do here."

"Have you tried yoga? That's where I met your mum."

Mac rolls his eyes. "Oh, get over yourself, Vikram. We can't all go out with a yoga teacher." He feels a little bubble of nausea rise in his stomach. "And I think the last thing I want to do is see you and Mum stretching in lycra. That'll damage my health faster than any drink."

"I'm sorry," says Vikram. "You know what your mum's like." He sighs and runs a hand through his thinning, greying hair. "I want you to think of me as a friend. Not your mum's little puppet. I must sound like she's sitting right here with her hand up my arse working my mouth."

Mac's lip curls. That's not an image he wants in his head either. According to one of the woman's magazines Mum likes to keep on the coffee table, the over

60s have pretty wild sex lives, and he does not want to hear any more about it than the thin walls at his mum's place allow.

"Where's my bag?" He doesn't mean to sound angry, but can't keep the impatience from his voice. "I better get to my round."

Vikram passes it over. "Trolley's out back. Already loaded." He takes a breath as if to say something more. Looks down. Lines up some of the letters on the countertop before him. Clears his throat. "I suppose you're right. The pub might be a good place to find you some friends. Maybe one drink after the shift?"

Inside, Mac's heart skips and sinks like a skimming stone. He doesn't want new friends. He'd had friends in uni and that'd been more hassle than it was worth. But at least he won't be drinking alone. The last time he'd done that, he'd been cornered by some local idiots and hadn't been allowed away until he'd recounted the whole dreadful affair of last year's show. He'd felt like a freak in a circus.

Vikram holds up a finger. "Just one mind, and then I'm driving you straight home."

Mac gives him a thumbs up and heads out the door.

One always turns to two, and two can add up to about four if you get them down fast enough.

It's not that he drinks because he wants to drink. Quite the opposite. It makes him feel disgusting. He throws up most mornings.

He drinks because he doesn't want to think. Thinking makes everything worse. Remembering what had almost happened to him, reliving that moment, that awful stomach wrenching feeling every night in his dreams, coupled with the helpless guilt in knowing what still went on behind the scenes, had been killing him faster than any addiction.

Ignorance had very much been bliss.

And today is no different. With that tipsy veil of drunkenness lifted, he sees dark figures with pale white faces watching him from the shadows in the corners of his mind. Creeping ever closer. The only thing holding them back is that blissful mind-numbing forgetfulness.

The drinking isn't a problem.

It's a solution.

Honeys In The Pub

If you were looking for a relationship, if you had courtship on your mind and wanted to find one with which to woo, The Nag's Head at 3 p.m., in the sunny village of Ripley, Surrey, is not the place to be. It is about as far from the place to be as you can get.

But there's beer there.

Mac stands at the bar, moving steadily from one foot to the other so he doesn't become stuck fast in the quicksand-like mix of stale booze and carpet, and watches as Vikram darts in and out of the other rooms scouting the place for what he calls "honeys". He comes back with disappointment on his face.

"Sorry Trent, doesn't look like there's anyone worth pursuing."

Mac claps Vikram on the back. "No worries, old buddy. All that getting a girlfriend stuff sounds like hard work. Chatting them up. Dating. Flowers. I don't know if I'm into it." He raises a hand to the bar lady. A tall, strong looking woman, with short dark hair and a black polo neck shirt. "Sandra, two of your finest pints..." he turns to Vikram, "... and for you?"

"I said one drink."

"Yeah, one trip to the bar. That's one drink."

"Trent, you don't have to hit rock bottom before you can start going back up again."

"I'm nowhere near rock bottom."

Vikram raises a single, worrying eyebrow, then looks to the bartender. "A coffee, please."

"A coffee?" says Mac, jutting his head forward in disbelief. "Not tired, are you? You and Mum had an early night last ni—"

He lets out a groan as Vikram raises his eyebrows and looks down with an unusual mix of reluctant embarrassment and brazen satisfaction.

"You are gross."

"Not what your mum said..."

The drinks arrive, and Mac carries his to the table furthest from the door, hoping it will suppress Vikram's need to escape.

Half a quiet pint later, Vikram speaks. "Did you see that girl in here last night?"

"Vikram, you are dating my mother. I don't feel it's right for you to talk about other women in front of me."

Vikram looks away, flustered. "Not for me."

"What did she look like?"

"Maybe a bit like that girl on your wall. In the poster."

Mac's bedroom remains unchanged from when he was a lad. His mother had kept all his old action figures and posters in the exact place he'd left them when he'd gone off to uni. This particular poster features his teenage crush, Ariana Grande.

"You might have been a bit blurry eyed, so you probably missed her, but I was sure she was checking you out." Vikram takes the biscuit from its plastic wrap on his saucer and dunks it in his coffee. "And I don't think it was just because you'd put Maniac on the jukebox and were shouting the words into an empty vase."

The disappointment of an opportunity missed floods Mac's stomach. "What girl?"

Vikram points to the table by the jukebox. "You and me were sitting there, and she was by the bar. Black sort of flared trousers, red jacket." He taps a finger on his chin and looks to the ceiling in thought.

"Blonde or brunette?" Blonde would be good. Either's fine. Anything's fine.

"Brunette. Now I remember it, she was definitely watching you."

Mac leans against the back of his chair and rubs both hands over his face. "Well, why didn't you bloody tell me?" He looks about the room as if to gather support from the empty chairs. "You're the one who keeps banging on about me getting a girlfriend. How am I supposed to do that if my wingman's radar isn't up?"

"I didn't recognise her. And you were in no fit state."

"No fit state?" He tuts. "What time was this?"

"Oh, I don't know. We left at eight, so must have been around seven?" Vikram shrugs and sticks out his bottom lip.

"Well, that settles it. We're going to have to pull an all-dayer in case this mysterious beauty returns."

"Oh right," says Vikram, giving Mac a bemused frown over his raised cup. "I thought you weren't really into all that dating and stuff."

"If she's already interested, then maybe we can skip that." Mac grabs a menu. "I think I might have the plant burger." He flicks to the mains then looks at Vikram with raised eyebrows and a sideways tip of the head. "Pint?"

Grown Wings Yet Macadamia?

By six, the place is packed. Despite it being a stereotypical teenage diatribe against their locale, there honestly is "nothing to do" in the village. Most of the 18 to 40 lot spend their early evenings having a drink and a chat at the pub.

By now, he and Vikram have moved closer to the bar. It's at least two people deep all the way round. The pub is loud and getting louder as the locals drink away their boredom and their money.

He hasn't seen anyone resembling the woman Vikram described.

"What I'm trying to tell you, Trent, my boy, is this," says Vikram out of nowhere, having not spoken for a good five minutes, "never settle." He thumps himself on the chest. Wobbles a little in his chair.

They've been seated for some time and the battlements of glasses between them has grown steadily, Vikram's promise to Mum a distant memory.

"Throughout my life I kept telling myself, things can be better, and don't settle for second best. All my mates, with their wives and their kids, all of 'em said, 'old Vikram, he'll be single forever'. Was I bothered?" He jabs a fork laden with peas dangerously close to Mac's left eye to emphasise his next word. "No. I was never settling. Then BAM!" He flings his arms out wide, peas flying in all directions. "Fifty-eight and I meet the love of my life. And with all that stuff you've been trying to tell us about growing old, and changing, looks like I've still got ages to spend with her, too."

He bangs his other fist on the table, causing Mac to jump, then places the pea-less fork into his mouth. Looks at it in empty mouthed surprise.

He turns his attention back to Mac. "All those smug couples from before, the ones who rushed into it, are stuck, unhappy, growing old and hating each other. Unless they've got the balls to fix what they have or get a divorce, they'll be miserable until they die."

Vikram often goes off on rants like this. Mac gets the impression he needs to confirm that his own life choices were correct with a little drunken monologue every now and again. He suspects this is a common trait in people who find success whilst on a different path to the norm. Thinks that it'd be nice to be able to make those sorts of affirmations, and not just live with the weight of constant and debilitating self-doubt pressing you into the floor.

"Wait a second... you and Mum are both trying to convince me to go out and get a girlfriend," as if it were as easy as that, or as if it were something he wanted anyway, "but now you're saying to wait?"

"All I know is this, I'm having a lovely time, and you appear not to be. That's the good thing about advice. Listen to me if you want." He shrugs and cuts into his olive and lentil pie. "Or don't."

Mac wipes a sliver of pea from the corner of his eye with a finger as the door to the pub opens, and two men his age enter. "Oh, bugger out."

Vikram shifts in his chair, but Mac grabs him by the arm.

"Don't move. It's John and James."

John and James were in Mac's school year. Both awful teenagers who grew into worse adults, and one of the many reasons why he'd left Ripley far behind. It had been John who'd posted about him on social media last week. The pictures had revealed him in one of his lower moments, passed out in the bush outside the pub. Mum hadn't been happy when she'd seen them.

He ducks his head down behind Vikram so they can't see him. Face almost touching the table.

"Macadamia," says John from across the bar. Red-cheeked. Wax jacketed. Wellied to the knee, despite the fact that he's probably never been near mud in his whole entitled little life. A voice so posh you'd vomit up plums trying to mimic it with any accuracy.

Mac hates the way he says Macadamia. As if it's a private joke.

They make their way over.

"How's Mrs Macadamia?" John says to Vikram, giving his shoulders a boisterous, though not particularly friendly jostle with both hands.

"She's fine," they both say.

Mac glances past and that's when he spots her. Brown hair. Tanned skin. Dark eyes trained on him. The white so white you could swear they'd been tippexed. She stands at the bar. She kind of looks a bit like Ariana, if he squints. She glances away when she spots him staring, then moves out of view.

"Grown wings yet, Macadamia?" says James, following John over with a pint in each hand. He passes one over to his comrade.

John snorts. And there's a titter from a few regulars at the bar who have picked up on the conversation.

"Why don't you ask your mum? I flew her to heaven and back last night," says Mac. "Maybe this time she'll get a child she actually loves." Zing! Wham! Pow!

Vikram's eyes go wide. Spurts of beer shoot out of each facial orifice and on to his navy postman's jumper. A few confidence boosting guffaws emanate from around the bar.

"What did you just say?" says James, stepping forward with grim menace in his eyes. His fists clench.

Buoyed by alcohol, Mac's blood boils. "I said—," he moves his hands to the arms of his chair, ready to stand. Ready to knock a couple of blocks off. All the blocks if necessary. Though block knocking isn't exactly his forte, he's tired of the constant poking, and the parasitic beer worm controlling his brain says it's time he did something about it.

Vikram puts out a hand. Wipes the beer from his face with the other. "Now, just leave it, fellas." He turns to John and James. "Why don't I get you two a drink?" He stands and corals the two Js back towards the bar. Looks over his shoulder and shakes his head with as close a thing to paternal anger on his face as a yoga loving postman can muster.

Mac leans back in his chair. A niggle in the back of his mind tells him he's forgotten something. That maybe he's seen something important, but can't quite remember what it was. He forgets things a lot lately so shrugs it off.

He forks a chip and swipes it through the gravy on Vikram's plate. Feels a tap on his shoulder. Turns with a mouthful.

It's her. The woman.

"I'm sorry," she says, taking a small step back and looking around as if to check no one else is watching, "but are you Trent Macadamia?"

"Depends who's asking," says Mac, chewing like a starved dog, the adrenaline from his previous encounter still pumping through his veins. He swallows. Clears his throat. His defences are always up now. "I mean, sorry, how can I be of assistance?"

"Can we talk in private?" Her stunning brown eyes glance over his head and around the bar. It looks to Mac as if she's worried about something. Nervous just talking to him.

He follows her gaze. Vikram is returning.

"Don't mind him..." says Mac, turning back, but in that split second, she's gone.

He stands and looks around the crowded bar, but can't see her.

"That was her," says Vikram. "Did you scare her off?"

"No, I didn't say anything."

"You must have." Vikram cranes his neck to look for her, then settles in his chair. "You're lucky that guy didn't lump you. Look, Trent, I know you've had a tough year, but you can't go picking fights with people. This is a small village. Everyone knows everybody here." He leans forward and whispers. "And no good will come of getting on the wrong side of those two. Bad eggs, the pair of them."

"They smell like bad eggs," says Mac with sullen petulance.

He scans the bar. Why had she tapped him on the shoulder if she wasn't going to talk to him? Who was she? And why was she looking for him?

Vikram leans back in his chair and sighs.

"I'm sorry, Vik," says Mac. "Look, I'm just tired of all of this. Tired of no one believing what happened to me, tired of the bad dreams, tired of keeping constant watch over my shoulder worrying about what might be there."

Vikram sort of smiles, but Mac isn't convinced. "I'm gonna head back. Your mum text me, she wants us home. I'm gonna be in the doghouse for sure. Are you coming?"

"Think I'm gonna walk back in a bit. Try and sober up. Maybe look for that girl." He hopes, with Vikram gone, she'll approach again. What had she been nervous about? "You should take my bike. That way, you'll be back way before me and can take most of the flak."

"Hm." Vikram raises his eyebrows and points a semi-threatening finger. "Don't be long."

After scouring the pub for a good ten minutes in search of the woman, Mac steps out into the early evening and crosses the road.

The cool night air smells of sweet smoke from the pub's wood burner. He loves that smell. It reminds him of warm summer evenings on the field opposite Mum's house with his only proper school friend, Carl, and a bottle of something they'd dubbed death mix. The recipe: A little bit of everything in the spirits cabinet topped off with fruit squash. Evenings when they'd experimented with drink and talked of everything they'd eventually do.

He doesn't see much of Carl anymore. Carl has a kid. A beautiful wife.

Mac doesn't.

He wonders if Carl misses him, too.

You didn't get to relax in the city. You never got that sense that time would wait for you to be ready to use it. Everyone was already late in London. You'd sleep when you died, which wouldn't be long at this rate. The smoky smell of calm nights replaced with greasy food, exhaust fumes, and the bodies of hundreds of people washing past you on the streets.

He looks up. The sun has almost set. A sliver of moon hangs above the horizon of red and gold, looking as though it's on fire. Black crows cross the sky, flying home for the day. He smiles, but it's not complete.

With his mind on the woman, he heads for home. Should he be worried because he was so easy to find? Or happy that someone has taken an interest in him? He looks inward and realises he doesn't know. Settles on the default: niggling anxiety.

Lost in his thoughts, he almost misses the glomp of two sets of rubber heels behind him on the cobbles. But, if years of bounty hunting on the mean streets of London have taught him anything, it's that two sets of heels often accompany voices, unless perhaps they are trying to be quiet. And if they are trying to be quiet...

His alcohol addled brain moves too slow.

The blow to the back of the head sends him flying forwards, and he barely breaks his fall with his forearms on the jagged cobbles that separate the road from the pavement. He's lucky he doesn't break something.

"Think you're funny, do you, Macadamia?"

Mac rolls over onto his side just as a welly lands in his ribs, pushing the air from him. "I've never been funny," he wheezes. "Least of all now."

Hands grab his pullover. The stink of alcohol and expensive cologne. It reminds him of London. They wrestle him into an alleyway between the butcher and the newsagent. It's dark and cold and damp.

He backs up as two shadows silhouetted in the streetlights follow him in. Their broad shoulders take up the full width of the slim alley.

Something cracks in his brain. He falls into the crevice. His breath catches in his throat and he staggers back. "No. Please."

His heart hammers in his chest. They've come for him. After all this time. They've come.

He takes the defensive stance of a startled hedgehog and curls into a face down ball with eyes closed. But unfortunately, he is spineless in every sense.

He holds his breath. But before more kicks come, he hears the swift sound of footsteps followed by a few guttural shouts and the thud of two well-executed punches.

"Who the hell are you?" says James or John.

"Get out of here," says a woman, followed by the galumphing sound of two welly boot wearing cowards heading in the opposite direction.

He waits a moment. Head still covered. Flinches as a gentle hand grips his arm and pulls him upwards. He stands. Hands poised over his face.

Striking brown eyes. They glow in the alley's dark. Like cat's eyes. It's her again.

"Are you ok?" she asks with eyebrows drawn together. She dips her head to look up into his downturned face.

"Fine. Nothing I can't handle." He pauses for a moment. Studies her features. She has a strange familiarity in the dark. Like he knows her from somewhere. "Have we met?" He pauses. "I mean before tonight?"

She shakes her head. "I need to talk with you. I have a case." She looks behind, to the mouth of the alleyway, then back at him. Grabs his hand. Stuffs something into it. "I can't stay long. It's not safe. I need you to meet me at this address. Midnight tonight. I'll give you all the information then."

"But—"

"I have money." Her eyes meet his. She looks desperate, to talk to him, but also to leave. Why do women always look desperate to leave? "Trent Macadamia, you are the only person who can help me." In the history of his life, no one has ever said that before. "Please. I only have tonight, then I must return to London. Meet me here." She holds his hand closed. Her skin is cool and rough. Her touch causes the tickling sensation of hundreds of feathers tracing up his forearm to his heart. She hurries back out of the alley.

For a moment, he stands there stunned. Then gives chase. Looks left and right, but there's only two people on the street, over by the pub, and neither are her.

She's gone. As if she'd just vanished.

With sceptical caution, he looks up at the sky. Just in case. But she hadn't had wings. And besides, she was too young.

He opens his hand and looks at the paper held within. A leaflet for a set of holiday cottages five minutes from his mum's. He turns it over. A single number. Two. No additional markings other than what's printed. Nothing to give him any clues.

He sniffs it. Smells like paper. Quelle su- flippin' -prise.

No sign of John or James either. Prrricks.

If only they'd have come at him from the front. He'd have given them what for. Or he'd have just been punched in the face instead.

There's movement in the corner of his eye. One of the two figures by the pub has turned to face him. The other stands on tiptoes peering through the pub window. The one facing him pats the other on the arm and points. They both stare. Each wears a long coat and a wide-brimmed hat that cast shadows over their faces. Both wear dark sunglasses despite the oncoming night.

For a moment they just stand there, watching him. Speaking hushed words between themselves. Mac hasn't seen them before. And he knows most of the locals from his route or from the pub. Not that he can really tell. They're wrapped up so tight.

The figures are unusually short. About five foot each. Their staring makes him uneasy, so he inches away along the pavement.

With strange jittering movements, as if floating or taking many small steps beneath their long coats, the figures follow.

They drop off the edge of the kerb, wobble and part, then re-join and continue their slow, floaty advance across the road towards him. Their gait is like that of a centipede. As if hundreds of tiny legs are going like the clappers to propel them along at a slower than human pace.

The hairs stand on the back of Mac's neck, and a chill runs down his spine. He shakes his head. Must be the beer. Bending time and space as it so often does.

The figures are halfway across the road by the time he decides he's had enough. Their uncanny whispering sets him on a knife edge.

"Go home," he says, most likely to himself. "You're drunk." And, with a dull ache in his ribs, he jogs for home.

Gems and Monsters

Lily paints gems. She just likes it. Likes the way they come out — imperfect, weird and unique. Likes the way they come to life with every stroke of her brush.

She has no idea why it's gems she likes to paint. It's not as if she craves real emeralds or rubies. She doesn't have a want for splendid jewellery. She just likes painting gems.

She never knows how they will end up when she starts out, but always knows when they are finished. Karen says they crystallise on the page. Lily doesn't really know what crystallise means, but it's something to do with gems. She paints blue ones, green ones, red ones. The white ones are called diamonds. Karen puts most of her pictures by the window. The thick paper slightly bent with the wet and dry of the water colour. Some of them, the ones Karen likes best, make it on to the fridge.

Today Lily paints a purple gem. It reminds her of the one her grandparents had on their window sill by the front door, back before she couldn't be with them anymore. A rough finger length rock with a forest of purple crystals standing on top.

She remembers their house. She'd liked it there. A clean, white bungalow with a big garden and a willow tree. She still doesn't understand quite why she couldn't stay with them. Mr Godfrey had said it was because they were getting old, and old people couldn't look after little children.

She looks at Finn's picture. He likes drawing monsters, although they don't look much like monsters. More like black sticks with wings. He's only four, so he's still behind her by a year. He says this one is The Nightmare Bat. It's got lots of teeth. Or at least she thinks they're teeth.

Some of the other children draw The Nightmare Bat too.

Lily doesn't. She doesn't know why you'd want to remember The Nightmare Bat. She's tried to forget. So she draws pretty things.

Monsters and gems were like good and bad. But sometimes you didn't know which was which.

Gems could be pretty, but on the TV sometimes the greedy baddies might cause trouble to get them. Beautiful gems could make people go a bit bad. And Monsters could be scary, but sometimes they might be nice, just misunderstood. Knowing what was what was hard. You had to be smart to tell the difference. Grandad used to say she was smart. And she was. She could even read a few words.

Karen always says you can never judge a book by its cover, which is a weird thing to say because how else would you know which book to read. Maybe you could never judge a monster by the rows of sharp teeth, or a gem by its sparkle in the sun.

Finn finishes his picture. It doesn't look very finished, but he's put his brush back in the pot of cloudy brown water. He holds the paper in both hands and looks it up and down.

"Oh, that's lovely Finn," says Karen, putting her phone on the table and clapping her hands together in her lap. "Bit spooky." She says spooky in a spooky voice that wobbles up and comes down again. It makes Finn giggle. Lily smiles.

The smell of chilli wafts from the kitchen and Lily's stomach grumbles. She doesn't really like chilli, but as Karen always said, "food is food".

Lily prefers fish fingers. And chips, but not broccoli. Maybe peas.

"Maybe we could show it to Mr Godfrey later." Karen holds her hand out and Finn passes the picture over. "He's coming tonight to help some of you find new homes. I think he's going to take two of you."

The other children start to whisper.

"Really?" says Lily, taking an interest. She puts her brush down carefully on her paper. Last week Noah and Ethan got taken to their forever homes.

Apparently they have mummies and daddies there. Good ones. Not like the ones they'd all started with. According to Mr Godfrey the mummies and daddies they'd started with had been nasty ones.

Lily hopes she's picked next to go. It'd be nice to have a nice Mummy. Someone to give her cuddles. Someone who'd make her fish fingers and chips, and maybe let her go to school or the park like the kids on the TV shows. She's the oldest here now, so it really is her turn.

Potential

By the time Mac is home, the beer has worn off, and his anxiety has him by the throat.

Not a case. He's not ready for a case.

Also, why him? There are hundreds of PIs in London. Why did she track him down to this small town? *How* did she track him down to this small town?

He expects it's not a coincidence that John had posted those photos of him last week and here someone was looking for him this week.

He crunches up the gravel path to the door of his mum's little cottage. Yellow light bleeds through a crack in the living room curtains. Not a good sign. Mum's yoga practice starts early, and as she has no need to stay up late, she gets up with Vikram and so goes to bed when he does.

He checks his watch. It's nine. If she's up, it means she's waiting for him. He feels fourteen again.

He slides his key into the lock, pushes the door hoping it doesn't creak, and steps into the dark hallway.

The house always smells of food. It's never hurt his waistline, but Mum's a feeder. Cakes, pies, huge Sunday roasts. It's been that way since he was young. He guesses it's something for her to do. Something so that she feels useful. To show she could provide for her children without their father.

And she could. She's always been an amazing woman.

He slips his shoes off and creeps towards the stairs.

"Trent," comes the voice from the living room, soft but cutting in the silent dark. "I know you're here. Vikram's asleep. Don't make me shout."

He sighs and slides his socked feet across the bare oak floorboards towards the lounge and pokes his head through the crack of the door – squints in the bright light like a new born panda.

"Sorry Mum, didn't think you'd be up."

She sits in her armchair. The muted television shows some celebrity couple being judged by a panel of glossy professionals on their proficiency in tap dance. The show ends and moves to an advert for the latest nutrient goop being offered by a faceless food corporation that seems to have risen in the power vacuum left by the now disgraced Di Blasio. It looks a lot like the pasty stuff Kenneth and the other influencers used to peddle.

"Coming Soon," the title reads ominously.

Mum leans forwards and turns it off, then pats the sofa next to her. Mac doesn't move. He knows what she's going to say.

"I should get to bed—"

"Sit." She smiles a little smile – a warning as obvious as a dog baring its teeth – and places her folded hands gently in her lap.

He crosses the room to the sofa but settles one cushion away just in case an ear clipping is in order.

"Where have you been?"

"Out."

"I can smell it on you from here." She raises her eyebrows and purses her lips. It doesn't matter how old he gets, that look still fills him with dread. "I thought I told you to stop this."

"I..." He looks down at his lap. He knows how disappointed she must be in him. Knows how much he must remind her of his father. But he can't talk. It's as if there's some sort of trapdoor across his throat. An invisible block that holds the words back. "I..."

Her face softens. "I can't help you unless you talk to me," she says. "What's all the drinking about? Are you depressed? Bored even."

He's never told her exactly what happened that night. All she knows is that she saw him about to address the world and then the feed went black.

It's not like he's refused to talk about it. More that he always steers anyone away from asking questions. Like those twenty minutes of mysterious radio silence had been some sort of universal blackout that no one will ever know about. It protects him to pretend those moments didn't happen.

He looks up at her. "You trust me, don't you?" It's not quite what he means, but it's the easiest thing for him to say.

"I've always been proud of you, Trent." She smiles. "I'm not disappointed, I'm not cross, I'm not sad about who you are. I'm just worried. I can see your future, and I think your potential is better than that."

There's that word – potential. It's been rearing its ugly head ever since he was a boy. Mum uses it. Teachers used it. Even his first and only proper girlfriend had managed to work it into her break up speech while he'd sat there in silence, wondering what on earth he'd done wrong, on the park bench where they'd once scrawled their names in marker more permanent than the love she'd told him she'd felt.

Potential. Apparently, he's never lived up to it.

"What do you mean, my future?"

She draws a quick breath. Opens her mouth to speak. Pauses. "Your father had troubles, too. I thought of them almost as stains on an otherwise beautiful soul. But over time, they became more than that. They swallowed him. Made him something he wasn't."

Mac can't meet her gaze. He feels sick. There are few people whose opinion he cares about. But sometimes he thinks he'd kill to make his mother proud. After all she sacrificed to bring him up, he doesn't want to let her down.

Is it guilt he feels or disappointment in himself?

He's always hated his father. Not that he ever knew him. But who could leave such a kind and gentle woman with two kids? What sort of person would just up and leave them?

"Am I really like him?"

"No."

She says it too abruptly. Is she lying?

"You're not quick to anger like he was."

"I never meant for things to go this way," he says. "I wasn't doing well for myself, but I was sort of happy in London. You know, before the..." He looks away. "Before that night, I felt I had a purpose. Or at least something to work towards."

"Have you ever thought about going ba—"

"I can't go back." He shakes his head. "No. No. It's not safe. Everyone knows me as the guy who ruined things. You don't go on social media, Mum, but I'm still all over it. They hate me."

A picture of him, right before his lowest ever moment, looking dishevelled and downtrodden staring into the camera, has become a joke, a meme often accompanied by witty text about the fall of industries like video rental or dairy.

He's stared at that picture a lot. A picture of someone about to scratch the surface of what true horror might look like. A picture of a young man not quite yet broken, but soon to be.

"You never knew how to take things on the chin, did you? Sometimes the best thing you can do is laugh at yourself."

"But nothing's funny anymore."

"Not everything that happens to you will be good, Trent, but the only way to make the most of a bad situation is to see the good that comes from it. This is just a blip in the great tale of Trent Macadamia. It won't last." She looks across the room at a picture of her and Vikram on the mantlepiece above the fake electric fire. "When your father left us, I had no idea what I was going to do. I had two young children, no job, no money. I thought if he was willing to leave you and Amanda behind just to get away from me, then I must be pretty terrible." She reaches out. He meets her halfway, taking her hand. "But turns out I'm alright. And I know it's not the same, I know whatever happened that night, you don't want to talk about, but you're alright too." She squeezes his hand and wobbles her head with a little self-assured cockiness. "I mean, *I* like you and I'm actually pretty special. I'm a yoga-teaching mother with a hot boyfriend who's a number of years younger than me."

Mac raises an eyebrow. "Do you have another boyfriend I don't know about?" He tries to look serious, but his mother's joy is infectious. He tightens his lips to hide his smile.

"Vikram, I'll have you know—" she goes for his ribs. He's been ticklish since he was a boy, and he squirms away with a pre-emptive giggle. "—has been chased by women across this village ever since he and his family moved here. And who did he settle on?" She pokes herself in the chest with a thumb. "Yours truly."

His ribs ache as he pushes himself back up to seated.

"What's up with you?" She says, wiggling her index fingers at him. "Can't handle a good ticklin'?"

"Thanks Mum," he says, thinking *'no, it's the good kicking I received I can't handle.'* But your mum is the last person you tell when you've received a good kicking.

"Anyway, turns out I'm not the only one who's getting a bit of attention from the opposite sex." She gives him that nosey mother look. Eyebrows raised, head turned slightly to one side.

"Don't say sex, Mum."

She chuckles. "Vikram told me all about that lovely lady you were talking to in the pub." She leans forward in her chair, with prayer position hands tapping together in an excited little Mum clap. "Who is she? I want all the goss."

Mac shrugs, remembering those pools of brown in the dark alleyway. Maybe he should give Mum something to hold on to. A bit of hope that he's not wasting whatever potential she thinks he has. "Just a girl." He tries to look coy.

"Anyone I might know?"

He slips his hand into his pocket and touches the leaflet. Should he tell her the truth?

After a moment's deliberation, he removes it. "She's not local or anything. She asked me to meet her here."

Mum leans back. "Say no more." She gives him a knowing grin, accompanied by an enthusiastic wink.

"Wait, but—"

"I know you haven't always had the best of luck with girls, but you're not happy here. You don't want to be stuck in Ripley all your life. You never have. Don't get comfortable with discomfort, Trent." She pats his leg and stands as if the conversation is over. The next thing she says is final. "Sometimes the path of most resistance is where we grow. You go and see this girl. Make her see who you really are inside. She'll be hard pressed not to like you."

Holiday Cottage

He climbs out of his postman's uniform and folds it away into the drawers by his bed, showers, then sits in his room eating coffee granules from an egg cup with a spoon. It makes the hangover worse, but is something he's discovered to be quite sobering.

Mum is right. He doesn't like it here. There was a reason he'd left. He has always wanted more.

But could this meeting at the holiday cottage be a trap? A way for The Guardians to get him out somewhere secluded so they can finally kill him?

The fact that she is a woman somewhat dampens his worry. He can remember Victoria had said women weren't allowed into the organisation.

But you can't have sons without mothers. They could have spies.

His eyes flick around the room, always moving back to the Lightning McQueen alarm clock on his bedside table as the hour ticks down.

When the clock hits eleven fifteen, he stands and moves to the wardrobe. Inside are his trench coat and hat.

He hasn't looked at them since he returned home. Had even made a statement by dumping both in the kitchen bin. Somehow, they'd ended up back in his wardrobe cleaner than they'd ever been.

He slips them on. Leaves. Returns. Sprays a mist of aftershave in the doorway and spins through it. (No spray, no bae.) Sneaks down the stairs and out.

The cottage isn't far. He takes his bike. Vik has cleaned it and oiled the chain. Good ol' Vik.

In the dark, and with his trench coat dragging perilously close to his gears, Mac doesn't rush the journey. It gives him time to think. At 11:45 he stops at the entrance to the winding country road that leads up to the trio of cottages and leans the bike against a tree. In his mind, it's a better idea to sneak up on foot.

The lights are on at number two. The other two cottages are dark.

He creeps up the garden path. A window sits on either side of the front door. He approaches the one on the left. Peers through. Just a kitchen. There's something on the dining table. A bowl of noodles. A fork. A book. Nothing out of the ordinary.

He moves across the path to the window on the right. A darkened living room. Nothing untoward here either.

Perhaps he's being paranoid. It could just be a case.

He takes a deep breath. Shakes his arms out and tries to relax his shoulders. No need to arrive at the door looking as stiff as a concrete slab.

"You can do it," he whispers to himself.

He steps up under the ivy covered porch, raises his fist to knock on the door, and notices that it is already ajar. The hallway light is off, hence why he hadn't noticed the two inches between door and frame running along the edge.

He pushes it open ever so slightly. Checks the locks. No sign of forced entry.

He slips inside, making sure to leave the door open behind him in case he needs to beat a speedy retreat. The hallway beyond is cold. Almost as cold as the night outside.

The heat coming out of the radiators suggests the door has been open for some time. He sniffs the air. Nothing strange. Maybe a musty, earth hint, but not unusual for a country cottage.

Pausing in the hallway, he listens. Only the sounds of cars driving away in the distance and the whisper of the wind through the trees nearby. Save the humming fridge in the kitchen to his left, and an old boiler muttering to itself somewhere, no sound comes from within the house.

He inches towards the kitchen. Brushes the door open and looks inside. Opens his mouth. Realises he doesn't even know her name to call out.

"Hello," he whispers. He doesn't want to scare her. That would be a bad first impression.

Maybe she's just left the door open.

He holds his breath. Listening again. A faint rustling comes from the dining table. He steps closer and has to fight the urge to throw up. The large bowl on the table is full of writhing earthworms. Pink and glistening in the bright white light of the kitchen. Like someone had somehow confused their fishing tackle and cereal boxes.

He covers his mouth as his stomach lurches. And backs out of the kitchen into the dark hallway.

Another sound. Crunching on the gravel path outside. Closing on the house. Two muffled voices.

Instinct drives him from the hall and into the kitchen. He passes the noodles from hell, and through a door on the far side into a utility room. He shuts the door behind him and stands in silence. The sweet clinical smell of laundry detergent fills the room.

The front door opens, and he hears the voices move straight into the kitchen. Both female. Both unknown. They sound old.

"Are you sure he came in here?"

"Yes, I saw him scamper across the lawn—"

Something smashes on the floor.

"Oh, what's that? Noodles?" There's a slurping sound.

"You can't just eat off the floor."

"Five-second rule." There's a wretch. "Unusual consistency for noodles. Must be a ramen."

"What's a ramen?

"It's something the kids say."

"What kids?"

"Where did he go?"

Who are they? And why are they following him? This can't be good.

"Listen..." There's a pause.

Mac looks down at himself. Had he moved? Had he made a sound?

"Do you smell something?"

The room goes silent save sniffing noses. The sound approaches.

"That is too much aftershave."

"He must be in the cupboard."

Mac doesn't like it. He scans the laundry room for some sort of weapon. Nothing save a box of Persil, so he picks it up. It's heavy. What's the best move? Let them come in or bust out on his own terms.

"Is it him? Do you think he saw us?"

"We should zap him. Have you got it?"

Bust out seems the best option.

"Oh, you know what, I think I left the zapper back in the car."

"You have a memory like a sieve. How on earth are we going to take him with us, Be—?"

He kicks the door open. Launches the open box of soap powder through the doorway and bursts into the kitchen shouting — half out of fear and half in a bid to shock whoever's there. He says no actual words. Just a guttural sort of snarl with a few extra choice consonants. The soap powder crashes to the ground and spills over the floor having done no damage at all to anyone.

The two coated figures from the pub stand there. Their hunched little bodies are all bundled up like big cloth balls. Mac can't see their faces beneath their hats, glasses, and scarves. He cringes in fear. They block the route to the door. One holds a long, hooked club down by their side.

The bowl of worms lies smashed on the floor. The sight of them wiggling their way across the terracotta tile snaps him out of his stupor. He should be escaping, too.

He jumps up on to one of the kitchen benches and clambers over the table past the pair, who rotate like rheumatic desk chairs to track him as he leaves the room.

Mac doesn't stop to see if they are following. Slams through the front door of the house and down the gravel track. Legs it all the way to his bike and pedals for home without looking back.

The ride is hell. Every tree, swaying and rustling in the wind, is a shadowy bat-like shape dropping from the sky. Every sound on those dark country roads - shrieking foxes, distant cars, night birds - is a threat of death.

He rides wide eyed, despite the cold sweat that pours from his forehead and into them. He shouldn't have gone. He should never leave the house again. At least not at night. The dark is not his friend. It is an enemy. Camouflage for everything that wants to kill him.

And *everything* wants to kill him.

He doesn't hear a vehicle giving chase. Were those things Guardians? Could they be stalking him from the sky? Who knew what they had wrapped up under those creepy long coats?

Mac doesn't know. Doesn't want to know. Doesn't want anything to do with this bloody case. He is not an investigator anymore. He's not an anything anymore.

There are no lit streetlights on his mother's road. No illumination radiating from the well spaced houses.

He looks back. Looks to the sky. Looks everywhere but ahead.

Doesn't see the pothole.

His front wheel falls in deep and comes to a complete halt, shooting him over the handlebars and into something hard. A fence post or trunk. Stars explode in the dark. He lies in a crumpled heap with the bike on top of him.

Had someone hit him?

He is too disoriented to think. Tries to fight the oncoming grey as a shadow looms over him in the dark. Something grabs his ankle, but he's too far gone to do anything about it. He passes out as he is dragged away from the crash site.

Mr Godfrey

Mr Godfrey comes for dinner while Lily sits with the other kids around the big table eating. There's twenty children in total.

"Good evening, children," he says, as he walks through the kitchen door.

He has a black suit and a black umbrella. He gives it a little shake. It's raining. It's always raining. Karen said that once upon a time it didn't rain so much. Global warming, she says, but it doesn't feel very warm. It's always cold in the home.

Mr Godfrey looks different compared to other people. Lily thinks he must be very old because his hair is grey and his skin is white like the inside of a fish finger, but his face doesn't look all wrinkly like her grandad's had. It looks kind of new. When he's not here, Karen and Sally talk about wanting some of what he's on. He talks a bit funny, too.

She sits up straight to make herself more noticeable. Usually the tallest get to go with him, and she's definitely nearly the tallest except Finn, who Karen says is big for his age.

"Who have we got here then?" he says to Karen, who stands by the sink washing up the pans. "Who do you think has been behaving themselves most this week?"

Karen wipes her brow with her arm because her hands are all bubbly, then gives her hands a shake and a rinse.

"Lily is about ready to go, aren't you Lily?" she smiles, but she looks a bit sad. She always looks a bit sad.

Lily nods. Grips her knife and fork tightly in her fists. "Yes, please. I'd like to go to my new home. My forever home."

Mr Godfrey smiles. His teeth are a bit of a jumble. A bit pointy. She guesses he's a bit like the monsters that you can't judge by their looks because he is a bit scary looking, but he's actually really nice. He sometimes brings presents. She wonders if he's brought presents.

"Oh really," he says, turning his head to look at Lily with dark eyes. "Well, then I would love to take you."

Lily's tummy jumps. She wonders what her new Mummy will be like.

"And what's the tall boy's name?" says Mr Godfrey, pointing at Finn with a long, thin finger. "Maybe he should come, too?

"Finn," says Karen. "Finn, would you like to go tonight?"

Finn hesitates and bites his fingers. Lily gives him a little kick under the table. He looks down at her foot, then into her eyes. She makes a face at him. Does he want to miss out?

"Um... yes," he finally says.

"Want doesn't come into it," says Mr Godfrey with another of his pointy smiles. "When it's your time, it's your time. Get your things packed. I already have some other boys and girls waiting in the bus. Your new parents are excited to meet you all."

Shoot High

With eyes still closed, Mac lifts his head. It aches like a mother. He touches a hand to his temple. Feels the soft linen of a bandage around his brow. The worn, familiar springiness of his single bed beneath him.

That means he's home. And not in the domain of some insane butterfly person. He opens his tired eyes. His room. As he'd left it.

Had it all been a dream? Perhaps he'd fallen asleep after his shower and never gone to the house at all.

Perhaps he'd hurt his head another way and just couldn't remember. He was always bumping things when he was drunk. He had been in a fight, hadn't he? In the alley near the pub. Maybe that was it. Maybe he took a harder knock than he thought.

He's safe at least.

He rolls over and slips his legs out of bed. Feels for his slippers with bare feet. The floorboard creaks.

"Trent, is that you?" comes his mother's voice from downstairs. "Terra and I are about to have brunch."

He glances at Lightning McQueen. Midday. Why hadn't it gone off for work? Had he even set it? Why hadn't Vikram or his mother woken him?

Wait, did she say Terra? Who the hell was Terra?

He crosses the room and grabs his dressing gown from behind the door. It's the same one he's had since he was twelve. Bright red. Man United. Bought by a great aunt who had absolutely no idea what a teenage boy was into, least of all Mac, bless her.

But who could it be? He ups his pace as he passes a pile of fresh laundry that his mother has left by the door. In his hurry, he almost trips over it and down the stairs. Crashes through the kitchen door whilst still tying the gown's rope around his waist.

"How are you doing, sweetie?" says Mum. She has an apron on. A tray of steaming American style pancakes held out before her. It smells amazing. Cinnamon and blueberry and maple syrup. "How's your head?"

"Who's here?" he says, looking around the kitchen. The room curves around to the right of the door so he doesn't see who else is there until he turns fully around.

The woman from the pub. Sat at his mother's kitchen table. As if she's been coming around for breakfast on the reg for months. As if she hadn't led him into some sort of trap at the holiday cottage. He gives her the evils. Tries to let her know with his eyes that he has her pegged despite not having her pegged in the slightest. In fact, she's about as far from pegged as a tent flying away in a hurricane. But she doesn't know that. Does she?

"Terra said you two were walking home last night, and you fell in a pothole and bumped your head." His Mum bustles past and places the tray on the table. "Gosh, you are clumsy." Then, with the casual ease only Mum's entertaining guests have, she pivots towards the woman. "I know you said you didn't want anything, my dear, but I had these in the freezer so I've just warmed them up. I have maple syrup. Or fruit."

"I'm fine, thank you," says this *'Terra'*, giving Mum the smile equivalent of birthday cake.

"Juice? Coffee? Cereal? I can't have you staying over and not being fed." Classic Mum — at her happiest forcing someone to eat.

Wait, staying over?

"Stop staring, Trent, and come and sit with us." His mum points at the chair next to the woman. "Jeez louise, what are you wearing? That dressing gown is disgusting. It barely comes past your boxer shorts."

"Um... Mum," he says without taking his eyes from the woman. "Can I have a word," he clears his throat, "in the hall?"

His mother frowns. “Let’s have breakfast first, shall we? It would have been nice to let Vikram know about the big trip you two have planned, but I’m sure he’ll handle being without you for a few days.”

That’s polite mum speak for *he’s never really needed you anyway*. Mac has always known he’d been a sympathy hire.

Mum takes a sip of her juice and looks at Terra. “So, my dear, how did you two meet?” Without waiting for an answer, she turns back to Mac. “And why have you been keeping such a lovely lady a secret?” She scoffs. “How long have you been together now?”

Mac shuffles across the room and sits next to his mother. Makes a quick and irreversible decision. “I don’t know, um... Terra, how long have we been together?”

“Oh, I’d say about three months.” She takes his hand. His whole body tingles. She leans towards his mum with a little laugh. “He is forgetful, isn’t he?”

What?!? Whaaaat?!

Mum notices the display of affection with obvious glee that at first warms Mac’s heart, then stamps on it. This is what she has always wanted for him.

“Isn’t he just?” Mum says. “This is lovely.” She pats her knees, then looks up. “Oh, I made coffee.”

“We can’t stay, Mum,” says Mac. He locks eyes with Terra. “Can we?” He has to get this woman out of the house. She might be dangerous. She’d certainly given James and John a good kicking last night. God knows what she could do to him and his mum.

Mum looks crestfallen but bounces straight back. “Of course. Your big trip. Back to London. And will you be returning to Ripley soon?”

Mac doesn’t take his eyes from Terra. Swallows. But his throat is dry. Big trip? Will he be returning at all? Why is he entertaining this madness?

He looks at Mum. He’s not seen her this happy, this full of life, since he returned home.

That’s why.

“We’ll be a couple of weeks,” Terra says.

"Weeks? Well, you better go get packed then, Trent. I doubt you've even started." Mum rolls her eyes with an amused exhale then gives him a funny look he's not seen before, a mix of mock exasperation and pride.

He takes a deep breath. "Sure." He stands. "Terra, care to help?"

"I'll make sure I have everything set in the car. It's not a long drive, but I want to check the route."

"Sure," he says in somewhat of a daze. "Absolutely. Good plan. Wonderful. I'll meet you out there when I'm done."

He lugs his suitcase down from the top of his wardrobe. Who knows why? He can't go. Can he?

A mysterious woman arrives out of nowhere, tells him she needs his help, saves him from getting a good thrashing, and then appears at breakfast pretending to be his girlfriend and offering to take him on a trip.

On paper, it doesn't sound too bad.

She hasn't threatened harm upon him. If she'd wanted him dead, then she would have waited for John and James to beat him up, then just come along and stabbed him. Easy. Plus, John and James would have taken the blame - the perfect crime.

Still, it's good to see Mum so happy.

He'd go along with it for now, but keep his guard up.

He packs. All his pants. Most of his socks. Two pairs of trousers. Three shirts. Old faded Iron Maiden hoody (as a disguise). Trench coat. Hat.

To be honest, it's all quite exciting. Packing a bag. Being whisked away on a surprise secret trip to London. A road trip in a car with a woman who has an unusual charm that he can't quite put his finger on. An unknown destination. Perhaps this is the very thing he's missed by never having a proper girlfriend. Well, almost never. He apparently failed to live up to his potential with that last one ten or so years ago. Perhaps it's all just quite normal, with the only caveat being he doesn't know the girl who is taking him on the surprise trip.

Internet dating has the same principle, and no one frowns upon that.

Maybe it'll be nice.

He humps his suitcase down the stairs. Terra and his mum stand at the front door nattering like old friends. Mum leans at casual ease against the frame, arms folded, like she doesn't have a care in the world.

What can they possibly be talking about?

"Well, have a lovely time," she says as she moves in for a hug.

He feels a bit like he's being sucked powerlessly down a drain.

"Will do," he says and kisses her on the cheek. He hugs her back like he may never see her again. In that moment, the realisation hits him that any hug could be the last. He squeezes a little extra tight. "I'll miss you." He smiles at Terra. "Come on then, you. Let's get on."

"Sure thing, hun," she says, keeping up this awful ruse. "Goodbye, Mrs Macadamia."

"Oh, call me Alyssa."

Terra smiles.

He follows her up the garden path with a single return look.

The beginning of all the questions smashing around in his head like bumper cars tumbles out of his mouth in one word as he climbs into the car beside her.

"What...?"

"Seat belt," she says.

"Oh." He straps himself into her white Kia hatchback. It's rented. It has that smell. And a little U-Drive sticker on the window.

Terra waves to his mum as they pull away.

"Thank you for saving me outside the pub last night," he says. He doesn't want to get off on the wrong foot. She might still be a murderer, and he doesn't want to sound ungrateful. "And I guess it was you yesterday who found me after I crashed my bike. You got me home, but..." He leaves it open, hoping she might fill the many gaps.

"I did." She concentrates on the road. More than a normal person would. As if she's not been driving long. She doesn't appear to want to talk.

"So..." He lets the word hang and leans back against the passenger side window to get a good look at her.

"I guess you're wondering who I am."

He lets off steam in the form of a raspberry, spraying a fine mist between them.

She frowns. "Well, that's disgusting."

"Oh disgusting, is it? You're the one who's basically kidnapping me. I'd call that pretty disgusting."

"Kidnapping? Hardly."

He wiggles his index fingers at her. "Getting all in my mum's good books with your womanly wiles. Pretending we're together. You saw how happy she was." He drops his hands on his lap and relaxes a little in his seat. "How could I have crushed her dreams by telling her that you were some sort of usurping psychopath? You had me between a rock and a hard place. And if it comes between seeing the joy squeezed out of my mum's face and going on a trip with some random woman who could potentially murder me, then I'm going on the trip."

"Sorry about lying to your mum," she says. "And don't worry I'm not going to murder you."

"I'd figured as much. If you wanted to, you'd have just staved my head in with a rock last night after I fell off my bike." He watches her a moment. "Which means you actually do need me to help you with something." He looks out of the window. Knocks the glass with a knuckle as they pass out of Ripley. "Early mornings and delivering letters were never going to be my thing, so I'm down with whatever you've got going on."

She pulls on to a roundabout, gripping the steering wheel at ten and two with white knuckles.

"But who are you and where are you taking me?"

"My name is Terra." She points at the glove box by his knees. "In there is an envelope. Take it out."

He waits a moment. Just to let her know he won't react well to such curt instructions in future. She doesn't say anything. The silence hangs like a held breath. Curiosity finally wins over, and he opens the glove box.

He takes out a brown unmarked manilla envelope. Classic detective stuff. Pours the contents out on to his lap. One piece of paper (waste of an envelope), a folded picture.

He unfolds it. It's grainy, a zoomed in screen shot, but he can just make out the face. It's one he didn't expect to see. One he'd almost forgotten. A face seemingly made for fading into the background.

"Terry?" he says, raising a confused and somewhat disappointed nostril. "This is that little cultist, right? From The Church of The Fallen Angels."

She smiles and her eyes glaze as if she's remembering a happier time. "Terry? Is that what he's calling himself?" She pulls the car on to the slip road of the A3.

"What do you want with him?" He looks her over. He somehow doubts she's a jilted lover. "Owe you money?"

"He's my brother."

This comes as a surprise. It takes him a moment to process that Terry, a man he remembers as something of a congested sloth, shares the same gene pool as the woman in the seat next to him.

"I need to find him, soon, and you're the last person to have seen him alive that I've been able to reach."

He wrinkles his nose. "So I wasn't the first person you tried to contact?"

He hasn't been able to reach the others either. Not since his last communication with Nige just before Christmas. And The Church of The Fallen Angels had fallen off his radar almost as quickly as they had shown up on it. He has no idea how to find them.

She shakes her head. "You're just the first person I found."

Still, there's always a way. Or at least there's always a bit of stalling he can do before he finally stumbles on to an answer or goes over his one week refund period.

He holds up the picture when she doesn't answer. "This is a very cold case. It's going to cost—"

"I just need him found. And quickly."

Shoot high, Macadamia. "I'm £250 a day while on a case."

"Money is no object."

Doh! Always. Shoot. Higher. MACADAMIA!

"Plus expenses. Um and... uh, VAT, probably." He holds his breath and his position while he awaits her response.

"Sure."

Yessss!

Negotiations negotiated, he pats his lap. "So, a few questions before we begin. Why weren't you at your house last night?"

She nods. "I thought I was being followed, so I hid outside. I saw you, and them." She looks out of the window as they sit in the slow lane heading north. Rolls her eyes. "It's my older brother, Gaspar. He didn't want me talking to you. He's a bit old-fashioned. Doesn't like me running too far from the nest."

"Your brother is creepy and short, and has a weird old woman voice." He's a little confused about what exactly he had seen. He remembers something about worms too, but the knock to his head (and possibly the earlier drinks) has fuzzed things up a bit.

She frowns a moment. "I can pay you double if we find Enki in the next week."

£500 a day! Phwoar!

"I have a contact in London who could possibly help," he says. "He's retired, but has kept his thumbs in the many pies of the underground." That phrase sounded better in his head. "Take us to Camden. He'll be in. He's pretty much housebound now."

The Oracle

Together, Mac and Terra climb the multiple flights of stairs in the huge grey block of flats. He's not been here before, but every bounty hunter in London knows where every other bounty hunter in London lives. It's kind of a given. If you are all chasing the same criminals, it helps to know everyone else's starting point. That way, if you're at a loose end, you can stake out a rival and, if you're faster and cleverer, second guess their destination and band the perp. Mac has tried it a few times, but has never been faster nor cleverer.

They cut out on to a balcony on the seventh floor which leads along the front of the building.

He looks out over what small portion of the city he can see. Three more tall tower blocks stand at the corners of a concrete, plant-less square. Several kids sit on bikes in the centre, drinking, spitting, smoking.

Despite his preference for isolation, he has missed the city. Millions of people huddled in close proximity. Cramped conditions. Dirt and grime and greedy pigeons. There was something about a solitary existence surrounded by other people. It felt like you were all paying your dues. Surviving loneliness, together.

Since last year, he wonders if that feeling is intentional. Tell people they like being alone, make them see the joy in it, or at least make them fear togetherness, and, suddenly divided, they become very easy to conquer.

Having knowledge of dark overlords controlling everything makes him question each decision he's ever made. Makes him question whether or not he actually has freewill, or whether he is just another pawn on a giant chessboard fulfilling his preordained part to the letter.

"What number?"

"708."

He knocks. Knows it might take some time for the occupant to come to the door. In the dead of night when he can't sleep, Mac often frequents the bounty hunter message boards, and from what he's heard, Bobby Feta's recovery has been slow and painful.

"Coming," comes the hoarse cry from inside. Shuffling footsteps. The click of a walking stick.

"Let me do the talking, ok?" There's no real reason other than he wants to impress her. And perhaps keep control of the conversation so that she doesn't become aware he's chasing smoke. To cover himself, he says, "he'll just get nervous if a girl talks to him."

The door opens. Still on the chain. A forehead and a pair of glasses. "Yes."

Will Bobby be glad to see him? "Hey bud," he says in his most sympathetic tone. Since when has he ever called anyone bud? "It's me, Mac. How's it going, old pal?"

The door slams. A frantic rustle on the other side as the chain is slipped across. Mac inches away, back connecting with the railing of the balcony. The idea of the seven-storey drop behind him sends shivers up his spine. He'd not thought if Bobby might kick off about Mac's part in his stabbing. Not that any of it was his fault.

A rush of wind passes and for a moment he wonders what it'd be like to be thrown over a balcony and fall all that way on to flat, unforgiving concrete.

Not pleasant.

The door opens. Bobby stands there in a dark green dressing gown. He is hunched to one side. The side Mac assumes had been stabbed.

"Mac." He has a wide smile on his face. "Mac, is it really you? I've been trying to contact you. No one knows where you've been."

Mac eyes Terra for a moment. Someone did.

"Didn't you get my emails?" Bobby continues.

He had. Read them all. "No. I changed my address." He hadn't wanted to entertain Bobby's incessant questioning about The Guardians.

"Bobby, I need your help with a case."

"And I need yours with mine." He grabs Mac's hand and shakes it. This is not normal Bobby Feta behaviour. But then again, being fierce bounty hunter rivals, they'd never found the time to sit down for a chat. Bobby then holds an arm out to guide them inside. "I'm so glad you're here."

Mac steps through, somewhat anxious. Bobby has never spoken to him with such warmth before. Independent bounty hunters had a fierce rivalry. The bigwigs that ran the charts heavily stressed the competition element, and so secrets were kept, fares stolen.

The flat reminds him of the one he used to rent. Though not as clean. The carpet, where once it could have been pink, is brown. It almost crunches underfoot, like walking on compacted sand. And the air is thick with the grease of sausages 'George Foreman'd' to within an inch of their life. Terra's nose turns upward.

"Terra, Bobby. Bobby, Terra," says Mac. "She's a client. He's an old... um... aquain—"

"Work mate," says Bobby.

"Work mate," says Mac. Maybe he'd underestimated their relationship. It was a lonely old life bounty hunting. Perhaps their rivalry had been friendlier than he'd thought. "Nice place."

"Oh piss off," says Bobby, with a wry smile. He throws up the hand not holding his walking stick. Leads them down the hall to the main living room.

They pass the open kitchen door. Mac glances in. It's bad. Like indescribable, Lovecraftian cosmic horror, 'don't look or you might go insane' bad.

"Sit," says Bobby, pointing towards a sofa that has seen far better days. "Can I get you something to eat?" he says, holding up an old pizza box.

Mac declines, and though he would rather not, perches on the corner of the sofa cushion so as not to be rude. He'll have to throw these trousers out. Terra hovers by the living room door, not daring to venture into a room that could give you tetanus just by breathing inside it.

"So what brings you to me?" says Bobby, sitting down in a reclining armchair. On the small end table next to him is a plate of pizza crusts, a pint glass covered in greasy fingerprints, and a battered PlayStation controller.

"Well, may I start by saying I'm sorry. For what happened to you." Mac pauses. "What exactly did happen to you?"

"Well, I tried to slap a bracelet on my assailant's wrist and rip it back off again. You know, to inject the poison. But unfortunately, in my panic, I managed to put my hand in the wrong pocket and pulled out a sausage. I must have looked like a complete twat."

Mac can't disagree. Before he'd been stabbed, Bobby had looked somewhat of an idiot, slapping the wrist of an eight-foot-tall winged ninja with a sausage. Still, it had been the influence behind the move that had saved them all.

He waves a finger. "Not at all. I understood what you were trying to do. It was next-level genius."

"It was." Bobby smiles to himself. "The blade severed a lot of crucial pieces that I won't bother to mention. I lay there for maybe seven hours, bleeding and holding as much of myself in as possible. Then the police showed up thanks to my tracker and whisked me off to hospital." He places his hands on his lap. "I was lucky to see another day. I had bounty hunter insurance, so received payment for what was a workplace injury. Not as much as if I'd caught you, but it has helped."

"I need you to help me find someone," Mac says, cutting straight to the chase. No more time for small talk. On a sofa as filthy as this, small talk will earn you a yeast infection. "One of the guys I was with that night. One of The Church of The Fallen Angels."

Bobby nods. "I might know some things. I've been keeping my ear to the ground. They call me The Oracle now."

Mac suspects perhaps just Bobby calls himself The Oracle now.

"I'm not much good in the field anymore, so I help other bounty hunters with their intelligence for a percentage." He digs his hand down the side of the chair and pulls out a wireless keyboard and mouse. Gives them a little sniff. Shrugs as if to say he's smelt worse corpses, and hits enter. The TV on the wall flickers to show a computer desktop with a picture of a loin clothed barbarian clutching his massive sword. "But first I want something from you."

"Sure, whatever you need," says Terra from the corner.

Bobby looks at her and freezes as if he's never seen a woman before.

"What is it?" says Mac, clicking his fingers to bring Bobby back from the dead.

"I want to learn everything about the ones who did this to me." He pulls aside part of his dressing gown to reveal a little pudding tummy with a large scar running across almost the entirety. The words "Hard To Kill" are tattooed above it.

Mac glances at Terra, reluctant to go into it in front of her. Doesn't want to look like a total nutcase. She nods and raises her eyebrows to tell him to go on.

"I suppose I can tell you everything I know."

It doesn't take long. There's not a lot to say. But laying it all out straight, talking about it for the first time in months, makes him realise that, even now, after having revealed the truth to the world, how little has changed.

"Hm." Bobby taps his finger on his mouse. He's written most of what Mac has just said down in a document on his computer. "And you're telling me the truth?"

"Why does everyone think I'm lying? You know me. I'm not working for BigFood as some sort of super executive marketing guy. I'm not even an actor. Have you seen someone's done me an IMDB profile? They even deep faked me into the latest Marvel movie." He spreads his palms to the ceiling.

"Are you sure that wasn't you?" says Bobby. "I saw it. You weren't great."

"I think I'd know." He pauses. "Everything I said was true. All of it. Everything I've just told you happened to me. And it's true that, if you eat well enough, do a bit of exercise, fail to get hit by a bus before your time, you'll pop inside a chrysalis for a couple of days and come out with wings." Wanting to burn off some of his agitation, he stands and paces to the window. Looks out at the houses and buildings that seem to spread out forever. Takes a deep breath and turns back to face Bobby. "Is that so hard to believe?"

"Well, it is actually," says Bobby. "And the way they've trashed you in the media hasn't helped."

Mac bomps a fist on the back of the sofa. "Of course the media is going to say, 'Macadamia is a fat liar'. It's controlled by the very people who I was trying to bring down. It's so super cliched, isn't it? Why don't people just believe the opposite of what the papers say?"

"That would be equally ridiculous though, wouldn't it?" says Bobby. "But your story of that night does bring us to how I can help you."

"It does?" Terra steps a little further into the room. She'd been silent while Mac told his tale.

He watches her a moment. Wonders what's going on in her head? What she thinks of him now?

"You know where we can find The Church of The Fallen Angels?" Mac skirts around the sofa and perches once more.

"I don't know exactly. But I do know this..." Bobby looks around with shifty eyes, as if anyone could be listening. "There are talks of a secret army. An underground militia. Men and women, tired of being oppressed. And you know who they say is bringing them together?"

"Of course I don't."

Bobby shifts in his seat and brings something up on the screen. It's that picture of Mac. The screenshot from just before the lights had gone off in Studio One. The moment before that Guardian had threatened to butcher three generations of the same family in front of him and let him take the blame.

He puts a hand to his brow. "Don't show me that. I've seen that."

But on closer inspection, the picture is different. It's been altered in some way. Or perhaps a different frame. He doesn't look scared or tired. Somehow he looks angry, defiant. In fact, he looks quite dashing. They've done something with his hair. Smoothed out the bags under his eyes. Minimised the yellow paleness of his skin. It's subtle, but he looks like quite the force to be reckoned with. Have they done something with his biceps? He looks quite good, actually. He gives Terra a look to say, 'hey, check that guy out'. Feels maybe he comes over a bit desperate. Reels it in.

"What is it?" he says.

Bobby expands the picture to fill the screen revealing a title above Mac's image. 'Join The Fight. Join The Army of The Fallen Angels Today.'

"They say it's you bringing everyone together, Mac. It's you."

Where Does Mac Keep His Armies?

Mac studies the digital leaflet thoroughly confused. "I've not been amassing an army. I've been delivering letters in rural Surrey and drinking a fair bit." He screws up his nose. "Mainly drinking, to be honest."

"I knew it," says Bobby, squeezing a fist. He bubbles with infuriating glee, then points a finger at Mac. "I knew Trent Macadamia never had anything like this in him."

"Well," Mac shrugs, sticks his bottom lip out, "never say never, Bobby."

"I'm guessing it's those cultists." Bobby picks up a pizza crust from the plate by his chair. Dips it into a plastic tub of mayo secreted down by his side. "How many of them did you say there was? Three?"

Mac nods.

"And this one is Enki," says Terra. She moves to the screen and taps a dark shape in the background of the leaflet. You can just make out Pete, Dave, and Terry there with Nige's granddaughter.

Bobby taps away at his keyboard. "I tried to find what I could about each of them, but there's not much there." The arrow for his mouse pointer circles Terry's face. "That one is somewhat of an enigma. Can't find birth records, or addresses, only that he worked a couple of places as a chef."

Terra glances up at Mac, but answers Bobby. "He's been missing a long time."

"Where did you get this?" Mac steps closer to the screen, fascinated by this stoic version of himself staring into the camera as if he's about to charge across a battlefield.

"A friend sent it. A lot of the bounty hunters have received one. I guess they think if they sign us up, they'll have less trouble to deal with if things go wrong."

He sits up pressing his chest out. "We're also the best investigators and fighters in the country. I've spoken to a few of the others and general consensus is we're in."

"Why's that? Isn't this the sort of thing you'd usually want to stop? Isn't there still a price on their heads?"

"There is, and it's a big one, but there's a reason we become bounty hunters."

"Not the money?" says Mac, but he knows somewhere deep inside that's not it.

"Yeah right, we're all out here kicking back in our luxury mansions..." Bobby snorts and holds two hands up to show off his one-bedroom flat. "We like the idea of fighting for what's right. Making a difference to someone in our own little way. We're not police - we're not nice, or in some cases, corrupt enough for that. We're chaotic good. We want to live our lives on our terms, and if someone is stepping on us, we don't hesitate to tell them to back off."

"So what are they doing, then?" Mac says, gesturing at the flyer.

"There are meetings. People who believed you. People galvanised by the story Kenneth Bailey and Victoria Desdemona told. It's a minority, sure. Or at least it's a minority who are happy to admit they believe. But there are enough. I'm guessing you've seen the division from wherever you've been hiding."

"Mm." One way to keep a population in check is have it fight with itself. If you have one half constantly ridiculing the other for their beliefs, then they can't unite. They police themselves.

Like hundreds of conspiracy theories that have come before, the efficacy of vaccinations, the shape of the planet, the existence of lizard people beneath the earth controlling everything above the surface, his little stunt has bred a conspiracy. But this time the tin foil hat wearing crack-pots who dub themselves critical thinkers, and anyone who doesn't go along with their ideals, that ever so grating term, sheeple, believe it's just a failed marketing ploy created by Di Blasio to sell more paste in a tube. And to be honest, that is what it looks like.

The truth, on this occasion, is the crazier idea. But there are some who believe. Maybe there are others. Normal, everyday people.

Unfortunately, it's the ones who shout the loudest who are heard. Those that do believe him don't make a big fuss about it.

And the media and the government do nothing to quell the fierce online rivalries. They don't say, "ok, some of us believe different things, but let's not fight about it, let's fight for truth," they say, "Oooo, isn't *that* half of the population stupid?" And the half they call stupid seems to flip daily.

"Where do these groups meet? Who runs them?" says Terra.

"I've not had the chance to go yet. I was considering it. Knowing what I know about The Guardians. Knowing that I'm one of the few that has faced them and lived, I'm probably well placed to guide them." He looks smug for a moment. "The leaflets have event times coded into them. There's one in two days. 9 p.m. The location doesn't get pinged across until about an hour before. It'll be local though. Somewhere in London."

Terra looks at Mac with hopeful fists clenched before her. He gives her a willing thumbs up.

"Well, we should definitely go?" he says. Although he is the face of the organisation, he wants to see what's going on from the ground level. Doesn't want to draw attention. "Can you get us in?"

Bobby nods. "I don't think there's any sort of invite only policy. They are trying to grow the membership. But they're trying to keep it anonymous. You can't wear anything branded. Nothing vibrant. And you have to take a balaclava. One that only shows your eyes."

"Why?"

"Isn't it obvious? They can't have someone going along and pointing out others who have been too."

"No, of course not. Thanks Bobby. We'll meet here. Saturday. 8 o' clock."

With a plan confirmed, they say their goodbyes, and Mac and Terra head back to the car.

"That's a better start than expected," she says, smiling as a chilly wind blows through her dark hair.

It is. Way better.

He looks out over the drab area of tarmac, those cold grey blocks of flats, and nods. Something tells him it'll be down hill from here, though.

Squillionaires

"You think Enki will be there at the meeting?" Terra says as she starts the car.

"Might be. Bobby didn't seem to know much more than he was telling us. I don't think your brother is likely to be the brains behind this little operation."

The Church of The Fallen Angels hadn't been the brightest bunch, but perhaps they weren't the top dogs. Could it be Nige running the show? Or Victoria and Kenneth?

He checks the clock. "There's a Travelodge around the corner. Think they've got a harvester. We can get a room each and something to eat."

"We'll stay at mine," she says, pulling away from the kerb.

After a few minutes, he breaks the silence.

"I need you to tell me a little more about what's going on here."

She turns her chin towards him to show she's listening, but maintains her focus on the road.

"So, Terry is your brother, you're looking for him, and I assume, you being willing to pay extra to find him quickly, means you have a very good reason... so I feel you're not being completely open with me."

"I'm not."

"Oh." He'd expected her to say something else. "Well, maybe you should be completely open with me?"

She glances at him as they creep through the London traffic. "I don't think you'd like what I had to say." She turns unsure eyes on him, then looks back to the road.

"Try me." What can be worse than what he already knows about the state of the world?

She purses her lips for a moment, then begins. "He was only a boy when we lost him. Very young. Seven or eight. We all thought him gone for good, if you know what I mean." Her eyes gloss over and in that moment, he sees the sadness on her face. The beginnings of wrinkles around her eyes. Furrows ploughed by tears.

Seven or eight? That meant they had lost Terry at least twenty years ago. He must look very different now. How can she be sure the person she'd seen lingering in the background on a television screen is actually him? What if it's not? Twenty years is a long time. People and faces change.

He tries to think of a tactful way to ask how sure she is, but she looks at him and reads the question on his face.

"I know it's him." She doesn't look annoyed. "His real name is Enki. We used spend a lot of time together. Just me and him. My Dad would sometimes call us Terri. You know, like a silly duo name. I guess he took to it to fit in better..." She trails off. Clears her throat. Stares out through the windscreen. "I just want to find him quickly. We've been apart for so long."

Mac watches her carefully. There's still something she's not saying.

He expects there's no point in pushing it. "And how did you find me?"

"Last week, when those guys doxxed you."

He inwardly groans. "You saw those pictures?"

She tightens her lips. "Yeah. I'm not going to judge. We've all woken up in a bush."

He lays a finger over his lips, his perception of her updated. Oh, have we?

Not long later, she pulls the car up to a smart looking residential building; expensive apartments surrounded by gentrification and luxury. This can't be where she lives. He'd once poked his head into a cafe on this road when in dire need of a breakfast after a late night working a case, checked out the menu, and more importantly the prices, and decided that even though he could claim the meal back on his tax, it kind of defeated the purpose if you had to take on a whole new case just to pay the expenses of the first.

"Here?" he says, examining the tower's glittering frontage with an impressed elevation of the nostrils.

She pulls the car up to a space just in front. A man pops up from behind a small booth situated kerbside. He wears a smart dark suit and black shirt. He is tall and slim, imposing.

"Miss Terra," he says, opening the door and offering her a hand.

She takes it and steps out. "Thank you." She moves around to the back of the car.

"I'll get that for you," he says, rushing to beat her to the boot.

She looks as if she's not comfortable with him doing it, but he is very insistent.

Another man stood in front of a set of revolving doors leading into the building, hurries over and takes their bags. One in each hand. Mac can't help but be impressed. He had struggled to carry his own in two.

Both the valet and the bagman look very similar. Same dark cropped hair. Same tall, slender build.

The valet gives Mac a stare, a head to toe once over, with a face as flat and as hard as rolled concrete. Then, somehow, without taking his death-ray eyes from Mac's, climbs into the car and pulls away.

The bagman hot foots it towards the revolving door. Terra follows with wide strides towards the apartment building.

Mac notices for the first time her unusual taste in flared trousers. Like really flared, as if her knees had their own special little skirts that hid her feet almost completely.

He'd never got fashion. And every year that went by, he felt further and further removed from it, which is why he'd gone safe with the private investigator starter pack - trench coat, wide-brimmed hat, shirt, suit trousers, tie, and all important sneakers, for a quick getaway.

He jogs to keep up. "You live here?" he says, catching up to her as she pushes through the revolving door. He jumps into her segment. "This place is... expensive."

"I know. I own it."

The foyer is large. Impressive. It stretches up two-storeys. The floors are heavy marble cut through with colourful patterns that writhe off in all directions as if someone had frozen a bed of snakes in transparent resin beneath their feet.

The bagman holds the doors of an elevator open for them as they cross the room.

Once inside, they ascend in silence. Nineteenth floor. Not the top, but close.

The doors open, and the bagman leads the way. Stops at the second door. Places Mac's bag down. Takes a key card attached to a retractable cord on his belt and swipes the lock, then holds the door wide. She thanks him.

Mac nods, tries a friendly smile, but the bagman's face, like the valet's, remains unimpressed.

He follows them into a large open plan lounge and kitchen. The apartment is dark and tranquil. A thick humidity hangs in the air. Like a cave. Somewhere, he can hear the trickle of running water, which he assumes is intentional and not a dire plumbing fault. The decor is lush. Large plants stand in corners and cover shelves. Curtains of leaves and fronds dangle from walls and sprawl on surfaces. The windows that take up one wall have rollers pulled down so no sunlight can come through. The only thing Mac can liken it to is a trip he and his mother and sister had taken to The Rainforest cafe, but a thousand times more luxuriant.

In the centre of the room is a large corner sofa placed opposite a series of screens. A grand parody of Bobby Feta's home.

The smell that permeates is interesting. He can't quite place it. It's like fresh soil. Pleasant though. Clean.

"Welcome," she says, placing her bag on the kitchen counter.

"Nice place," he says, meaning it this time.

"Oh, piss off."

His heart skips a beat, then she gives him a playful wink, before turning to the bagman and thanking him again.

Jokes aside, Mac admires how polite she is, not like other London high-fliers he's come into contact with in the past.

"We are going to a meeting tomorrow," she says to the porter. "We need two full face coverings. Any chance you can organise that?"

A brief frown crosses his brow and he glances at Mac, but without question, he nods.

"And..." She looks back. "Trent, are you hungry?"

"I am."

"Could you arrange some suitable food?" She tips her head towards Mac as if to say 'something this idiot will eat'.

The bagman nods and leaves in continued silence.

Mac jumps over the back of the corner sofa and digs in. "So what's our plan until Saturday, then? Chill out? Catch a movie? Not really much point in doing any more detective work until the meeting. We know where Terry is likely to be, we just have to wait." He folds his hands behind his head and leans back.

"You're not going to lie around here if I'm paying you £500 a day," she says, taking a small water vaporiser and giving something that looks like a hunk of reconstituted sawdust covered in tiny mushrooms a spray. "We're gonna get settled in tonight while we wait for the food. Then tomorrow I'm going to look for my older brother and find out why he sent those guys after me. Can you tell me anything more about them?"

"Not really sure." He hadn't got the best look. He'd been too busy launching laundry detergent and running for his life. "They were a bit small. Wobbly." He sits up. "I'd seen them at the pub, too. Outside. I thought they were drunk. They were coming at me." He moves a clawed hand sharply towards his own face.

Her forehead creases into a frown. "That doesn't sound like my brother's men." She gives her fungus another few sprays. "I'll talk to him tomorrow. He'll know." She moves to the front door to retrieve his bag.

"That's heavy." He stands and rushes to meet her. "Am I coming with you? To see your brother."

She picks it up with ease. "No. He wasn't keen on me coming to find you. It'll just annoy him."

"So what should I do in the meantime?" He takes his bag and holds it down by his feet.

"Investigate some other avenues. I'm sure you have ideas."

Right now he doesn't. "Oh yeah, lots."

"Your room is up here." She steps towards a short corridor leading away from the living space. Opens the door onto a small bedroom. "You get settled. Food won't be long."

He drags his bag after her. Almost trips over it trying not to touch her as he brushes past in the slim corridor. He tries to apologise, but just splutters with embarrassment.

She giggles and leaves him to his room.

Inside is a bed, chest of drawers, and an en suite with shower. He could do with a wash. Yesterday's pub session and blow to the head have left him feeling quite groggy. He swears he can smell the beer leaking out of his pores.

When he re-emerges dressed and fresh, the food has already arrived. The smell calls to his rumbling stomach. It answers with a groan.

"It's funny," his mouth waters as he dumps a snarl of greasy noodles on to his plate, "falling off my bike might have wobbled my brains, but I could have sworn there was a bowl of worms on your table back at the cottage."

She laughs, covering her full mouth. "What are you talking about?"

"Oh, nothing." He changes the subject. "Terry liked noodles. I think they were his favourite food."

"Really?" She smiles, once more covering her mouth. "Tell me about him." Her eyes stare into his across the small kitchen island where they sit. Brown paper bags loaded with great smelling Chinese food stand between them.

"I only knew him a few days. He's nice. Selfless." He remembers Terry on the table at the church firing his rifle, and again willing to stay with Alan so that they could all get away. He wants to say more but feels nervous talking about The Guardians in front of her. People treat him differently if he mentions it. Like he's plagued. "Terry always looked out for his friends."

Her eyes shine a little more under the bright kitchen light that hangs above them. She looks down at her plate. "That sounds like him. He was a good boy. I can't imagine what it's been like for him, alone all these years."

There's a moment's silence while they eat. Mac wants to fill it, but for once doesn't know what to say.

"And this church, they were good to him?"

He nods. "They were like a family of lost souls looking out for one another."

"I can't wait to meet him."

"Your other brother, why would he send people after you?"

She rolls her eyes. "Gaspar is just being overprotective. I don't get out much, really. He doesn't think it's safe for people in our situation to go out on quests looking for little brothers that may or may not be."

"Your situation?"

She holds her hands up to indicate the room, and furthermore, the building where they currently sit.

"Ah, right, squillionaires."

She laughs again. The sound lights a little fire inside of him. A feeling he could become addicted to.

"But you're sure it's Terry, er, Enki?"

"Positive, and I think Gaspar knows it, too."

Fairy City

Lily doesn't have many things so packing is quick. Just her toothbrush and Bear. It's lucky because there's not much space in the back of the mini-bus.

They leave their clothes. Mr Godfrey has brought new ones. Grey trousers. Grey long sleeve tops. Grey shoes. She and Finn had needed to change before they'd left. They look a bit boring — she prefers her blue cat T-shirt — but they feel soft. The shoes are funny, squidgy.

There are eight other children already inside the van. Her and Finn makes ten. The other kids wear the grey clothes, too.

She hopes they aren't all going to the same Mummy and Daddy. She doesn't really want to share. She's done enough sharing at the home to last her a lifetime. But maybe Finn could come with her. It'd be nice to know someone at least. She might get nervous otherwise. She touches his hand while he sleeps next to her in the van. She's older than him so she has to look after him. He might be scared, but she's not scared.

She hasn't been on such a long drive in forever. The other kids are all asleep, but she's too excited. She's never been this far from the home. They don't go out much. She doesn't get to see the roads at night. The streetlights. The passing cars as they whizz by. She watches the race of the rain drops as they judder and slide down her window. Smiles when a big one crashes into a small one, picks it up, and they speed down the glass together. It makes her happy, but she doesn't know why.

Mr Godfrey sits up front with another man, Mr Ackerman. Mr Ackerman drives. They don't talk much. They don't smile much either.

She's not sure she likes Mr Ackerman. He'd called her a bit short. Mr Godfrey had said, "yes, but she's getting old." Which had been a funny thing to say. She was only five and a half. That's nearly grown up, but it's not old.

Ahead is London. She knows it's London from the TV. It has the tallest buildings she's ever seen and there are millions of bright lights. It's so pretty. Sparkly, like a fairy city. All it's missing is toadstool houses. She smiles. Imagine toadstool houses as big as the London skyscrapers. That would be fun. She'd love to live in a fairy kingdom.

"Are we nearly there yet?" she hisses to Mr Godfrey in the front, hoping not to wake Finn who's head rests on her shoulder.

"Not far," says Mr Godfrey without turning. Then he looks back. His eyes travel over each of the sleeping kids before stopping on her. "Fifteen minutes, maybe. Are you excited?" The streetlights cut a diagonal line across his face hiding his eyes. His smiling mouth seems to jump as the lights pass.

"I am."

"Close your eyes," he says. His voice is very quiet. "I'll wake you when we get there."

She does.

Terra?

Mac wakes early. Automatically. His brain stuck in the sleep pattern of a postman.

He lies in the guest bedroom and ponders his new predicament. It's funny how quickly things can change. One minute you're living a provincial life, the next whisked away on an adventure.

He thinks of his mother. Is she happy with him now that he's out here? Is this what she wanted?

He hopes so.

His bed rests alongside the blinded window in his room. He opens the shutters. A shot of vertigo runs like lightning from the tips of his toes to the top of his head. The waking city stretches out before him. A pale, clear blue sky in the East suggests a beautiful, crisp winter's morning is on its way. A single plane leaves behind a silvery white contrail. The streets below move slow like a gentle river. From up here he can imagine the low call of the pigeon, the hum of the automatic street sweeper, the familiar astringent, cloying odour of exhaust and concrete and all things man made.

It's inspiring. A new day. A new start. He thinks of the story Nige told him about the dog on the nail, and how it fits with what Mum had said the night before last. He was comfortable at home in Ripley, but he would never be happy unless he got up and made himself so.

This is exactly what he needs.

He sits up and reaches for his bag by the side of the bed. Takes the fresh notepad from the outside pocket. Slips an unused pencil from the ring binding and lies back down. Taps it on his nose while he goes over what he knows.

More than one mystery surrounds the case.

The first is simple. Is Terry Enki?

He hasn't quite decided if he believes they are the same yet. He doesn't hold much hope. What if Terry is just a figure whose image Terra has spun in her mind to look like someone she lost long ago?

Either way, he has to find him to answer the question… and get paid.

Then there's the army of the fallen angels.

What are they up to? Are Terry and Dave and Pete behind this new underground movement? If so, will they all be there on Saturday? Or perhaps the organisation has grown beyond its originators? There's a chance, after having seen last year's show, someone else is using The Church of The Fallen Angels' name.

And the final case - who is Terra?

What did he know about her? Not much. Despite trying to get the information out of her over dinner, she had been particularly cagey about her origins. It's clear she comes from wealth. Her family were connected. But how far up did those connections go? She didn't seem familiar with The Guardians. But that didn't mean her family wasn't in some way linked.

And she could fight. She'd saved him in the alleyway when James and John had ambushed him. Was that important? Or was it just a case of rich kids excelling at everything because they had the best tutors money could buy?

He has decided he trusts her. Can't quite put why into words. But she seems… nice, genuine. He hopes he's not being swayed by that slight kindling of warmth he's beginning to feel towards her, but, if he's being honest, he has a sneaking suspicion that might play a part. It's difficult to distrust someone you fancy a little bit.

The way she'd spoken about her older brother suggested a split in the family. A divide potentially caused by the loss of their younger sibling. Perhaps there was some blame held there. But which way did it go? Could she be the one out looking for Enki because she felt in someway responsible?

He writes this all down, populating three separate spider diagrams in his notepad. It wouldn't do to lose track of his thoughts. And with so much going on, he might.

The hand holding the pencil tremors as he sits there resting the pad on his knees. He watches it. Tries to steady it with his mind. It's been a while since his last drink, although while his head is on task, he doesn't want it. Edges are becoming more defined again. Perhaps being active — doing what he does best — is what he needed all along.

He opens his laptop. How can he find more about her?

Doesn't know her last name so can't search it. Should really have asked. Chalks this failing up to being out of practice.

Finds the address of the building. Finds the name. *Who owns Ashnah Court?*

Ashnah and Ashnah Holdings Ltd.

He does a little more digging. The holding company is linked to a tech company called Source. He's heard of it. It's big. Multi-billion pound big. They built robots and communication systems, as well as planet friendly building materials using fungus. They'd been groundbreaking at one point. Not so much now.

He trawls the company's records. A man named Saurian Adler had started it in the '80s.

It's strange. If Terra owned the building like she said, then what did she have to do with Source? Surely, if you or your parents had the sort of money and resources that came from owning a global tech giant, then how could you ever just lose track of a family member? Why hadn't they contacted the news? Why no record of a global search?

Could she be lying to him about how Terry disappeared?

A groggy sort of nausea sits in his stomach that at first he'd put down to lack of sleep. But maybe it's some sort of hangover. He's coming down after months of hitting it hard.

He keeps digging. Finds an interesting article from 2014, around the time she said they'd lost Terry. It says that the CEO and founder, Saurian Adler, passed away and the company was sold. It doesn't say who to.

There's a link to another article. This one talks of Terra and Gaspar Adler. It says a few weeks after their father's passing, before they could claim their inheritance, both were killed in a fire.

He stops reading and stares out of the window. What? A question he's asked himself countless times in the last twenty-four hours. If Terra wasn't Terra, then who was she? But if she was, then what did that mean?

He scratches his head. His hair has grown rather shaggy over the last few months.

The news article must be wrong. And, besides, he's not being paid to find out who his client is. He just needs to find Terry. Doesn't matter who's doing the paying, as long as he gets paid.

He dresses and leaves his room. Moves to the kitchen. It's quiet. The sounds of the city outside dampened to an almost imperceptible hum by the altitude and what he expects is expensive sound proofing.

He opens several cupboards before he finds a big enough glass and runs it under the tap. Takes a long refreshing drink until his head feels like it's about to burst.

A piece of paper is stuck to the black fridge with a toadstool magnet. A note.

"Trent, I've popped out to see if I can find Gaspar. Should be back by late afternoon. I've left a per diem for you on the counter. Dial zero on the phone if you want a lift somewhere."

He leans to the side and sees a wodge of notes. Nice. Looks like she's good for the money, whoever she is.

He puts all he's learnt to the side. The sooner he can find Terry, the sooner he can get paid and the sooner he can move on. Maybe he should take the day to find out a little more about the army of the fallen angels before the meeting on Saturday.

The old church would be the place to start. Time to unearth some of that deep-rooted trauma.

Take Me To Church

"Wait here, will you?" says Mac, as he climbs from the car outside the old church.

The driver — the valet from the previous night — grunts to suggest he will.

"Good man."

It's strange to be back. Not just at this particular building, but in his old neighbourhood. His office was only a short walk around the corner. His flat, not far from there.

A '*Sold*' sign stands outside the block of flats to the left of the church. Alan and his boys had owned it. Pete and Dave must have sold up.

Across the road are more residential blocks.

The church itself looks as worn and disused as it had those months back. Creepy, he'd called it. But it had been home to a loving family. A group of guys put through the grinder, making the best of what they had.

He pushes the gate. It's rusted shut. With a little extra force, something cracks and it shrieks open.

Yellow police tape criss-crosses the large wooden doors, faded and hanging loose. Must have been here since that night. He doubts anyone has been here in a while. What could the police do? No insurance meant no case, and if no one was paying them to investigate, then the place would be left, forgotten. Another abandoned building littering London's already overdeveloped streets.

He pulls the tape away. Screws it into a ball and throws it to the long grass that surrounds the pathway. Pushes the door open. To his surprise, it's unlocked. Saves him having to pick it.

He steps inside. The air is stale. Still. Dust particles stirred up by the winter breeze through the open doors drift in shafts of sunlight that stab through the broken stained glass windows.

Gloomy shadows hug the corners of the room. He swallows. Last time he was here, those shadows hid the creatures that had haunted his nightmares ever since.

He drags the door open behind him, hoping that more light will come through. It helps a little.

The statue of Saint Michael stands with sword raised to his right. Beneath it, a dark stain where Bobby had fallen. He'd lost a lot of blood. His tattoo wasn't an exaggeration. Bobby 'Flippin' Feta was indeed very hard to kill.

Graffiti covers the walls. Gang signs and tags of locals he was once familiar with. Smashed beer bottles and other assorted trash litters the floor. It's sad to see the place gone to ruin like this. A place where a good man had died. A place where people far braver than him had fought the enemy of every man, woman, and child...

He walks to the centre of the room. Past the overturned oak table where they had shared great food and great company. The table they had used as a shield. He considers standing it back up. Doesn't.

The bank of servers has gone. Either taken as evidence or ripped out and sold by local hoodlums. The image of the angel has been defaced. A massive pair of blue boobs sprayed on her chest. A triangular penis comes off her head like a party hat.

He sighs. Why are they always triangular?

What did he think he would find here? Did he think Pete and Dave and Terry would just be here sitting at the table eating stew waiting for him? It's been so long, anything of use has been stolen or broken.

He crosses the room, heading for the stairs leading down towards the basketball court. They plunge into pitch black. He takes out his phone. Turns on the torch. Begins his descent. The light surrounds him with a circle of white. In it, he can see the door at the bottom stands wide open. Black, ashy stains cover its back and some of the wall. Had the fire been left to burn or was this a direct result of Alan's explosion?

He steps through. The cracked and burnt court crunches beneath his feet. The room smells of smoke and ash. He covers his mouth.

He swings his torch around. In the centre of the room is a sort of crater. Darker than the rest. The point of detonation.

Alan had been so brave. Did Mac have that in him? Could he give it all up for his family? He didn't so.

The JCB stands like a sentinel by the back wall. Bucket up. Melted remnants of the basketball net dangle from it. He crosses towards it. Drawn by the memories of their escape. Not knowing what he'll find.

He passes the digger. Ash and months of neglect have discoloured its yellow chassis, but other than that, it seems unaffected by the detonation. The rear two tyres are buried in earth. The roof of the tunnel behind having collapsed around it.

To the right is an opening. Small and rough. Maybe something The Guardians had dug to try to give chase?

But, as he kneels to inspect, the cool dirt crumbles between his fingers leaving a hint of moisture that suggests perhaps the hole has been dug more recently. He holds his torch at arm's length. Beyond is a corridor under the earth. Another part of the catacombs. Brown bricks make up the floor and walls. It continues out of sight in the blackness.

He takes a deep breath and looks back towards the charred basketball court. Last time he'd been here, he'd been with people. And he'd been running from something. Perhaps if he hadn't, he would have realised how creepy the tunnels were.

He directs his hearing down the hallway for a moment. Nothing. Although it's scary, there isn't anyone down here except him. And it's not like he believes in the supernatural. No such thing as ghosts or ghouls. The monsters in the night are tangible and real and there's no reason for them to be anywhere near here. Nothing else can scare him.

It's a tight squeeze, so he crawls through on hands and knees into the catacombs. The smokey ash smell changes somewhat. Damp and dirt overriding it. A more ancient odour.

The brick beneath his feet crunches a little as he stands. The sound sizzles off down the echoing hall ahead. If there were anyone down here, they'd hear him coming.

He could either go left down a dark corridor or straight on down another. He holds his light close to the ground, looking for footprints or something to suggest where whoever had dug the hole had gone.

There's nothing obvious, but there is something. Each brick here is so old, so caked in dirt, he can see a difference between those that haven't been stepped on in decades and those that have. The difference is slight. More a lightening of colour than anything. Many criss-crossing lines of faint footprints lead straight ahead. Nothing to the left. He has nothing else to do until he sees Terra again tonight so decides to follow them, if only to warm up his investigative skills.

He steps forward. After a few metres, seeing the difference in colour becomes second nature. He takes a left a little further on and then passes through a wider space. He is so intent on following the marks he doesn't realise there's a door ahead until he almost walks into it.

It's wooden. Splintering. The foot eaten away by the damp rising from the floor. He tries the handle and it opens into another room.

He enters some sort of storage area roughly five metres by ten. Built into the opposite wall is a brick archway that looks like a fireplace.

To his right is a small single mattress on the floor. It's uncovered. No blanket. No pillow. Did someone sleep down here? Buried away from everything in the dark? From what he knew about the Camden catacombs, there were lots of routes in. Someone could have been living here right under the cultists's noses.

There's a wooden chair next to a table with lots of little knick-knacks on it. Tucked away in the corner and facing the wall is another smaller chair. Perhaps one for a child. There's also a bookcase by the bed.

The bookcase is stuffed full. Some sections of it are two books deep. With more resting on top. He steps closer. Removes one. '*Peepo*'. A children's book. One his mother had read to him when he was young.

There are other kid's books. Then more adult ones. Cookbooks, biographies, all sorts of fiction. A seemingly random selection. All thumbed to within an inch of their lives.

He moves to the table to see what's there. A handful of bottle caps. A few old coins. Five little figures made from screwed up tinfoil. Two tall and slim, and three smaller ones. The foil is brittle and has that off-yellow colour that comes with age, and when Mac scoops the larger two up, they disintegrate in his hand. They look like they've been here for some time.

Also on the table is a faded plastic bucket and a kid's spade. The spade is broken and worn. Dirty. Too small to be the tool used to dig the tunnel into the basketball court under the church.

He flips out his pad and starts a fresh page. Lists the things in the room. Is it connected to anything? Doubtful, but worth bearing in mind.

He writes the thoughts as they come to him.

Possibly someone homeless living in the catacombs near the church. With a child? Did they dig into the church by accident?

He crosses the room to look at the other side. There's a pile of old clothes. He does a quick sift. An assortment of male and female and adult and child. Though that doesn't tell him much. He supposes if you have nothing, just staying warm is enough.

He taps his pencil on his lips. It's all very unusual, but not something uncommon. London can be a tough place to live. Better to be underground where it's safe and warm than above on those long rainy nights where anyone could pass you by. Especially if you have a child with you.

What was it they called homeless people who lived underground? Mole people. He lets out a short laugh that reverberates under the fireplace. The things people come up with.

The only place he hasn't checked is under the darkened archway opposite the entrance. He flashes his phone light beneath. The archway slopes downward for quite a way. Within a few metres, the brick floor gives way to bare earth.

He steps over the lip of bricks, stooping to fit under the arch. Crouches low and moves along the decline. The space soon narrows to not much wider than his shoulders. The temperature drops, and when both his head and shoulders scrape the ceiling and walls, kicking up decades of what could be toxic dust and grime, he stops.

"What the hell am I doing?" he whispers to himself. His voice reverberating, returning as a vicious hiss. All he can see ahead is the brown descent into the earth. This is a waste of time.

He tries to turn but is wedged, and for a second panic nearly overcomes him in a wave like so many chattering rats covering his flesh. One step at a time, he backs his way up to a place where he can turn. With visions of groping, icy fingers chasing him from the shadows behind, he breaks into a run back up to the little room.

He takes one last look at that little chair in the corner. The single mattress. And leaves.

In Da Club, Again

Terra comes back around eight. He hears her key in the lock and she calls his name as she enters. He likes that she calls him Trent. It makes him feel more like a human being.

'Mac' is so playground.

He steps out of his room. She stands with the porter who is loaded with arms full of bags from clothes shops.

"We're going out," she says. She thanks the bagman, who leaves.

"Are we?"

"My brother has been eluding me all day. We're going to his club tonight in Mayfair. He'll be there." She lets her hair down. The colour is almost blue in the kitchen light.

"But you said that I'd annoy him."

With a devious flash of the eyes, she smiles. "That's the idea." She ties her hair back up into a ponytail. "How was your day?"

He eases closer, giving himself a moment to wonder what it would be like if this were a romantic relationship. Thinks about the things he's missed by never really having one. Him working a case all day. Her working her cool job all day. Both returning home tired but looking for fun. Heading out to a swanky club in Mayfair.

"Good thanks, hun..." he says, half-joking. Instantly regretting it. "... gry? Cus I missed lunch. Did you miss lunch? I could go for anything. Chinese? Indian? Pies? Oh, I've had such a busy day."

He sprays words like bullets, trying to put enough of them between the 'hun' and this moment in time, hoping to water it down to nothing, to scrub it from the record, then moves to lean on the kitchen countertop. "You?"

Slick.

"Busy? Where did you go?" she says, brushing over his embarrassed waffle.

"I went to the church. The place where they used to hang out."

She leans both elbows on the worktop opposite. Rests her head on the heels of her hands, mimicking him. "And did you find anything?"

"Most of their stuff is gone. Either seized by the police or stolen." His hands begin to shake again so he stuffs them in his pockets before she can see. "It's been months. I don't know what I expected to find. They were hardly going to be there."

Maybe he'd gone to refresh the memory. Or to prove to himself that what had happened had actually happened. When enough people call you a liar to your face, you start to believe that maybe you're just making things up. Your experiences and memories take on a different hue. Like the recollection of a dream, or something you saw on TV.

"Still, worth a look though?" she says, clearly sensing the drop in his mood. She raises her eyebrows. "Worth the money I'm paying."

He blows air through pursed lips and nods like a jackhammer. "T'oh yeah."

"Good." She claps her hands, and does a quick big fish, little fish, cardboard box. "Now, clubbing." She bends and dumps one of the clothes bags on the counter top. "I didn't know your size, but you can't go wearing that." She leans a disapproving nod at his loose-fitting suit trousers and terrible shirt and tie combo.

He strokes his tie. "I'll have you know, this is the height of private investigator fashion."

She smiles. "I'm sure it is, which is another reason you can't go looking like that."

After the last club he'd been to, an under 18s night in Camden, and the location of a multiple homicide, Mac has since decided going clubbing in your late twenties is a bad idea.

But he's interested to meet this Gaspar.

Her driver, the valet from outside her building, drops them off right outside.

Mac wears clothes he couldn't afford in his wildest dreams. A pair of black jeans, with so many rips he looks like he's been mauled by a lion, stick to his legs like clingfilm. On top, a navy silk shirt, and a dark, slim fitting suit jacket. The name on the tag by his neck isn't one he's heard of. He feels a bit like burger meat dressed as Japanese kobe.

She wears a deep blue sort of catsuit thing that hugs her slender frame on the top half, but flares out like her usual trousers from around mid-thigh. And, despite the average level of attractiveness in the queue being way above the norm, he can't take his eyes from her as they wait to enter.

"Why didn't you just call him up? Get us on the VIP list?" he says, shivering. For some idiot fashion reason, the buttons on his shirt end mid-cleavage. He wishes he'd brought his hoody. He also wishes, looking at some of the other men in the queue, that he'd spent more of his life doing press-ups. Maybe he should hoick up his trouser leg to reveal a little of that fabled postman's calf. It's poppin'.

"I didn't want to give him the opportunity to bale on us. If he knew we were coming, he might find an excuse not to be here. He does that."

Mac raises an eyebrow. "So you guys are close, then?"

"Hardly. Gaspar's a bit of a prick, to be honest."

He laughs. "You're good fun, you are."

Her eyes dazzle. "I am."

"Ah, Miss Terra," says the doorwoman as they come to the end of the queue. She glances past her at Mac, her face unimpressed. He rubs a hand across the back of his neck, feeling somewhat out of place.

"Does Mr Adler know you're joining us tonight?" continues the bouncer.

"No. I'd like to surprise him if possible."

The doorwoman nods and ushers them inside.

The club is huge. Yeah, it's sophisticated, with its giant chandeliers dominating the centre of the room, and stunning aerialists swinging and spinning on hoops suspended from the ceiling, and yeah, it's stylish, with its blue and white

LED lighting and bright strobes flashing like alarms through discharging smoke cannons, but people getting down and dirty on the dance floor always look the same to him despite the level of expense on show.

Once again, sweating gyrators sweat and gyrate on sweaty gyrators at every turn.

The music is percussive, tribal. Like an electronic version of what he'd expect cavemen to dance to. A blend of rhythms that resonates somewhere deep inside, making him want to lower his brow and say, "ook", before grabbing a fallen tree branch ready to do some real clubbing. His head bops in response.

"We'll head straight upstairs." She points up to a small viewing gallery seemingly suspended above the extensive lighting rig. It's hard to see with the flashing strobes and swarming lasers. "We need to get up there fast before someone alerts him."

She pushes her way through the crowds towards a flight of stairs blocked by a bouncer dressed all in black. He nods when he sees her, steps aside, and holds out a hand to show she's free to go up. The bouncer glares at Mac, giving him the feeling that he's stepping past the human equivalent of a hungry rottweiler on a short leash.

He smiles and says, "Hi," which comes out as a squeak, then drops his head and follows Terra upstairs.

Another man in black stops her at the top. They exchange words while Mac stands behind her on the stairs. He can't hear a thing they say. She doesn't look happy.

She turns back to face him. "He knows we're here. One of his minions must have radioed up."

She talks once more to the man who leads them towards a lift door. He pulls out a keycard, holds it against a reader and the door opens. It's dark inside. Mac guesses so as not to disturb the carefully curated club atmosphere. He holds the doors open as Terra steps in, follows her and allows the door to shut, which severely dampens the sound of the music.

Before the lift rises, the lights come on. Mirrors cover the walls.

She stands in front of him, facing away. She is his height. Though the way she stands means the top of her head comes to just below his nose. He can smell her from here. Something floral. A scent that relaxes him and makes the hairs on his arms prickle.

For a split second, looking at the pair of them there in the reflection, he has another flash of what it might be like for this to be a genuine moment in his life. Him, a nice lady, dressed in fine clothes, spending the night out somewhere together, drinking and dancing like exciting people with exciting lives.

An opportunity missed. A potential unfulfilled.

A cavern of regret opens deep inside of him.

Somewhere in the back of his mind, he's always had this thought that one day he would be cool, one day, he would start doing things for himself. Dressing well. Styling his hair how he wanted. Getting his own place with nice furniture and nice things. Going places that others only ever dreamt about. Like here.

One day.

One day, when he had the money and the time and the courage, he would be something... special.

But every year that passes, the chance to be something special slips further from his grasp, not nearer, and he tries to convince himself that being special isn't really what real people do. This sort of well manicured exciting life is only seen in films and carefully constructed social media posts. And behind all of that, he tells himself, people are just as unhappy as him.

But he still yearns for it.

He notices she's looking at him in the reflection, then spots his own expression. He has a pained frown of discontent on his face.

"Are you ok?" She raises an eyebrow. "Did dinner disagree with you?"

"I'm not trying to hold something in," he says. Nothing digestive anyway.

"Good. This lift is airtight."

He laughs, and that regret crumbles away. She smiles at him in the mirror. They hold each other's eye for a moment before she looks away.

The lift stops. The door slides open, leading into the viewing area he had seen from below. One wall is all glass. It overlooks the club. The carpet is plush, white, spotless. If someone were to pass him a cup of coffee here, he'd spill it immediately.

Several velvet sofas make up the centre of the room. To one side rare alcohols and cocktail making apparatus top a dark wood drinks cabinet. White and blue mood lighting gives the place a cosmic yet lavish sort of ambience.

One man sits on the sofa. He has his back to them. Dark hair. Dark suit. Arms spread across the back. Watching the floor below.

"What a pleasant surprise," he says. He glances back. "And who might this be?" He fixes Mac with cold blue eyes. Turns his head slightly. "Do I know you from somewhere?"

Mac doesn't know what to say. His trademark greeting caught at the back of his throat. Somehow, the man's arrogant confidence has cast a spell on his tongue.

Terra steps forward. "You know very well who it is, Gaspar. I told you I was going to find him to help us."

"Ah, Trent Macadamia of The Church of The Fallen Ange—"

"I'mnotreallywiththem." The words drop out of him like potatoes from a sack. He's not a crazy cultist. "That was all a ploy."

"Really? I'd love to hear all about it one day," he says, in a way that suggests hearing about it one day is literally the last thing on Earth he'd ever want to do. "But first things first, what brings you both to see me?"

"I went to Ripley to find Trent, but someone followed me." She looks at him. Her eyes are slits. "Only a handful of people knew I was going, including you."

Gaspar slides from the sofa and stands. Steps around it towards them. Mac sees now that Terra's brother also wears wide bottomed flares. Chalks it up to some sort of cultural thing. Or perhaps disco is just back in style for the squillionaires of London.

Now he's viewing them both together, there's definitely something different about the way they look. A flatness in the nose, perhaps. A blue suggestion in their dark hair.

"You realise that by telling a handful of people within our community, you might as well have told everyone?"

He saunters closer, almost threateningly, like a monitor lizard sizing up its prey. He looks several years older than Terra. Maybe ten. Mac doesn't like him already.

Mac repositions himself to put his body between them. More in reaction than with intention to stand between the siblings.

"You said yourself you didn't want me talking to Trent," says Terra.

"I said we could handle it in house." Gaspar's face is serious. He looks as though he's trying his best not to say something. "I want to find our little brother as much as you do. But he is not our priority right now."

Terra grips Mac's elbow before stepping in front of him. "He's never been your priority. You've been too busy with—"

His face tightens and his eyes flash. "You know exactly what happens with every day that passes. It's my job to protect you, Terra. To protect everyone. Dad left me..." He growls in frustration and his fingers tense. His voice rises and points at Mac. "Why did you bring him here?"

"Why have you been avoiding me?" she snaps back.

"Because I didn't want to have this conversation in front of an outsider." His lips tremble as he suppresses his anger.

"Well, it's too late."

"How much does he know?"

"Nothing."

What does that mean?

"Did you send someone after me to Ripley or not?" Her voice is flat with impatience.

Gaspar shakes his head. "No." He takes a breath and lets it out in a long, calming exhale. "Look, I don't want to stand in your way if this is how you want to do this. But there are reasons we don't leave the city. We're safer here, together."

"Well, there was someone there."

"Are you sure they were looking for you and not—" He nods towards Mac. "What exactly did this someone look like?"

"Short," says Mac. He is numbed by everything that seems to be going over his head. Tries to flick the switch on that sharp part of his mind that used to excel at tracking details and working things out, but his habits over the past few months have blunted it. "There were two of them."

"If you are going to be in our employ, and there is someone following you, I don't want you taking my sister along on your investigations." Gaspar's jaw juts with menace as he stares at Mac. "She is to stay in her building at all times."

Terra scoffs.

Mac nods. Under Gaspar's hard gaze, he can't do anything but.

Gaspar makes his way towards the drinks cabinet. Takes out a bottle and throws a couple of ice cubes into a cut glass. "Can I offer you a drink, Mr Macadamia?" He smiles. A Cheshire Cat grin, as if he knows the inner turmoil such a question will cause.

Mac can't help but feel he's being tested. He swallows. His mouth is dry. It's been forty-eight hours since his last drink. Should he? It might help calm his nerves. Terra's hand brushes his stomach as if to hold him back. He clears his throat. "No. No thanks. I'm working."

"Of course you are." Gaspar pours his own. Lifts it to his nose. "And what have you found out about our brother's disappearance? Do you know where he is? Do you know if that person we saw last year is in fact him?"

Mac takes a breath to answer that as a matter of fact they do have a hot lead, but decides against it.

"We've asked a few questions, but nothing concrete yet," he says instead.

"No. Of course not. People who have been missing for twenty years don't suddenly pop up on national TV, do they?" He steps away from the drinks cabinet.

Mac moves further into the room, as if to assert some dominance. Steps closer to the window and looks out over the club floor. He's sure all those people dancing below earn more in a month than he could earn in a year. It's that sort of place.

He tries to think of something else to ask, but the thought of a drink has brought him to a dead end.

"Are you two staying on for the evening?" Gaspar asks. "You really ought to. We've got some great DJs on tonight." He takes a credit-style card from his inside jacket pocket and holds it out to Mac. Another test. "Mr Macadamia, drinks on me."

Mac's fingers twitch. He runs his dry tongue over the roof of his mouth. Out of the corner of his eye he can see Terra watching him. No. He's come this far. He moves to stuff his hand into the pocket of his skinny jeans, a show of willpower and strength, but as the trousers are so tight, he misses the opening and roughly caresses his own leg.

Gaspar frowns, then tucks the card back into his pocket. Mac watches it go almost regretfully.

"Suit yourself." Gaspar swirls his drink.

Terra steps into the elevator. Mac follows her in. She doesn't speak. Just presses the button and shuts the doors with arms folded.

"You were right?" says Mac, hoping to lighten her mood. "He is a bit of a prick."

She snorts, amused. "Do you think those people at my accommodation were perhaps looking for you?" She tucks a loose hair behind her ear.

He hopes not. "If it wasn't Gaspar, is there anyone else who might send someone after you?" He observes her in the reflection of the lift's mirrored interior.

She shakes her head, unsure. Her eyes catch his. "Maybe, but there isn't anyone who knew I was going to Ripley."

"Then yes, I think," worryingly, "perhaps they were looking for me."

Your Turn

Lily doesn't know if she's been asleep, but when she opens her eyes again the mini-bus has stopped. Parked inside a very bright room. Mr Godfrey gets out.

Outside the window are more men wearing dark suits, two other vans with their doors open, and around twenty other kids.

Finn lifts his head from her shoulder. His hair sticky and matted to his red forehead.

"Are we there?" he says in a sleepy croak.

"I don't know."

Mr Godfrey pulls open the side door of the van. It clanks and clunks hurting her ears.

Cold air enters.

"Undo your belts," he says. "We're here."

"Are our mummies and daddies here?" says Lily. Mr Godfrey doesn't look at her. Maybe he didn't hear.

The other kids remove their belts. One by one, they climb from the van.

Something low hums in the room. It's louder than the clank and clunk of the van door. It makes her tummy feel funny, but her tummy already felt funny. She doesn't feel so excited anymore. The children already out of the van all look to the same thing. Something she can't see yet. Purple light washes over their faces, over Mr Godfrey, over everything. The kids' eyes widen. Finn, who's already out, has his whole hand in his mouth.

Lily scrambles out of the van to see what they are looking at.

At the far end of the room is a door in a wall that looks like it's made of mud. But it's not really a door. It's like a tall purple TV, but standing on its side. It shows a picture of another room. A dark room. She can just make out two long windows through it.

"Um..."says Lily, but she doesn't know what else she wants to say.

The men in the room start funnelling the kids towards the purple door.

"Come on, children," says Mr Godfrey. He puts his hand on Lily's shoulder and guides her and those she came with after those from the other vans. "It's your turn."

Brunch

"Will you tell me a little more about yourself," he says, as they sit together the following morning in one of the small cafes near her building. Singles on laptops sip frothy lattes and nibble on cronuts, while gaggles of glamorous women giggle over mimosa brunches. Two elderly ladies having tea and cake seem a little out of place for the trendy surroundings. They glance at him as he looks over and he offers them what he hopes is a friendly smile. *Yes, come, enjoy the trendy young people place. All ages welcome.*

Terra doesn't speak for a moment, as if she's preparing to defend herself.

"What would you like to know?"

"I've done some digging and—"

"Ok," she nods and looks down at the fried mushrooms on toast in front of her. "You want to know what I'm not telling you?"

"I understand you don't want to tell me everything about who you are. And that's fine, unless somehow it will help the case. If we don't find Terry tonight, we're going to have to start somewhere else."

She waits.

"You said you lost Terry twenty years ago when you were evicted. But Source has been a wealthy company since the early noughties. And it looks like it's been going since the nineties."

She leans forward. "How do you know about Source?"

He raises a single eyebrow in a sultry smoulder. "I'm a very good PI." With a very good grasp of google.

She squints at him a moment, then looks around. "We've always had wealth." She puts her hands together in front of her chin. Chooses her words. "It wasn't an eviction. Father made some people angry." She picks up a fork and pokes at her breakfast. "He was supposed to do something for some very bad men, and in the end he didn't."

"Your father being Saurian Adler?"

She nods.

"What happened?"

"They killed him. Knowing we weren't safe, our mother hid us away."

He presses his lips together. "That must have been tough."

"Yeah. It was a long time ago. I was still pretty young." She sits up straighter. "I've been without them longer now than I was with them."

"Did she fake your deaths? The fire?" He doesn't like probing, but needs to know.

Terra's dark eyebrows draw together. "How do you...?"

He tightens his lips into a sorry smile. "I'm a very, very good PI."

"Mother organised some of father's people to hide us. The bad men were coming for us all. Money was transferred. Fake names. Fake IDs. Enki was with her coming to meet us, but something happened. They never showed up. We thought they'd got them both. We grieved, we healed, but I never forgot, until I saw him with you on that show."

"Who was it? Who was your father supposed to do something for?"

She sends a furtive glance around the cafe, then leans even closer. "I think you can guess. You met them last year."

A part of him relaxes. So she knows. "What did you think when you saw us last year on the show?"

"After the initial shock of seeing Enki, I thought finally The Guardians were going to get what was coming to them. Finally something was going to happen." She looks around the cafe and hums in her throat. "Stupidly, I thought people would rise up. But... You know..."

"Mm. Too busy with their mimosa brunches and their cronuts."

"Exactly." Her eyes linger on his a moment. Searching his face for something. "I remember thinking how sad you looked."

"What?" He hums through his nose. Not what he'd been expecting. "On the show? Or just in general?"

Her lips curl into a half-smile.

"It had been a bad few days," he continues in defence of himself. "I thought I was about to die."

She leans forward. "Sorry, I didn't mean it in a bad way. I thought, there's someone who's been through a lot to get to where he is. Someone who's trying something. I thought you looked sad. But I…" She hesitates. "I also thought you were brave."

He waves a hand to brush it off. "Oh, stop it you." His cheeks warm a little. "I just kind of fell into it. If I could have been anywhere else, I would've. That's not brave."

She smiles. "You should give yourself more credit."

"Hm." He ponders as he takes a bite of his toast. He smiles back. "Alright, maybe I will."

Fallen Angels Anon

Saturday night they meet at Bobby's at 8 p.m. Mac wears dark jeans and his Iron Maiden hoody. It's turned inside out to make it less noticeable.

"The location came in," says Bobby, as he opens the door. Without so much as a greeting, he brushes past, leading the way back downstairs. "A trading estate in Tottenham. The instructions say we have to arrive at exactly 20:50. They won't admit us if we're too early or too late. It'll take about half an hour on the tube and walking."

Mac had hoped to avoid public transport while he was in town. Sitting on the underground with hundreds of other people who might recognise him doesn't sound like a great way to spend an evening. But it's the fastest way to get there.

Riding the train, he pulls his hood up over his head, and gazes out of the window, pretending to be watching the stations and tunnels zip by.

"Are these meetings well attended?" asks Terra as they rocket out of Angel tube station.

Bobby grips a bar with one hand and leans heavily on his stick with the other. "I don't know. I've not spoken to anyone that's been. Everything I have heard could be recruitment propaganda. You know, saying it's an army to try and drum up support for something that is, in fact, just a couple of guys running around wearing balaclavas."

She nods. "I guess it makes it easier for us to find Enki if there's not many of them."

"I'd feel a little better about myself if it was packed though," says Mac, turning away from the window. "It's my face on the flyer."

Although he catches one or two people watching him with questioning stares, there aren't any confrontations on the tube. At first, he's happy about that. People are forgetting. But, if he thinks about it, it's a bad thing. It's just what The Guardians want.

They cross through busy streets to a small industrial estate much like the one where he'd first met Nige.

"Unit 5E," says Bobby, as he studies a map of the estate. "That's where they'll be. We should don our balaclavas now."

Mac looks around. "Won't we look kind of suspect walking around with balaclavas?"

Bobby points deeper into the estate. "I don't think those guys are going to mind," he says.

Several small groups and duos, all dressed in plain clothes with balaclavas covering their faces, move towards the centre of the site. All going the same way. All heading to the meeting. Mac counts ten individuals.

"Come on," says Terra, checking her watch. She pulls her balaclava over her head. Her hair pokes out through the eyeholes and she tucks it in. "We don't want to miss it."

The trio jog after the others. Bobby does his best to keep up with his limp.

A clamour of anxious voices leaks from an alleyway, and when they arrive, they see a group of people wearing face coverings gathered outside a set of doors into a small warehouse.

They join the back of the group. Those there talk and joke about nothing and spout exciting suppositions. Nervousness bubbles in his stomach. Have all these people been to a meeting before? Or are they all new like them?

Looking around at the eyes of the people present, he feels like an imposter. Though there's not many, they are all here for something he and Nige and the others had started. A real movement. Something greater than himself. Something that, if it grows big enough, has the potential to shake the very bedrock of a sick and oppressed society. There's that word again - potential.

A light comes on above the doors. The crowd hushes into a worried silence of held breath and anticipation.

The doors open and a masked man steps forward. He's quite tall. Could it be Pete? Mac isn't sure.

"Is that him?" says the woman stood just in front of them to the man with her. "Is that Trent Macadamia?" He shrugs.

Mac feels a warm glow ignite in his stomach. People are here for him. He's a bloody rockstar. He looks to Terra, who doesn't seem to have noticed. Shame. CUS HE'S A BLOODY ROCKSTAR!

"Welcome," says the man. His voice a slow boom. "Thank you all for popping along. Come on in. Find a chair and the meeting will start ima— um... imani-manently." Definitely Pete. "Please move quickly. We don't have a lot of time."

The crowd files in. Mac catches Terra's eye as she shuffles in front of him in the queue to enter. Those behind push him up against her.

His pulse quickens. There are two reasons.

"Sorry," he says.

The room isn't large. The size of a tennis court, perhaps. Foldable chairs sit in a semi-circle in the centre lit by several halogen lamps on stands.

It looks a little like some sort of illegal fighting ring. Everyone sits in a silence cut by the occasional burst of nervous chatter. He joins them, sitting between Terra and Bobby. Looks around at the others present as the room falls quiet.

The blinding light of the halogens blocks out the sight of the surrounding walls, as if they sit in the middle of a never-ending room. The only thing spoiling the illusion is the streetlight through the open door they've all just come through. Pete stands silhouetted in the rectangle of orange light. He glances left and right outside of the door, then shuts it behind him.

His footsteps echo across the bare concrete floor as he approaches the centre of the room. He enters the circle and stands there for a moment. Another set of footsteps come from the other direction, and a shorter man joins him. Dave?

People look to their neighbours.

"Thanks for taking the risk in coming," says Dave. "I know two things. You're not necessarily here because you believe everything we had to say last year, but... you have a notion that something is wrong in the society we live in, like the odds are always stacked against you, like no matter what you try, or how hard you work, nothing improves." He pauses a moment to nods and words of agreement. "And you're here because you want to do something about it. You want to level the playing field for yourselves, for your children."

He removes his balaclava. Gives Pete a little nudge to remind him to do the same, then continues. "You may have seen my brother and I on television last year. Twice actually. Once calling for the deaths of Kenneth Bailey and the other influencers, and then another, that same week, when we revealed the greatest secret the world has ever known. For the first we can admit we were wrong. Kenneth, the influencers, even Di Blasio, they were not the enemy. The enemy was a higher power. A tyrannical group dictating every government, in every country, on this planet. A group that calls themselves The Guardians." He rubs his hands firmly together cracking his knuckles. "These Guardians killed our father and were responsible for the deaths of our sister and mother. We thought when we exposed them last year that things would change for the better, but they have such a tight grip on everything that even outing them in front of billions was not enough. Our story has been ridiculed and filed away as the conspiracy of lunatics at best, or a failed Di Blasio marketing attempt at worst. But I assure you it is not. What you saw that night was all true. Everything. And we want to prove it to you. If enough people know and believe the truth, then we can change things."

Mac looks once more around the group. He sighs. He had expected more. This isn't an army. It's not even a squad. And these soldiers don't look ready to fight. They are all very normal, very average people, like him.

Dave and Pete, on the other hand, look good. He remembers them as skinny, lanky little things, but each appears to have bulked up. Pete's tall build looks almost athletic under the all revealing glare of the lights. His posture is now changed, proud and upright.

"We're going to ask you to move to the next room where others like you are gathered," continues Dave. "This is our fourth meeting of the night. You are the fourth fifteen. We have three more groups coming. By the end of the night, there will be over one hundred more of us. And we will show you proof that what we say is true, so that while you do believe, you can believe with absolute conviction." He raises his hands. "So, friends, stand, and follow my brother towards the door to the next room." He motions with a hand as a door on the other side of the room opens.

Mac cranes his neck to see if it's Terry. Terra is the first to stand, neck stretched, checking the same thing. With the halogens burning bright, it's difficult to see. She walks towards the doorway, and Mac hurries to follow her. The rest of the group drift with them. Nervous, quiet talk starts up again.

The figure that opened the door beckons them over. It's a woman. Well built, like Pete and Dave. Not a profile he recalls.

Could Nige be here?

They spill through the door with their group. Beyond is a large room. A crowd has gathered inside. All wearing balaclavas. All looking at them as they enter. It takes a moment for the two groups to merge. He can sense the unease in the air. It's all very strange.

To their left is a large stage. Several more athletic and balaclava'd figures stand on it watching the crowd. Not so much to attention, but ready for action if action is required. Between them, in the centre of the stage, is a large cube with dimensions a little bigger than a man. It's covered in a tarpaulin.

"What do they have in there?" says Bobby, nodding to the box on stage.

"I expect we'll find out in the next hour," says Mac, stepping further into the room so he can get a good view for when they do.

It takes a little under an hour for the next three groups to come through the doors. One hundred people wait for what is to come.

And it doesn't disappoint.

Once the last group has entered, their number mixing with those already there, Pete and Dave hurry to the front of the stage. They are the only ones not wearing balaclavas. Mac guesses it's because everyone already knows what they look like having seen them on the show last year. He also expects it's to build some sort of trust.

Dave approaches the podium at the centre. It has a microphone connected to a small set of PA speakers on either side of the stage. Nothing fancy. A quick setup.

He clears his throat. The whispers that were developing at the sight of him on stage die out.

"Once again, thank you for coming. We don't want to waste your time, we know it's a risk being here, so we're going to get straight on and show you the proof we promised." He holds up a hand to indicate the box.

What's in there? Could it be Kenneth or Dawn or Victoria? Or another changed person? There must be others out there. If there were, they would have seen the show and come out of hiding. Or perhaps they were too scared of the persecution they might face from The Guardians, or from an unbelieving society as a whole.

He knows he would be. Better to stay low and wait for something to change. No one wants to be on the front line. But you can't get anywhere without innovators.

Perhaps some had tried.

"Spoony," Dave says, and a large man holding what appears to be a cattle prod steps forward. He grabs one corner of the tarpaulin that covers the box.

Spoony Phil. Another blast from the past. Does that mean Nige is here too? His broad silhouette isn't amongst those on stage, though that doesn't mean he's not somewhere else nearby. Mac's just as excited to see him as to see what might be in the box. The cattle prod suggests something bad.

Phil pulls the tarpaulin. It falls off the container and pools in a heap on the floor.

For a moment, both Mac and the crowd don't see what's inside. The figure so gaunt and haggard as to almost not be visible. Then shocked gasps come out of the crowd as his brain agrees that what he's looking at is real.

Terra covers her mouth. "It's true," he hears her say.

Bobby grits his teeth. Lets out a little growl.

It's a Guardian.

It stands there. A permanent leer on its pale white face. Black wraps cover its tall body. Its huge, leathery wings dangle from its back.

"Go on. Take a good look," it says, but its voice is lost as the crowd's shock turns to anger. Their suspicions are confirmed. Their hate has a target.

Dave raises his hands for quiet. "This is one of them." He looks back at the thing in the box. "One of the caste that crushes us beneath its boot heel. One of the members of the elite that hold us down for their benefit. They have convinced themselves they are doing it for the greater good." He shakes his head. "That humanity would not survive if allowed to continue as nature intended, but that is a lie. A lie they tell themselves so that they can live out their decadent fantasies."

For a bit of a cretin, that Dave can sure talk a good talk.

"This thing was there that night. It would have massacred me, my brother, and our friends — including very young children — if we had not fought and escaped." Dave pauses for a moment and looks out over his hushed audience. "Think about that. Some of you have children. Think now of your love for them. He would kill them for his own benefit without a moment's hesitation, without a thought for their innocence. What kind of a monster would do that?"

Mac senses a shift in the crowd. A low murmur of seething anger builds. His own breath catches at the back of his throat at the thought of what might have happened to them all back then, of what is still happening behind closed doors even now. Every angry eye in the room is on The Guardian. How could someone born a human become such a beast?

Dave raises a hand. "They are hateful and cruel and have no pity. We would lock away petty criminals for less. And this thing has lived decades longer than most men or women. Think of the atrocities it has committed in the name of keeping its filthy little secret."

The crowd is stunned. One woman shouts out. "But what can we do? Nothing is changing."

"Everything appeared to return to normal after our broadcast," continues Dave, "but did it? We put a dent in their armour. A shard of glass under the skin. It festers even now. You are here. That's a start. We are building to something. We have a plan. Tonight is one small step in helping you believe. Helping you have conviction in the cause. A cause that will help change the futures of you and your children and even your children's children." He smiles. "Now you know the truth. Now you've seen it with your own eyes, go home. Tell two others about it. Two people that are uneasy like you. But only two. We must build slowly, only with those who truly want to change things." A set of double doors opens at the back. A cool breeze of fresh air blows in to the room, stuffy with the respiration of one hundred people whose breath has been taken away.

"That is all we ask of you for the next phase." Dave points to the back doors. "I know you'll want to stay, see more, ask questions, but it's not safe for all of us to be grouped like this. We have questions too, and in time we hope they will be answered. We will contact you with further instructions using the same number we used tonight. Thank you for your bravery in coming." He turns away from the mic.

Spoony Phil pulls the tarpaulin back over the box as the crowd shuffles out through the doors.

"We should talk to them," says Mac, and he approaches the stage.

Phil stiffens at the sight of them. He moves towards the edge. "Doors that way," he says.

"No wait," says Mac. "It's me." He cups a hand over the side of his face and lifts his balaclava.

Phil acknowledges him with a nod of the head and looks over to see how many people are left in the room. He hops down from the stage. Whispers, "when you go out, come back around the front again. I can't be seen to be giving you any special treatment in front o' that lot." He nods to indicate the people leaving. "Come round, and I'll let you back in."

Mac nods.

He, Terra, and Bobby are the last to leave and the woman on the door closes it behind them. Most of the crowd are halfway up the road when they get outside. Drifting home in duos and small groups. He can't imagine what must be going through their heads. Those first conversations between friends or lovers as they make their way home. It's enough to think you know something. But to see unequivocal proof is another thing all together.

The trio skirts back around the building. Phil is already standing at the door when they arrive. He scans both ends of the alley, then beckons them inside.

Once in, he shuts the door. The room is still lit by the halogen lights.

He whips off his balaclava and holds out a hand. "Mate, good to see ya."

Mac shakes it. "This is Terra, and this is Bobby Feta," he says.

Phil greets them and shakes their hands, too.

Mac looks towards the double doors that lead back into the room with The Guardian.

Phil follows his gaze. "You wanna know how we got it, don't ya?"

"That was one of my questions," says Mac. He pauses a moment. Feels awkward asking, like he's some sort of fangirl. "Is Nige here?"

Phil shakes his head. "Sadly not. He's over at the colony. He's good though."

"Colony?" asks Bobby.

Spoony eyes him a moment. "I'll fill you in. But we're moving out asap. Can't stay in one place too long, just in case." He moves his head toward the doors. "Come on, Dave and Pete'll be glad to see ya, and there's space in the trucks. You can come with us."

He leads them across the room as three other people enter and start to pack away the halogen lights. They have removed their balaclavas. There's a spring in their step and a lightness to their speech as they work. It makes Mac smile.

Something good is happening here.

Back To Base

As they enter the main room, a white Ford Luton van reverses through a huge set of doors with a squeal of wheels. It parks close to the riser with the box on it.

"Hold on," shouts Phil at those still on the stage, "I'll help you out." He jogs over as Mac, Terra, and Bobby watch on.

He pulls open the truck doors and lowers the tail lift. Another two men join him. One of them lifts a heavy rack mounted unit attached to The Guardian's box with thick cables. The other helps Phil shove the cage on to the lift. He then raises it and manoeuvres the box into the back of the truck.

Mac looks at Terra and Bobby. "Are we doing this?"

Bobby nods. "I'm in."

Terra looks nervous. "Do you think they know where Enki is?"

"I haven't seen him here, but if anyone knows, it'll be them."

She nods. "Then I'm in."

"Mac," Phil shouts as he gathers up his cattle prod and throws it into the back of the van. He climbs up after it and pulls the gate shut behind him. "You and the bird up front with Pete. Fatboy, you jump in one of the cars outside." He gives a thumbs up to one of the men that helped him a moment before and without another word, they shut and lock him in the back of the truck with The Guardian.

Everyone else clears out towards the back door. There's an urgency to their movements that sets a little train of unease going in the back of Mac's mind.

"Bobby, you ok to go with them?"

"Oh, I'm Fatboy, am I?"

"Well, you're not the bird."

"Charming." He shrugs, then limps away.

Mac and Terra head to the truck. Pete waves with visible joy as they pass the front.

"Hey Mac," he says, having reached across to open the door. "Hop in."

"Good to see you, Pete." Mac hauls himself up. "This is Terra."

She reaches a hand up for him to help her in. He takes it. Once again he's aware of how cool her skin his - how rough - not unpleasantly so. It's like sand on a morning beach.

Once they are seated, Pete cranks the van into first and pulls out of the warehouse. Ahead, a convoy of three cars waits by the chain-link fence that borders the estate. Bobby stands by the door of one. Upon seeing the van with Mac and Terra inside, he climbs in.

The cars pull away, and the van follows.

"Where are we going?" says Mac, strapping himself in.

"We got a place just west of London. It's safe."

"Seems like you're in a bit of a hurry to leave."

"It's not a good idea to hang about after the rallies." Pete glances in his side mirror. "It's not a good idea for us to hang around anywhere but back at base, really. Not when *he's* with us." He looks at Mac. "How did you find us?"

"A friend showed me a leaflet." Mac is aware that the brothers might have some animosity towards Bobby. The former bounty hunter being the one that had given their position away, which had ultimately led to their father's death. He'd not thought about this before coming. He hopes it doesn't pose a problem when they arrive at their destination. They'd only had a brief altercation, so perhaps neither Dave nor Pete will recognise him.

"Is he that one from the church?" says Pete, pointing towards the car ahead.

Bugger.

"Uh huh." Mac studies Pete's face. There doesn't appear to be any anger there. "He was just doing his job at the time."

Pete waves a hand. "Oh, no hard feelings from me. I get it. We were breaking the law, and he was upholding it. Good vs Evil. I know he's not the enemy. And Dave will understand."

A little hatch opens just behind Mac's head. "Still, bit of a prick thing to do, though, yeah," says Spoony Phil.

"Yeah, no one's refuting that," says Mac. "But he did get nearly stabbed to death for it, so maybe he's learnt his lesson." He leans forward and looks back to address both Pete and Phil. "Where did you guys get it? The Guardian, I mean."

"The TV studio," says Pete. "We killed most in the fighting. They have this thing which burns them up after death. It's why you'll never find a body if they die while out of hiding. Terry, Dave, and me stayed in the room while the rest of you ran out."

Terra shifts next to him at the sound of Terry's name. He glances at her hoping she'll wait a moment before asking about her brother, he wants to hear what Pete has to say.

"You got the fuckin' bloodlust, didn't ya?" says Phil, his voice taking on an aggravated tone. "You was on a kill frenzy. I was impressed."

"That's right, Spoony. The fu- the fu-" Pete looks a tad embarrassed. "Mm. The f-f-f-flippin' b-bloodlust."

"Oh yeah!" Spoony Phil gurns. "It's why I went back in." He reaches through the hatch and taps Mac on the shoulder as if to single him out. "You know that feeling where you're so ramped up the only thing that'll cure it is smashing a bunch of fucknut's heads in."

He and Pete share a look suggesting they aren't quite sure if they do know that feeling. Terra looks out of the window.

"Oh yeah," says Mac. "Get that all the time."

Phil continues. "When I saw you and Nige was out safe, standing in front of all those bloody coppers, I dived back in for round two. And these three were blasting those pricks to bits. We grabbed one who was out cold and legged it. I had some GHB in my car, so we kept him out until we could get him somewhere and tie him up."

"And now you use him to prove what we said was true? How many of these have you done?"

"We done five this week." Phil holds up five sausage-like fingers. "But it's only the first round. We're gonna do loads more."

Mac whistles. "So you have about five hundred who know, who are out there recruiting two more?"

"That's right. And there's about forty of us back at base too." Pete grins. He looks very excited.

"Nice work." Mac nods, impressed.

Terra elbows him.

Mac clears his throat. "You mentioned Terry. Where is he? Back at base?"

Pete's arms lose some of their rigidity. And he shakes his head. He stays silent for a moment and Mac begins to fear the worst. Had Terry died in battle at the TV studio?

"Terry, left us," Pete says. "Just up and disappeared one night. He helped us set-up the new base. Helped us get The Guardian put away. Used to take all the guard duties he could. A real team player. Then one night he just left. Didn't leave a note. Didn't say where he was going." He sighs through his nose. "I'm a bit sad about it, actually."

Terra makes a noise, and in the close confines of the cab, Mac feels her body tense.

"I reckon this dickhead back here said something to him." Phil disappears from the hatch. Bangs something in the back. "Didn't ya, ya dickhead?"

"Maybe," says Pete.

"Do you have any ideas where he might be?" says Terra, leaning forward to look at Pete around Mac.

He shakes his head. "Sorry, I don't."

"Did he leave anything behind, perhaps?" asks Mac. "Or does he have a room we can look through?"

"He didn't have much stuff. But there might be something. We kept his room vacant in case he came home."

Mac turns to Terra. "We'll find something, and if we don't we'll try something else."

She nods. "Ok."

"This is Terry's sister," says Mac to Pete. "She's looking for him."

"Oh." Pete purses his lips and lowers his eyebrows. "Didn't know Terry had a sister." He passes a few short glances to her whilst trying to keep his eye on the road. Smiles. "You look a bit like him. Same eyeballs."

"Did he ever say anything about his family?" asks Terra.

"No, he never really talked about his life before we met him. Just said he was on his own."

Terra's lips tighten and she nods. Passing streetlights glint in her eyes like the moon on the ocean.

"You can use whatever we have, and we'll do our best to help. At the moment, though, our goal is recruitment, so we can't set aside much time to help you look."

"Anything you can do will be great, thank you," says Terra.

It's late by the time they arrive. Gone midnight.

They pull up a long gravel track which ends in a circular drive in front of an old hotel. It doesn't look in a great state of repair from the outside. Almost abandoned. But there's something beautiful about it. Heaps of purple wisteria sprawl up its red brick frontage and the knee-high grass that borders the gravel path appears green and lush with wildflowers in the headlights of the truck.

It's sort of the opposite of the church.

Two slim white pillars stand on either side of big black double doors at the front. A light comes on above the door as the first car pulls up ahead. The occupants get out. Their faces turn to the truck as it approaches. Bobby waves.

Three figures, silhouettes in the bright light hanging over the door, break off from the others and head around the side of the house. The rest climb up the front steps. When the door is opened, a warm glow emanates from inside.

Pete drives the truck past to follow a route around the side of the house. The trio wait outside a large wooden barn-like outbuilding. One opens a set of tall doors as Pete pulls the van around and then reverses it up to the barn.

"Got to put him away first," he says, nodding back towards The Guardian in his box. "You two should head inside." He glances at Terra. "He can be quite rude. Some things he says really stick with you." His arms flop down from the steering wheel to his chair and he stares with lips pressed closed out through the windscreen into the night.

"Um..." Mac glances at Terra while Pete reminisces about something that looks to have potentially damaged him somewhat. "OK. Do we just head back around the front or...?"

Pete shakes himself back. "Oh yeah, head through the front doors. There's a room or rooms for you to sleep. I don't really know what yours twos sleepings arrangements are." He waggles a finger around to indicate Mac and Terra.

"Oh no," says Terra, sitting forwards straight backed. She shakes her head. "I'll definitely need my own room."

Although he hadn't expected anything, Mac can't help but feel a little pain at the abruptness of the dismissal. As if sharing a room with him is nothing short of insanity. Despite the way he's starting to feel about her, he needs to remember he's working for her. He'd be stupid to think she saw him as anything more than an employee.

Spoony Phil chuckles in the back.

"No problem. We have loads of space."

They agreed they'll look through Terry's room in the morning, so Mac and Terra are shown to their very separate lodgings.

The halls are quiet. Most of the others who had come from the warehouse have gone to bed. Those he has seen appear to be from all walks of life, all ages and cultures. A common thread runs through - they are all physically fit, not overtly muscular, but strong, solid, well trained.

On the short walk from the van to the front door, Terra had asked him whether Pete and Dave and their followers could be trusted. He thought so, but she had a point. Brought to the middle of nowhere with a group she'd never met before. A group who were building a secret army with the sole aim of smashing the current system of government. Who knew what they could be capable of?

He assured her that there was nothing for her to worry about. Although, he is very aware that in bringing her here, someone that he barely knows, he may have put them all in danger.

Despite his tiredness, this thought keeps him awake.

Can he trust her?

His room is small, sparse, spotless. A desk. A built-in wardrobe. Bed. The bathroom is shared with the room next door. It appears they have split each of the rooms in the hotel in two to make more space.

He takes out his notepad and looks at what he has. He's already answered some of his questions. He knows where Terra's family got their money. Knows who Saurian Adler was. Knows what happened to him. Murdered by The Guardians for upsetting them. But what did that mean? Had Terra's father and The Guardians been in cahoots?

Perhaps they'd threatened his family first, and that's why he'd been expected to work for them. But in the end he'd sacrificed his family's safety because whatever The Guardians had asked of him had been too much. That sort of thing took a great man.

Mac places the pad on the little table by his bed. Rubs his eyes, turns out the light, and lies back. Sleep doesn't come quickly. The same two questions keep bubbling to the surface.

What had The Guardians asked of Saurian Adler? And, had they achieved it without him?

Through The Door

She can't remember actually walking through the door. It had all happened so fast and something about it had really confused her. It had prickled, like a million little pins when she'd gone near it, and then she was through.

And now her legs feel all wobbly.

The ceiling of the new room is high. A bit like a cathedral she'd seen on the TV once. It slopes into the walls and the walls into the floor. It's pretty and has funny swirly snail shapes in it that she likes. Some of the children with her stare up at it, their exposed necks stretched. The floor is a bit squishy like her shoes. Other kids giggle as they try bouncing.

Finn takes her hand. She doesn't really want to hold hands — his fingers are a bit wet — but she's the oldest so she has to look after him.

To their left and right are two sets of staircases that sweep down to the middle of the room like hugging arms. She and the other children gather within their embrace. Ahead, two towering windows stand at the front of the hall either side of a large wooden door. Through them she thinks she can see London. The twinkling of purple lights high up in the night sky. They look like gems amongst the towering buildings.

She looks back. She can still see the other room through the door with the vans and men moving around. Again, it looks like the room is on a purple TV screen. Mr Godfrey watches them for a moment from the other side, then turns and walks away.

"Mr Godfrey?" she says, moving back. "Are you coming?"

He doesn't seem to hear her. He doesn't turn back. Her tummy does a little dance. He's the only adult she knows.

Something whooshes overhead. Her loose hair flickers around her face in the breeze and she looks up. The other kids stop their bouncing.

Finn inhales sharply and his hand flies from hers up to his mouth as something large and black lands ahead of the thirty or so children stood in the hall. The kids push back, crashing into her and Finn. She pulls him close to stop him from falling. Fights to stay upright as others trip around her.

One boy screams. Then another.

"What a beautiful selection of children." The flying thing's large, pasty white face splits with a sharp toothed grin. It looks up to the sides. Lily follows it's gaze. Standing on the steps either side of their group are several more black shapes. Tall thin figures. "And just in time to celebrate the cull." He throws his arms wide. "Welcome to Racken, children."

Finn whispers something, and although she thinks she knows what he's saying, at first she doesn't hear it. When he turns to look her in the eye, she reads the words on his trembling lips.

"The Nightmare Bat, Lily." Tears fall from his eyes, and his mouth crumples together. "The Nightmare Bat."

Nuts And Necks

Mac wakes to the thump of feet. He checks his phone. Seven. He jumps up and pulls on a T-shirt from his bag, then sticks his head out of the door.

A couple are passing outside his room.

"What's happening?" he says, his voice coming out in a sleepy growl.

"Training," says the woman. She is red-haired. Mid-twenties. Wears a loose pair of jogging bottoms and a vest top. The man with her also wears gym gear.

"Can I watch?"

"You can't watch, but you can join in," says the man. He grins wide and gap toothed. A hump in his nose suggests it's been broken at least once. He places his hands on the woman's shoulders like they are doing the conga. "We'll go easy on you, seeing as it's your first day."

Mac shrugs. Why not? "I'll just get dressed."

"It's not raining, so we're meeting on the front lawn. Be down in five. Spoony gets grumpy if he's interrupted."

The woman laughs. "Yeah, and no one wants a grumpy Spoony Phil."

"I can imagine."

Mac shuts his door. He hadn't expected a trip and only has the clothes he came in, so chucks on his suit trousers.

When he exits his room, the couple are gone.

He jogs through the hotel. The cheap thin carpet does nothing to silence his heavy footsteps. Follows a brass sign on the wall that points to a long-gone reception and heads down a flight of dark wood stairs into the foyer they'd entered through the night before. A worn rug of swirling gold and red covers the floor. The edges fray into cream tassels.

Others are heading out of the front doors, and he tags on the back of the queue. Excited chatter fills the air. He feels a tap on his shoulder.

"Trent Maca-fuckin'-damia." The accent is American, although Mac has a sneaking suspicion it's fake. For some reason, and despite the biting morning chill that comes through the front door, the man wears no top. His upper body a hairless hunk of dense muscle. His dark hair as hard and pointy with gel as his nips with cold.

It's a face Mac knows very well from his time as a London bounty hunter. They've never met, but Mac has seen that cheese-man grin riding high at the top of the bounty hunter charts ever since he'd become one.

"Hollywood Johnson?"

"I've dropped the Hollywood," he says with a modest nod of the head. He smiles wide. His teeth are so bloody snow white it hurts to look. He hurries Mac out of the front door with a dancing shimmy of his shoulders.

"Nice to finally meet you," says Mac, before being caught up in the maelstrom of people leaving the hotel.

It's still a little dark out, but in the early morning light the size of the space the hotel rests in becomes apparent. There must be over a hundred metres of lush, blue-green lawn between the circular gravel drive at the front of the building and a large shadowy forest beyond. The tips of leafless trees and dense, dark green firs are crosshatchings of charcoal against the pale skies. A low mist hangs over the dewy grassland, giving everything a dreamy grey tint as the landscape fades into the distance.

Mac takes a deep, relaxing breath as a calm breeze crosses the long grass like a wave, stirring up hushed whispers before softly caressing his face.

He follows the others to the space between the hotel and The Guardian's barn. A large concrete courtyard spread between a few other out buildings he had not seen in the dark the previous night.

Spoony Phil stands before the barn in front of a group of about thirty men and women. Several stations with mats, weights, and boxing utensils... (utensils?

apparatus?) are spread around the courtyard. Nervous, Mac joins the back of the group.

"Alright, I know some of you were up late last night with the rally," shouts Phil, his voice echoing across the courtyard in the still morning air. He folds his arms across his chest, then shrugs. A small, quick movement suggesting no flips are given. "I don't give a shit." He pauses, looks at the faces of the others and prods a meaty finger into his palm to punctuate his words. "We train. When it comes to the fight these flying pricks ain't gonna care if you had a late night or not. Chances are they'll come at night while you're all tucked up in bed. Stab you up while you're fast a-peeps." He moves his arm in a circle indicating the mats set out around the edge of the courtyard. "There's fifteen stations. If your station don't have equipment, you're sparring. Four minutes on each station. You and your partner are on for as hard as you can go. Thirty-second sprints. Thirty-second rests. Any questions?" He gives less than a second, then claps his hands. "Get sweaty."

Dave stands nearby, next to a rather large boom box. He hits play and 2Unlimited start pumping out their unique blend of intense synth hits and 90s club beats.

Johnson grabs Mac's arm. "You're with me, Macadamia," he says, as the others pair off and hit the stations.

Mac looks around. "What?" He shakes his head. This all looks very involved. "I wasn't planning on—"

"I wanna see what you can do. Maybe you can show me a few things." He wiggles his hips like a sexy snake over to the nearest mat. Kicks off his shoes. Throws several high round house kicks, does a back flip — a warm up that, after at least a decade of practice, Mac might be lucky to use as a workout — then stands with feet apart and hands raised eyeing Mac over fists that look like they'd have no trouble punching out a bear.

Energetic movement in all the other stations starts up around them.

"I'm not sure exactly what I'll be able to show you?" says Mac, wandering over less than enthused. His fists float around his stomach. He doesn't know whether or not to put them up. Raising them may be seen as some sort of invitation he doesn't want to give.

He steps on to the mat and before he knows it, is lying face down.

Johnson pulls him up. "Hm?" he says, leaning his head to the side with a jerk. "I thought you'd be better?"

"Uh... why?"

"How did you survive?" Johnson says it with evident disappointment.

Mac shrugs. "I don't know."

"Alright." Johnson steps back. Raises his hands in loose fists. "Never mind. I obviously caught you off guard."

"Wh—?"

"Come at me again."

Mac raises his hands. "I hardly came at you the first time." He circles around. Johnson moves with him. It's like a dance. A dance between a cobra and a mole.

"Keep your centre of gravity low," comes a voice from behind. Mac looks back. Terra stands with Bobby watching him. She smiles and waves. He likes the way she looks at him. It makes him feel unique. "And try to be a little looser."

"Yeah, rather than a little loser." Bobby leans on his stick. "And always keep an eye on your opponent."

The world flips, and he's on the deck again. "Why don't you give it a go?" he says, spitting out a mouthful of salty mat.

"Alright." Terra kicks off her shoes and steps up.

"Hey," says Hollywood Johnson to Terra with a smouldering raise of an eyebrow.

Mac crawls away to stand by Bobby.

"Well done," he whispers. "Really showed that dickhead who's boss. Now sit back and watch the one and only Hollywood Johnson take your woman."

Mac can't help but screw up his face. His gut twists, primarily because he's worried what Bobby says will come true. Not that she's his woman or anything — she's like totally her own person and everything — it's just he kind of wishes she was, a bit, perhaps... Oh, who knows?

"She's not my woman."

He feels like giving Bobby a solid clip around the head, but is aware that will likely result in another meeting with the floor. More embarrassingly so, considering Bobby's injury ravaged body. He doubts hitting Bobby and then hitting the floor will make him feel any more hopeful, so instead he folds his arms and watches.

Spoony Phil calls time and each of the pairs move around. Johnson motions for the pair from the station before his to skip on to the following one, so they do.

Phil's voice booms out over the courtyard. "Remember their weak points. They are all blokes and they are all tall as fuck. So nuts and necks, people. We're aiming for nuts and necks. We don't fight honourably. We fight to win." He throws a couple of dummy punches into the target zones of an unsuspecting Dave to demonstrate. "Boom boom bosh."

Dave lets out an involuntary "gaah" and hunches to protect himself.

Terra rolls her shoulders and moves her head from side to side. She widens her stance and beckons Johnson closer. He shrugs and moves in with a quick attack, stopping just short of hitting her. She slaps his hand away without blinking.

"Don't go easy on me," she says. "Give me your best shot."

To his detriment, he does. She spins him around and lands him at her feet.

Mac claps excitedly before catching himself.

"Nice," says Johnson. Flipping back up to stand. He strokes his perfect length stubble on his perfect square chin. "Where'd you learn to fight like that? Maybe you could give me some private tuition."

Ignoring him, she turns to Mac. "Your go," she says. "Come on. I'll be gentle."

Mac's stomach drops, and with a shiver, he moves forward as Terra motions with her head for Johnson to step away. He moves to stand next to Bobby.

"Just show her what you learned in bounty hunter school," says Bobby.

"There was a bounty hunter school?" Mac looks back, but Bobby just grins.

"OK?" she says, as he joins her. It sounds like a question, but he's not sure. The part of him that would prefer to remain comfortable than live up to its potential is definitely not, but he nods anyway. His heart is racing. Mouth dry.

He clears his throat and glances around. Those resting on the other stations nearby are watching. He doesn't like the attention.

"Your stance is the most fundamental thing. Start from a bad place and you're always going to be on the back foot in a fight. Show me what you got."

He raises his fists. Looks down at his feet. It was much easier to just whack people who didn't know you were coming with a cricket bat. How he missed that cricket bat.

She moves closer to him. Her hair tickles his cheek. He looks down the length of her body as she moves his back leg with a sweep of her foot. Her legs seem to bend at impossible angles beneath those flares. His body tingles with their proximity. She smells wonderful. Natural. Something between lavender and vanilla. She grabs his hands then repositions them. Squeezes his fists shut.

"These are your spears and your shields. Never forget that."

"I don't really fight." He whispers it so that no one else will hear. She has a way of making him want to be himself around her. "I'm more of a..." He considers, 'lover', but immediately shuts that idea down as something a buffoon like Hollywood Johnson might say. He settles on, "... a thinker?" But it comes out as a question, as if even that's not right.

"We all have our strengths. And if you can think, without judgement of yourself, without letting emotion in, you can be better at anything."

The stations swap again. The pair before them skip over.

"Where did you read that?"

"It's something my dad used to say." She beckons him closer. "Try to hit me."

"Uh?" Mac is unsure.

"Don't worry, you won't. But try."

He punches straight forward. She doesn't even move.

"Why do you boys think you're going to hurt me?"

"I don't. I just saw you throw that mega-hunk Hollywood Johnson to the floor like he was a sack of feathers. It's me who'll get my butt kicked."

She laughs. "You're good fun, you are."

"Oi, you two," shouts Spoony Phil. "Stop holding up my stations. Either get on, or fuck off." He jerks a thumb behind him.

Mac raises a hand. "Sorry Phil." He steps off the matt. "We'll get off."

"Good." He gives them a glare. "And just so's you know we've got songs round the campfire tonight, so don't go too far. I'm doing marshmallows, and Rosie's doing coco. It's set to be delightful. Now, off you fuck." He claps his hands. "Everyone, back to it. Not long 'til breakfast."

As he and Terra step away from the training area, a family of four appears around the side of the hotel. Nige's son's family. He recognises the kids first, as he hadn't much time to talk to Lewis last year before the police had cuffed him and dragged him off.

Lewis's face softens as he recognises Mac. He raises a hand. "Mac?"

Mac smiles. "I didn't know you were here."

"Got in yesterday morning."

The little girl, Katy, he thinks, runs across the gravel drive to play in the long grass opposite the hotel. Her brother jogs after her, and Lewis's wife steps away to watch. It's nice to see the little ones having fun.

"I never thanked you," says Lewis, his eyes glitter as he watches his children play. His gaze shifts to Mac and he reaches out and places a hand on his arm. "You're the reason they are alive."

Mac clears his throat. "I don't know about that." He'd only acted as anyone would have. Just done what the moment had called for.

The little boy falls, disappearing in the grass, then emerges a few paces further along giggling.

"How's your dad? I haven't heard from him."

"You haven't?" Lewis looks surprised. Then rolls his eyes. "I expect he'll be out here in a couple of days. He doesn't like that we're here and not on the island."

Mac feels a drag on his mental state. Why hasn't Nige just checked in? Called to see if he was alright.

"Which island's that?" says Terra, suddenly attentive, breaking Mac out of his thoughts.

Lewis eyes her a moment. "We haven't met."

"This is Terra," says Mac. "She's looking for her brother, Terry. You don't know where he is, do you?"

Lewis shakes his head. "He was one of the guys who helped us that night, right? Like I said, we only got here yesterday, so I don't know." He looks again at Terra, squinting in the early morning sun.

Mac looks at her too, though she's now watching Lewis's kids as they shriek and dive through the long grass with their mother chasing.

"We'll talk later, Lewis."

"Yeah, we will."

The Search For Terry

All members of the army have their meals together in the hotel's restaurant. Instead of the fancy dinner tables for twos or fours that would have passed for seating at the hotel in the past, two large trestle tables span the length of the room with a bench running parallel either side.

Someone has cut a long hole through one wall into the kitchen. It's patched up but not repainted. The light grey plaster repair spreads like cream cheese over the restaurant's expensive looking, paisley patterned, navy wall paper.

Large canteen style hot plates steam along the worktop that runs between the rooms. Lightly steamed vegetables, mashed sweet potatoes, some sort of lentil and bean mix, sausages.

Sausages. He looks around for Bobby. Sees him in amongst some others at the far end of the table. Leaning in and listening to something a slight, middle-aged woman has to say. A small frown sits on his brow.

The food choices aren't exactly what he's used to for breakfast. It smells great, though. High calorie.

"Nutrient-dense foods for building better warriors," says Dave as he joins the queue behind Mac and helps himself to a large scoop of the beans.

Mac doesn't feel like eating a lot. He spoons some mash on to his plate. Picks out some sweetcorn from the steamed veg.

He follows Dave to a seat, where Terra and Pete are already eating. Hollywood Johnson sits on Terra's left trying to engage her in conversation.

"So," says Mac, placing his plate opposite Terra and squeezing in. "What's the big plan then?"

"Plan?" says Dave, meticulously chopping his sausages into bite-size pieces.

"You said at the warehouse that you were building something, that you have a plan."

Dave squeezes out a mountain of ketchup, then places the bottle down between the glasses and plates on the slim table. He steeples his fingers in front of his chin like a wise man and rests his elbows on either side of his plate. He glances at Pete. "We-"

"We haven't quite figured it out yet," says Pete, through a mouthful. He lifts his arm and does a circle with his finger, indicating everyone present. "We've all been thinking a lot, though." He taps his temple with the same finger. "But coming up with a plan to take down The Guardians without leaving some sort of major power hoover is hard."

"Vacuum, Peter," says Dave.

"Alright, but after lunch," says Pete, looking down at the carpet.

"Have you even got a plan to take them down?" says Mac. Perhaps it's best to start with a first step. "What *do* you know about them?"

Pete scrunches up his nose. "That's a little bit of a sticking point as well. For a secret global power, there's not much about them on google. And that one we've got in the shed isn't really that chatty about the organisation's inner workings."

"No, I didn't think he would be." Mac glances at Terra, who ignores Johnson's advances and watches Pete and Dave with clear interest.

"So you're building an army," she says. "But you don't know what to do with it?"

"We'll get there," says Dave, dipping some sausage into his ketchup. "It's better to have an army and not need it, than need it and not have one."

"Mm." Terra nods. A glance to the side and downwards suggests a deeper thought going on behind those eyes.

"Like a condom," adds Hollywood Johnson, cutting into the serious atmosphere like the slutty ball of slime that he is.

"Or a gun," says the red-haired woman Mac had bumped into earlier. She stabs a piece of broccoli on her plate and jams it into her mouth as though it represents all of her hate for the world.

Mac looks up the line of chatting people. "So you guys are lying to the people you're trying to recruit?"

"Course we are," says the woman. "We're all in this together. You can come up with a good plan like that." She snaps her fingers. "It's the years of preparation, recruitment, training, that you can't do overnight." She gives Dave a reassuring smile, then sips her water. "Get that right, and once you've got the plan, you move on it."

Mac places his fork next to his plate. Is giving hope to people when there is none better or worse than giving them no hope at all?

"You might not like it," says Dave, sensing his unease. "But it's the way it has to be. There's a tipping point and we'll never get there if we don't rock the boat."

After breakfast, they head to Terry's room. It's the same layout as Mac's. Pete unlocks the door and steps back. Mac enters first. There aren't any personal effects on show so he opens the desk drawer. Empty. Completely.

"Anything?" says Terra from the doorway.

"Not in here." He gives her a tight smile. Shuts the draw. Doesn't want to admit that already, only a few days into the investigation, they've hit a dead end. He doesn't have any other ideas.

She moves around the door and checks the wardrobe which stands behind it. Mac moves back from the desk so he can see. Spots the familiar burgundy of Terry's old robe hanging from a rail.

"Do you still wear those?" he asks Pete.

Pete pokes his head around the door to see what Mac is referring to. "Not really. We don't call ourselves The Church Of The Fallen Angels anymore. Not since Dad... um." He looks down.

"No. I guess it might be a bit of a hinderance to the cause if people thought you were some sort of religious cult."

Pete nods. "I didn't really see it before. You know, when you're in something, you can't see that maybe it might look a bit weird to people on the outside. Bless Dad, he'd had a bit of a rough time of it, but he did go off the rails a tad, didn't he?"

Mac stops himself from agreeing outright. Tact may be required here. Or is it worth just being honest? He holds his breath a moment too long.

Terra looks up from her search, sensing the awkward silence drawing longer.

"Yeah, he was pretty bloody mental." The words slide out, riding his held breath like crazed jockeys.

Terra leans her head back a little.

"Uh... I mean maybe he did go off the rails, but look where it got you." Mac raises his hands to indicate the hotel they stand in. He feels he needs to say something more. Something philosophical. He lifts a hand again, this time like a Shakespearean actor holding a skull. "Maybe the rail, the path that everyone else takes, isn't always the right one for you, so it's a good thing to hop off every now and again..." He glances at Terra who offers no support. "Hop off so you can check if you are really heading where you want to go..."

Pete closes his eyes and nods sagely. "Wise words. Wise words."

Terra raises an eyebrow.

"There's nothing here to suggest where he might have gone, Trent," she says, shutting the wardrobe.

"Sorry," says Pete. "I wish we could be more help. None of us here really have much stuff. It's all training and recruiting and watching The Guardian. We don't really have time for anything else."

"That's ok," she says. "You're his friend. What's he like?"

Pete smiles. "He's like another brother to me. Quiet outside of the church. I think he just liked it being the four of us. Me and Dave and Dad and him. Like he'd been alone a long time and could only cope with a few people that he liked. You know, he never mentioned a sister. He never really mentioned anything from before. Where have you been?"

"We didn't know he was alive." She glances at Mac then back at Pete. She touches her thigh. "Do you know... um." Her lip twitches. "Do you know *about* him?"

She puts a strange emphasis on the word about. A widening of the eyes. She leans forward a little.

Pete lowers his brow and purses his lips. Glances at Mac questioningly. "Um—"

"I mean was he happy?" she says quickly.

"Yeah, I think so. He never complained."

"You mentioned before that Terry took a lot of guard duties with The Guardian." Mac squeezes around the door to join Pete in the hall.

"He took any shift he could."

"Maybe it's worth having a chat with him."

Pete makes an unsure hum. "I wouldn't recommend it. He's not the nicest person to talk to."

"I don't expect him to tell us the truth, but he might have said something to Terry to make him leave."

They cross the courtyard towards the barn. Two men stand outside the huge wooden doors. One has a break-action shotgun draped over his arm. There's a shining brass bell attached to a wooden strut on his left with a thick, knotted rope hanging from it.

The men nod as Pete approaches with Mac and Terra in tow.

"Coming in, lads," says Pete, giving them a thumbs up.

The unarmed man lifts a large wooden bar from the door, then drags it open and hooks it up to a concrete post. He does it with such efficiency that Pete doesn't even slow his pace before heading inside.

The tarpaulin still covers The Guardian's cell. The room is quiet. If you didn't know there was someone inside, you would think the place empty.

Mac spots two security cameras. Blinking red LEDs aim at different sides of the box. "Do you have audio?" he says, nodding at them. "Might be good to check Terry's convos with him."

Pete looks up. "I can get it."

Mac spots a chair in the corner. Drags it over and flips it backwards. He straddles it and leans his forearms on the back with what he hopes is intimidating animosity. He gets Terra's attention, pokes a thumb into his own chest, and mouths the words. 'I'll be bad cop.'

"What?" she asks.

He leans towards her and jerks his head towards the cell. Whispers, "I'll be bad cop?"

A short bark of laughter comes from within the box.

Mac's posture falls. "Alright," he waves a hand at Pete. Tries to get back into character. Squints at the box and moves his head from side to side, trying to find his most menacing position. He waves a hand. "Pull it off."

"The tarpaulin?"

"Yes, the tarpaulin." Jesus Christ, does no one know how to intimidate a perp? "Pull the tarpaulin off."

Pete does so.

Mac leans back with a gasp. The Guardian stands with its head right up to the other side of the perspex. A cold smirk on its white face beneath staring pinprick pupils.

"Trent Macadamia," it says. "I wondered how long it would be before I saw your face again."

At first his heart flutters and he loses control of his breath, but in no time at all, the fear evaporates. Now he sees it in the light of day, rather than creeping out of the shadows with glinting knife in hand, it's not so bad. Although it looks strong, tall, winged, it's just a person. Not the invincible, deathless creature that his mind has painted over the last few months.

"I'm sorry, have we met?" Mac says, with a tweak of a nostril. "All you Guardians look alike."

"We first met in an alleyway in Camden the night I killed The Twins. I nearly got you then."

A shiver runs up Mac's spine and the hairs on the back of his neck stand. Every Guardian he'd ever met had wanted to kill him. But this is the one who'd come the closest. He can still feel the blind fear that raced through him as he ran to escape. He can't count the times he's woken, bathed in sweat, from dreams of endless alleys, of descending nightmare shapes.

Terra slaps a hand on the perspex right in front of The Guardian's face snapping Mac back with a bang. "Where the hell is my brother?" she shouts.

Her breath comes fast through flared nostrils. It blinks and turns its attention to her.

Guess she's going to be bad cop then.

"So..." Mac clears his throat. Tries to get into character. "Are they treating you well? Feeding you?" Although, actually, he hopes not. Guardians eat kids. He nods towards Terra. "You better do what she says." He twirls a finger around his ear. "She's loco..."

The Guardian says nothing. Its body shifts like a cobra spotting a mongoose, backing up so it can get a better look at Terra. A small smile splits its face. "How delightful." He nods towards Mac. "Does he know?"

Terra's eyes shift to Mac. She looks scared. But of what? What does The Guardian mean? Have they met before? Did he know her father, Saurian?

"He doesn't, does he?" The Guardian's smile grows. "Of course not." It leans its head back and stretches its arms overhead as if showering under perfect temperature water after a hard day. "How delicious. Don't worry. I won't tell him. I'd prefer to have his heart break when he finds out for himself."

"What do you mean?" she says in a small voice. He's not seen her like this before. She's usually so confident.

"Look at the way he's standing. He wants you." Its eyes travel over Mac. "He wants you, badly. You should probably warn him." It cackles.

"Shut up," she shouts. Her lips twitch with fury.

"Now, your brother, he wouldn't be the one that used to come see me, would he? Terry was it? There's definitely a..." its eyes glint, "family resemblance. Haven't seen him in a while. He is deeply missed." The Guardian's eyes flick to Pete. "Any idea where he got to? Maybe he's gone to be with your father." It laughs again. A horrible, mocking sound.

"Oh, you are the worst," says Mac.

"I'm not, believe me, but I've done some things that would put me up there."

Mac turns to Terra. "What does he mean? Who are you?"

"He's just trying to distract you." She moves to the door. "We're not going to get anything out of him."

"Deny it all you like, but you are who you are," calls The Guardian as she disappears outside.

"Help me with this," says Pete to Mac, holding up the tarpaulin.

Mac does and together they pull the tarpaulin back over the box.

"She's not who you think she is," The Guardian says, as it disappears under the plastic sheet.

Mac wants to ask what he means, but that feels like it would be a betrayal.

Pete exits as he returns the chair to the corner. Something on the floor glints in the sunlight from outside. A piece of metal poking up from the gathered dust and dead leaves under the chair. He kneels and brushes the dirt away. Picks it up. It's been there for some time. A little figure. Long and thin with wings.

Made of tin foil.

The Lizard Lady

It's dark down here. And it smells funny. Lily thinks it could be the water, but it could be her or the other children. They haven't had a bath since they got here. Not that she'd want to have a bath in the pool just outside of their cell. It looks like oil.

Across the water is another cage. Inside are ten other kids, the same as them.

Men in strange suits had brought them here and put them inside. They wore masks that covered their faces. It made their breathing sound really loud.

She doesn't know how long they've been here, but she's starting to get hungry.

The door to their prison cracks open. Someone in a light grey cloak pushes a trolley in front of them. Their head is covered, but something is wrong with their face. Their nose is stubby, and a strange dark and scaly sort of colour, as are their hands, like the wizard lizard from Lily's favourite book. They don't speak as they push the trolley towards the cage on the other side. But they sniff. Lily thinks it's a sad sniff. It's a sniff that reminds her of Karen, who now she thinks about it, always seemed a little sad. It sounds like a lady's sniff.

The children in the other cage stand back against the wall and silently huddle together. The figure takes bowls from her trolley and places them through a small gap in the bars on to the floor on the other side. Steam rises from each. Maybe it's food. Lily counts nine bowls, but there are ten children.

The figure then pushes her trolley back towards the door. Lily sees her face, though it is dark in the shadow of her hood. The lady has funny brown and yellow eyes. A wide mouth. She doesn't look scary. Just different.

Curious, Lily steps closer to the bars as the lady pushes her trolley towards their cell. She can smell the food from here. Her mouth waters and her stomach grumbles. It smells like mushrooms. She likes mushrooms.

The lady catches her eye and she tries to think of a question to ask.

"Can..." she begins, but she doesn't quite know what to say.

The lady pauses. She looks surprised to see her. She takes one bowl and slowly passes it through the gap in the bars. Lily accepts it. The contents is a brown mushroom stew. It smells savoury and salty.

"Thank you."

The lady looks at her for a long time and Lily thinks for a moment that she's done something wrong. That the lady is cross. Then she sniffs again, presses her lips together, and says, "you're welcome."

"I'm Lily."

Those yellow, diamond-shaped eyes blink.

On the other side, the children in the cage start to come towards their bowls to investigate. They each take one. One girl is left out. She begins to cry. The lizard lady starts at the sound.

Finn and the others in Lily's cage stand back as, with head down, the lady places more steaming bowls on the ground inside. Each has a small wooden spoon. There are ten including Lily's. She then pushes her trolley back to the other cage. She takes a key from her pocket and unlocks the door then gently takes the hand of the girl who isn't eating. She leads her from the cage and out of the room.

Winter Oasis

Terra doesn't make it to dinner. In fact, Mac doesn't see her for the rest of that day. After their meeting with The Guardian, Pete had taken him to a small outbuilding nearby to find the security camera footage of when Terry had been on guard duty. Expecting Terra to come and find him, he'd become engrossed in the video and lost track of time, only emerging bleary eyed like a mole from its hole once night had fallen.

Hours and hours of footage had been clocked, so after a couple of hours of wading through it and not finding anything, Pete put together an algorithm designed to find Terry in the video and edit together a reel of when he and The Guardian were speaking. It wouldn't be entirely accurate but would save them a lot of time flicking through looking for anything meaningful.

"So how long have you been with the organisation, Macadamia?" says Hollywood Johnson, gravitating towards him at dinner. He places his tray down next to Mac at the table. The evening meal is a health inducing mix of tofu, rice, and vegetables. It's actually pretty delicious.

"What do you mean?"

"I saw you on the show last year? Your take over. That must have been in the works for quite a while."

Pete, sitting opposite, glances up to see Mac's reaction. For a moment he considers making something up, but doesn't have the energy for it.

"I planned that while driving a supermarket delivery truck on the way to the BBC because the grandkids of a man I'd met several days earlier had been kidnapped."

Johnson nods with a raised eyebrow and hums a little impressed noise. "I can see why she likes you."

"Who?"

Johnson smiles and forks in a mouthful of tofu. He says nothing more.

Mac clears his throat and fills the threatening silence. "Why did you decide to join?"

There's a thoughtful pause while Johnson finishes chewing. He points out different people around the room with his fork. "A lot of the stories here are the same." The American accent slips a little from his voice, and he rests both arms on the table, his fork hovering over his food. "I had a younger sister. She was four when she went missing. I still think of her every day. I don't know if *they* had anything to do with it, but I know how much it hurt our family to lose her. It'd make me feel better to know I'd done all I could to stop that happening to someone else."

Mac looks around at the others present. Now he knows, he can see the tell-tale signs of grief. Lines on young faces. Smiles that don't quite reach tired, down turned eyes.

He spots Bobby with a few other bounty hunters that he recognises. He notices Mac watching him, smiles and waves. They haven't spent a lot of time together since their arrival, but Bobby seems to be having a pleasant time catching up with old rivals.

Thinking about it now, there had always been a camaraderie in the bounty hunter rivalry. And remembering what Bobby had said back in his flat, that they were all out there fighting for what was right, makes him feel good about who he used to be and who he's trying to be now.

When most plates are empty, and the room is noisy with chatter, Spoony Phil walks in through a pair of French doors that lead out into the gardens. He wears his moleskin coat. With him comes the smell of wood smoke and a bite of chilled night air. He claps his hands together in woollen, fingerless gloves. The room hushes.

"Fire's burning and the night is clear. Wrap up warm. Dave's got the mulled wine on. And for those of you not drinking, Rose's got that sweet, sweet coco."

Well, doesn't that sound lovely?

Chairs scooch as some stand.

"That's my cue," says Johnson. "Talk later." He stands and grabs an acoustic guitar that leans against the wall, gives it a test strum, and with the verse to 'Brown Eyed Girl' sung in a dreamy boy band tenor, leads those who've finished their meal out after Spoony Phil.

"Are you coming, Mac?" asks Pete, standing.

Mac nods. He scrapes the last of his food into a large bin and places his empty plate into a plastic tub at the end of the table.

"Where's your friend got to?" says Pete, as they leave through the French doors. "Not hungry?"

"Um, I'm not sure. I haven't seen her since we spoke to The Guardian earlier." He hopes she hasn't gone home or something.

"Ah." Pete nods. "I told you he wasn't very nice. When he first woke up after we got him in the box, he was very rude about Dad. Apparently he was there." Pete's face stiffens. For a moment, he looks gaunt and pale. "He said it was funny watching him burn."

Mac presses his lips together. Takes a long breath through his nose. "That's..." There are no words. He pats Pete on the shoulder. "Alan was the bravest man I've ever met."

Pete smiles at that.

Mac digs his hands into his hoody pockets against the cold night air. The silence between them extends as they follow the small crowd and the sound of Hollywood Johnson's irritatingly beautiful singing.

"Still, let's not let the past ruin what fun we might have in the present." Pete points ahead.

A bright bonfire burns near a solitary and towering oak tree. Several large logs are placed around it for seating, and to one side, two foldable tables are each topped with three large canteens.

The fire illuminates the scene with rippling amber light. Laughing couples dance in comfy, warm clothes to the sound of Hollywood Johnson, who has moved into something a little more upbeat. A mini-band of fiddle and cajon have joined him. Mac smiles. It's a cosy oasis of winter hygge in the cold, dark night.

As they step closer, Pete throws himself with carefree abandon into the mix of dancers, leaving Mac alone on the edge.

He spots Bobby holding a ladle and talking with Dave over by the tables. Somehow, he's got himself roped into serving up the drinks. Deep frown lines streak Dave's forehead. What are they talking about? They both glance at Mac with straight faces, then share another word.

As he nears, Bobby raises a hand and Dave stalks off towards Spoony Phil. Bobby passes his ladle to the woman next to him and limps over with a pair of steaming cups.

"Here you go. Something to blow away the cobwebs." He smiles.

Mac smiles back. "Cheers." He lifts the cup in thanks. Looks inside. Wine. He shouldn't drink it. "I'm probably gonna sit this one out," he says.

"Suit yourself," says Bobby. He looks Mac in the eye for a moment. "I've been chatting to some of the guys. Your woman..." Why does he insist on calling her that? "... I've done some digging, and I don't think she's who you think she is. There's not much about her online. And none of the other bounty hunters here have heard of her or know anything about the building you say she lives in."

Mac rubs the back of his head. He feels a bubble of anger rise in his belly. Why is Bobby trying to undermine his trust in her? He knows what he's doing. "Right? So..."

"So, I'd watch her if I were you."

"Sure."

Bobby watches him. A beady eyed squint. "Anyway, if you're not going to drink with me, I better find someone who will." He waves over Mac's shoulder to one of his bounty hunter friends. "Logan," he shouts, then, after giving the international hand tipping sign of 'would you like a drink?', moves back to the tables for more.

Mac shakes his head and passes the fire to sit under the tall oak tree. He finds a flat space in amongst the roots and settles on the soft loamy earth. Places the cup down next to him. The smell wafts up. A warmed, spiced mix of cinnamon, cloves, and wine. He notices he didn't give it back, but he doesn't want it. Doesn't feel the need for it here.

He scans the scene, hoping to glimpse Terra. But she's not there. A small emptiness opens inside of him. It's not a sensation he's felt before. A mix of worry, hope, nervous anticipation. What he'd give to share a moment like this with someone like her, with someone like who he hopes she is.

Not like anything could happen between them. Who is he to dare to think there's a chance?

He feels vulnerable, like a private part of himself is out on show.

He closes his eyes. Feels the warmth of the fire on the exposed skin of his face. Takes in the smell of smoke and spiced wine. Hears the laughing, singing people. Even if the army never did anything, could he stay here? Could he be happy? Could he be safe? Are these people finally free? Just knowing the truth could be enough. Or was it worse?

"Trent."

He opens his eyes. It's her. Sitting right next to him. He hadn't heard or felt her approach. His heart skips.

"Where have you been?"

"I needed some time alone." She lifts his cup. Takes a gulp. "To think."

"What he said in there—" Though the building isn't visible, Mac nods in the direction of The Guardian's barn, "—you know that means Terry is your brother?" He's thought some about it. Gone over the conversation in his head. Everything The Guardian said. About Terry. About Terra.

"How so?" A tumble of dark hair falls over her shoulder as she turns to look at him. It casts one eye in shadow.

"You didn't have to tell him it was Terry who you were looking for. He just knew."

She smiles and brushes the hair back behind her ear. In the fire light, she is lovely. He's growing to think her lovely in any light.

He's not wrong about her, is he?

He coughs. Catches himself before he stares too long. Looks down at the bare earth and pokes at a root with his foot. "I should have all the footage from when he was with The Guardian tomorrow. We could go through it together. See if we find anything that'll give us a clue."

"Sounds like we'll be spending a lot of time together." She places the cup down and takes his hand. "Come on, if we've got such a big day tomorrow, you can have the night off."

She stands and pulls. For a moment, he freezes. A flash-flood of memories of high school disco failures come to drown him. "I..."

"If you don't dance with me, I'm going to ask the hunk with the guitar." She raises an eyebrow.

Without another thought, he's up. Nervous. Excited. Mentally scraping together every dance move he's got in his limited arsenal.

She drags him into the circle.

And they're spinning. His hands in hers. Her eyes on his.

And she smiles. He raises his arm. She twirls beneath.

And for a moment, it's just them. In the firelight. In the crowd.

And for that moment he forgets anything, or anyone else, exists.

A laugh escapes him. Loud and free. The first real one in a long time. It feels like a floodgate has opened. Armour removed. Tension released.

He grips her hands tighter. Pulls her closer. She doesn't fight it. In fact, she seems to like it. Does she?

He twirls her again. This time she laughs.

His heart thumps, large and full in his throat.

He's never done this before.

"Thank you," he says.

"For what?"

"For finding me."

A Great Night

Time slips away. As do the odd couple here and there. Terra blinks tired eyes as the fire dies.

Hollywood Johnson announces the end of his last song. Looks a little disappointed when no one calls for more. The flames dwindle along with the music. The last of the dancers totter back to the hotel.

"I think maybe I drunk too much," Terra says to Mac. She pulls him towards a log and plonks down.

"Shall I get you some water?"

She shakes her head. "No, I think it'd be best if I just went to bed."

"Oh, ok." Were there any hints in there? Maybe she wasn't having as good a time as he thought? Or maybe she was, and this was one of those moments that the rest of his life might hinge around? He watches her carefully.

"I'm sorry." She brings a hand to her forehead. A pained frown crosses her brow.

What should he say? "I could um… walk you back?"

"Thank you."

He stands, and pulls her to her feet. She links an arm with his. Leans on him for support. That smell again. Lavender and vanilla mixed with the alluring hint of sweet alcohol on her breath. She hadn't drunk that much, had she?

He'll just get her back safe. Make sure she doesn't wake up in a bush or something.

He glances back at the fire. Wanting to remember the evening just as it was. Everyone's gone except Bobby who lies up against the tree asleep and alone with a large tankard gripped in his fist. Someone has placed several blankets over him up to his chin.

"Bobby," he calls, but his friend doesn't stir. "Bobby." He says again, louder. Bobby lets out a grunting snore. Smiles in his sleep.

For a moment, he considers waking him, but then Terra starts trudging away on her own. He looks cosy enough, so Mac decides he'll be ok in the cold. The fire still has some warmth, and he's wrapped up well.

"I don't know what's come over me," Terra says as he catches up and helps her back to the hotel.

"It's been a busy few days. Emotional. Maybe you're just tired."

She hums in possible agreement. But doesn't say any more as they cross the courtyard and enter through the double doors of the restaurant.

He's eager to fill the gap in conversation, but can't think of what to say. Doesn't want to talk about work or The Guardians. Doesn't know how to talk about anything else.

She's almost asleep on her feet by the time he gets her back to her room. Her eyes are half-lidded.

"Sorry," she says.

"What for?" He opens her door and helps her inside. Pulls the cover of the bed back with one hand and lies her down. Considers removing her shoes, but doesn't know if he should. Decides against it. Just pulls the duvet back up to her chin.

"Sorry for who I am," she whispers, eyes still closed. The moonlight streaming through her window gives her skin a blue tint.

"You rest up. I'll see you in the morning," he says, but she's already asleep.

He walks on air all the way back to his room. His mind races. This was a good night, right? They'd had fun together. Right? The excitement swells his chest. He wants to sing, to dance, to laugh. Woozy with the possibilities, the potential.

As he turns the corner onto the corridor with his room, he sees Pete outside his door.

"Good night?" Mac asks.

"The best!" answers Pete. "We work hard. We play hard." He pauses. "Although shame everyone was so tired."

Pete points to something stuck on Mac's door with tape. A little envelope with his name written on it in biro. "This is a drive with all of Terry's video. I got it all backed up on the computer, but didn't know how long you were staying, so made you a copy."

"Thanks."

Mac remembers his earlier thought about staying here. Might Terra stay with him if he did? Or was he getting way ahead of himself?

"I was wondering if um... maybe once my case is finished, if I could stay here? With you lot?"

Pete's face lights up. "You mean it? You'd stay? The room's yours if you want it. And Terra. And Bobby too, if he wants. This is great."

"I'm definitely considering it." Mac takes the taped envelope from the door.

Pete bounces from foot to foot, making excited little "oh" noises.

"In the morning," says Mac, "if I don't see you at breakfast, me and Terra will meet you in the computer shed and we'll go over the footage. That is, if you're free?"

"I got a bit of time. We don't have another recruitment drive for a week, so it's just training and planning until then."

They bid each other goodnight and part ways.

Mac enters his empty room holding the envelope. He slips it into his pocket. At the moment, he has no intention of leaving the hotel. Not until they've found out as much as they can about Terry.

He checks his phone. 11 p.m. Not as late as he thought. The dancing had started straight after dinner finished at 7 p.m, and had ended all too quickly. Still, there was only so long you could just dance with a girl, wasn't there? Sooner or later, you had to come up with something witty to say to move things along. Probably best to leave it with the night unsullied by his lack of witty things to say.

He grins to himself, remembering the way she'd looked at him as they'd danced. Looked into him. Those eyes, with the flickering orange flame reflected in them, like pools of lava. It had been a good night.

A great night.

No Bodies, Perfect

A rough hand shakes him awake, but before he can say anything, he feels a salty finger pressed to his lips.

"Sh!" Bobby stands above him. Eyes wide. Frightened.

He moves across the room. Eases the curtain back a fraction. Silhouetted by silvery moonlight, he looks up to the sky. "It's out. It's gone."

"What?" Mac sits straight up. "The Guardian?"

Bobby looks back to him and nods.

He swings his legs out of bed. "We need to warn everyone!"

"No." Bobby returns to his bedside, shaking his head. "We can't. It was her. It was Terra."

The words don't compute. "No."

"I saw her. She let him out, then he picked her up, and they were gone."

"But, she wouldn't. They killed her father." He rubs his eyes. It's still dark outside. He checks the time on his phone. 1 a.m.

"Who told you that?" Bobby grabs Mac's bag and starts stuffing what little he brought with him into it.

Mac squeezes his eyes shut and rubs his forehead.

"What are you doing?" he says.

"Don't you understand?" Bobby throws him his trousers. "We have to go. If they wake up and find that the woman you brought with you has freed their prisoner and compromised their entire operation, what do you think they are going to do to you?" He crosses the room to the door, but before he gets there he looks back. "What do you think Spoony Phil will do to you?"

"No, they..." Mac drags himself up. Stats to dress. This can't be right. Had she hired him just so that he would bring her here? "They'd know it wasn't my fault? I'm on their side."

"How? You brought her here. The Guardians never came for you after what you did last year. What reason can you give for that?"

Mac can't find the words. Can't get her face out of his head. Was everything she'd ever said a lie?

"There is none," continues Bobby. "They'll think The Guardians are letting you live because you're working for them. You'll be a traitor in their eyes."

"But..." Mac finishes dressing on autopilot.

Bobby opens the door and scans the corridor. He looks back at Mac for a moment with scrutinising eyes. "It *is* a little strange that you are still alive, don't you think? When everyone else who's ever found out about them has been swiftly erased."

He knows it is, but is too groggy to think of a come back. Too hurt. There's something he's missing. He rubs his face. "You're sure it was her?"

"Yes, I woke up under that tree with the biggest headache, and when I was coming back across, I saw her take out the guards by the barn, go in, and come back out with that bastard." He closes the door. "Coast is clear. We need to leave now."

Mac can't think. He's dazed, like he's been hit with a brick. He blinks as he crosses the room.

Bobby leads him out. Then hurries along the corridor towards the steps heading down to reception.

Mac hesitates. He has to warn the others.

"Come on." Bobby beckons from the top of the stairs.

"They're all still asleep." Mac looks around. "What if The Guardians come here now?"

There's a glass fire alarm a little further along the wall. He reaches out.

"Don't—" Bobby limps a step back.

Mac smashes it.

A piercing klaxon fills the air.

"Come on!" Bobby's voice rises. He disappears down the stairs and Mac rushes after him, out on to the gravel outside the front of the hotel, and towards several parked cars.

Bobby takes out his phone. Taps it a few times. The lights flash on one car. He jumps into the driver's seat, taps his phone again and the car starts.

Mac had deleted all of his hacking apps when he'd given up bounty hunting. He'd wanted to leave everything about that life far behind.

He dives in beside Bobby and they race away as lights blink on throughout the hotel behind them.

"Who is she?" Bobby says after nearly ten minutes of silence. They head south towards London. The motorway is empty save for the odd driverless truck and sleeper rental.

Mac opens his mouth. Stutters. Closes it again. He doesn't know. Not really. He only knows what she's told him.

Bobby snorts. "I can't believe you didn't do any sort of checks on her. What sort of a PI are you?"

"A bad one, it would seem." He stares out of the window, face pressed up against the cool glass.

"Amigo..." Bobby pats him on the shoulder. "We all have our blind spots. Yours, it seems, comes in the shape of weird-looking brunettes."

Weird-looking? Mac's lips stiffen into a fake smile. "What do you know about her? Did you find anything?"

Bobby nods. "I've been talking to some of the other bounty hunters. They've been gathering information. Have you heard of Saurian Adler?"

"Her Dad."

"Thought so. He worked for The Guardians. I don't know in what capacity, but my guess is something to do with the acquisition of children." He stares straight through the windscreen as he says it.

Mac frowns. "Why didn't you tell me?"

"I wanted to make sure first." Bobby glances at him then back at the road. Sweat glints on his brow in the muted glow from the dashboard. "So, what do you want to do now? Should we look for the other guys? Nigel Davies? Kenneth?"

"I wouldn't know where to start. I haven't heard from any of them in weeks."

"But you must know something." Bobby looks at him again. "You know The Guardians are likely to come after you. Now they have their man back, there's no reason to keep you alive. Your best bet is finding Davies and the others, right?"

Mac eyes Bobby warily.

"Think what those bastards might do to your mum. They must know where she is if they sent Terra to find you in Ripley. If Davies has found somewhere to hide, we'd better find him, right? It'll be safer there."

How does he know Mum is in Ripley?

"Um..." Mac realises his mistake. How could he have been so stupid? "Can you pull over I might need a pee?" He points out the window to the hard shoulder. Beyond is a large open field. Maybe he could make a run for it.

"Can't you hold it?" Bobby points ahead. The capital looms bright in the distance. "Not far now."

"I think I might actually be bursting."

"You're alright."

"Not alright."

"There's a bottle in the back."

"It'll go everywhere."

"Doesn't matter. Not our car."

"I uh... can't do it while you're watching." Mac reaches a hand up towards the wheel, not quite sure what he's planning to do.

Bobby stuffs a hand into his jacket pocket, and before Mac can pull away, slaps a tracker bracelet over his wrist.

"What are you doing?" Mac says, snapping his arm back. He studies the bracelet. It's a little different from the ones he used to use.

Bobby tuts. "I pushed too much, didn't I?"

Mac sits up, straight-backed, and eyes Bobby. Vocalises like a robot, "I do not know what you mean. I just need to go to the toilet. Like so bad." Beep. Boop. Beep.

Bobby shrugs. "Sure," he says, and slows before pulling over to the hard shoulder. He stops the car.

A moment passes in which neither of them speaks to nor looks at each other.

"Go ahead. But if you go further than ten metres from me, that bracelet will detonate and you'll be nothing but a red smear all over the side of the motorway."

Mac looks at the bracelet. It's an old one. One that explodes rather than poisons.

"It wasn't Terra who let The Guardian out. It was you."

"You are correct." Bobby stares through the windscreen. Taps his thumbs on the steering wheel.

"Everything you said was a lie."

He doesn't deny it.

"Does that mean she's still back at the hotel?"

"I hoped they'd all sleep through the attack. I put enough sedative in those canteens. But maybe your alarm woke them. Maybe they got out."

"Attack?"

"Once I'd freed him, the others were going to come. Mop up that little army." He looks sombre. A car speeds past, silhouetting his face in the moving white light. "The Guardians were always going to find them. You should be thanking me for getting you out."

Mac pats himself down for his phone. He has to warn Terra.

"Looking for this?" Bobby pulls it from his jacket pocket.

Mac puts his back against the window, wanting to see Bobby as best as possible. Gauge what he's thinking. "What did they offer you?"

"My life," he says. "Find Davies, find his father's colony, find the army of the fallen angels, and then maybe I get something else."

"His father? I thought he was dead. Lost at sea, Nige said."

"Oh yeah, which sea?" Bobby leans closer.

Mac buttons his lip. Has he said too much already?

Bobby smiles. "There's a colony somewhere. The Guardians are looking for it. It's the only reason they let Davies live. But then they lost him. And the only reason you're alive is because they think he'll contact you."

"Well, he hasn't." Mac scoffs and flaps a hand in annoyance. "Why didn't you tell me? We might have been safe at the hotel. I could have helped you."

"I've been emailing you for months. If you wanted to help me, you would have come back to me." Bobby laughs, but it's not a happy sound. "Besides, you can't even help yourself. I woke up in that hospital bed knowing I'd come to the end. I was tired of living the same thing, day in day out. I worked hard. I got nothing. I worked harder. I got more nothing. I have no future. No woman. No prospects. Nothing to look forward to. And then, when I was at my lowest, that's when one of their representatives came to see me. He promised me more. I find the colony and I get to join them. I get to *be* one of them."

Mac grimaces. "You do know how they become what they become, right?"

"I've heard."

"And you're ok with that?"

"You remember when I said we all became bounty hunters because we like the idea of fighting for what's right? You know that's total BS."

Mac frowns. "I thought it was nice. I felt inspired."

"You're lying to yourself, Mac." Bobby shakes his head. "We become bounty hunters because we don't mind profiting from others' pain."

"No... I—"

"You slap a bracelet on someone and get paid, who cares what happens to them afterwards? Who cares if they're innocent or not? They're hunted down like dogs and thrown away. A face to go with a crime, quickly and cheaply. That's all the insurance companies want. A quick end to it so they don't have to pay out for months of police work."

"The people we put bracelets on get a trial. They go through the system and if they're innocent, they get out."

"Do they?" Bobby raises smug little eyebrows. "Don't pretend you care. You just take the money."

"So you're saying you'll happily benefit from the deaths of children?"

Bobby shrugs. "Nobody's perfect."

"Nobody's perfect?" Mac sits for a moment wide-mouthed. Stunned. Sizes Bobby up with a scowl. "Nobody's perfect?" His voice rises to an unbelieving squeak. He would have been no match for Bobby when Bobby was in his prime, but now, with that limp, he might stand a chance. "Bobby Feta," he says, taking hold of the car door handle. "I am going to fight you now."

Bobby, quivering with what Mac hopes is fear, undoes his seat-belt with trembling, frantic movements. "Good, because I want to fight you." His lips tighten to a thin white line.

"Good, because I'm *gonna* fight you. "

"Good."

"*GOOD*!"

Bobby checks his rear-view as light from a passing truck fills the car. "You get out, I'm just—"

"Oh, I'm getting out." Mac doesn't move.

"—waiting for the truck... Ok." Bobby snaps open his door and scurries around the front of the car.

With a significant amount of rising horror, Mac notices Bobby's limp-less strut. He throws open his own door and clambers out. Backs away on the hard shoulder as Bobby strides towards him with guard up.

"Don't go too far." Bobby taps his pocket as Mac retreats.

"Where's your limp?" Mac points.

Bobby mimes a stiff leg for a few steps. "It was all a ruse, something to make you pity me."

"And I did as well, with your banged up leg and your hideous flat." He keeps shuffling back.

"What was the matter with my flat?" For a moment Bobby looks genuinely confused.

"New life forms were evolving in your kitchen."

"Oh shut up." Bobby scoffs. "What's the plan, Macadamia? If The Guardians aren't there already, then they're on their way. They know everything about the so-called army of the fallen angels."

Mac's stomach shifts. That nausea brought about only when someone he cares for is in trouble.

"Look, just give me the phone. I can try to call Terra. The Guardians don't have to know you let me warn them."

Bobby slows. Shakes his head. "That's not an option for me. It's either knock you out, stick you in the car, and take you to them, and live like a God, or I work myself to death as a bounty hunter for the rest of my life. That is, if they don't just kill me first. There's no way out for me except through you."

Mac takes a few careful steps back. "How many metres did you say?"

"Ten."

"So what happens if I go past ten, die, and then you have no way of finding Nige's dad's colony?" He takes a step back.

"Uh..." Bobby takes a cautious step forward.

"You've got nothing they want then." Mac takes another few steps back.

"Wait," says Bobby, making up the lost ground. "I..."

"So is it best for you if I don't bite the dust right now?" Mac taps a finger on his lips. "I think maybe it is." He turns and runs.

"Wait, I didn't think this through," Bobby shouts as he gives chase. "You don't want to die, do you?"

"Rather that than give you Nige Davies and his family. How long do you think you can keep up with me?" He looks back. Bobby is hot on his heels. Just where he wants him. He slows a little. Baits him. "Come on, Fatboy."

"Wait, why don't we just have that fight?" There's a breathless panic in Bobby's voice. "You were up for it a minute ago."

"I still am," says Mac, whirling around. He launches a fist into Bobby's unprepared face, and with the momentum of his run, it knocks him flat.

"I've always thought you were the worst Bobby 'flippin' Feta, but now I know you're worse than that."

He puts a well-aimed sneaker into Bobby's stomach, right in the stab scar. It's a low blow, but he knows Bobby would blow lower. He groans and curls on to his side.

"And you shouldn't call people weird-looking."

He dives on him, reaching for the pocket Bobby had tapped earlier. Removes a tracking device of some description. “I trust this is the transmitter that I can’t go ten metres from.”

“No,” splutters Bobby, still cradling his side.

“Oh shut up, of course it is.” Mac removes his phone from Bobby’s other pocket and runs for the car. As he does, he keeps a close eye on his bracelet. Nothing happens. No vomiting up of the molten intestines. No explosions.

So that’s good.

Bobby struggles to his feet as Mac reaches the driver's side door. “Maaaaac.” A blood curdling scream that echoes across the empty motorway. The scream of a man who knows his number is up. “It’s suicide to go back. They’re already coming.”

Suicide or not, he has no choice. He doesn’t look back. Just guns the engine and races for the nearest off ramp to get back to the hotel. He phones Terra’s number.

Hopes he’s not too late.

Squaring Up

Mac pulls the car through the two brick pillars that mark the entrance to the hotel's gravel drive. He doesn't have the key, or a hack app to start it again, so leaves it running on the grass by the side of the track and jumps out. Tries Terra again. She's not picking up. He runs through a small copse of trees, the soft mossy ground dulling the sound of his feet.

On the other side of the large stretch of thigh high lawn that he emerges on to, squats the hotel. A dark square in the quiet night. The wind rustles through the grass, bowing it in dense waves like the ocean.

He crouches and watches from within that dark sea of blue-green. Nothing moves. The cars that were parked out front have gone and so has the truck. Had they got away ok? Had the alarm been enough to wake them in time?

He was an idiot to leave. How could he have not trusted her? He shakes his head. Angry at himself. Squeezes his hands into fists. Wishes he'd hit Bobby Feta at least once more.

Could she still be here? What if they had her? What if they were torturing her? Asking questions about him she couldn't possibly answer. He wouldn't let them hurt someone as wonderful as her for him. Not for him. He wasn't worth it.

He snarls and stands. Forces his fear deep down inside. Takes the path of most resistance and strides across the open field towards the hotel.

They'd only known each other a week, but already his life meant nothing if she wasn't in it. It was crazy to think it, but Terra was the only thing that had made sense to him in a long time. Even before the events of last year.

Tension builds in his shoulders and forearms. The anger, the worry, the fear that he's held on to for months, comes out of him like some sort of power. Lurking as a constriction at the back of his throat. Pouring from him into the air with every breath.

He breaks into a run.

A tiny, very minuscule, almost atom-sized voice in his head suggests the folly of such a move. Running towards danger isn't what Trent Macadamias do, it tells him. Unfortunately, this is his brain talking, and he doesn't hear it over the kick drum pump of his valiant heart and the pulse of rampaging blood in his veins.

He slams across the drive. Feet crunching on the gravel. The front door of the hotel hangs open.

He steps through, wondering if he'll see bodies.

There are none. The reception is empty. He listens to the building around him for any sign of movement.

Nothing.

Perhaps they all escaped. Perhaps Terra went with them. The Guardians have been and gone having found no one.

Above him, something blinks red. A camera. They are placed all over the building. He could use the footage. See what happened.

He races back outside and around to the courtyard near The Guardian's barn. An unusual smell, like discharged electricity, hangs in the air with the scent of wood smoke as he passes the still smouldering embers by the large oak tree.

He enters the slim shed that contains all the security equipment. A room of monitors and computer hardware. It surprises him to see it still intact. For a moment he considers why The Guardians hadn't ripped the equipment apart looking for all the information they could. They must have come in and gone out fast, maybe, he hopes, because everyone had already left.

The computer is still on. The wheelie chair by the desk overturned and abandoned. He picks it up and sits.

When he grabs the mouse, Bobby Feta's bracelet catches on the edge of the table. He reaches into his pocket for the receiver. Turns it over in his hands, looking for a failsafe. There's a small key attached. He uses it to deactivate and remove the bracelet, then places both pieces into his pocket.

He rolls back the video to the moment just before Bobby woke him almost forty minutes ago. Watches the little creep take out the guards and let The Guardian go. Goosebumps appear on his arms as that slender black shape flits out of the barn and flies up and away.

He fast forwards. Finds himself hitting the alarm. Finds the corridor outside of Terra's room as people stagger from their doors.

Sees her rubbing her eyes, lost in a panicked mass of people she doesn't know.

Sees Spoony Phil race down the corridor shouting a warning. "It's escaped. They'll be coming. Meet at the emergency rendezvous. Leave everything and go, now."

Sees the fright take hold of their groggy faces as they realise what has happened and what it means.

Terra pushes her way through the crowd heading towards his room. She bangs on his door. Pushes it open. Returns to the corridor realising he's gone. His heart sinks. What must she have thought of him?

She's alone now. Everyone else having already gone downstairs. She moves back. Takes out her phone. Speaks to someone. Though there is sound, she's too far away to hear.

Mac changes camera for a moment to see what's going on outside. Everyone is running from the hotel. Jumping into cars. Racing away down the gravel track. No thought or care given for anything.

He skims through. Doesn't see her get into a car. Did they leave her? He finds her outside by the oak tree. Can only just glimpse her in the dying light of the fire and the glow of her phone held to her ear.

He checks the video timestamp. Everything has happened so quickly. It's less than twenty minutes since he set the alarm, and ten minutes before he returned.

He lets the video run. With frantic movements, she pulls several pieces of metal out of her bag. Each about a hand's length. They look like knives. She comes off the phone, then stabs them into the trunk of the tree. Presses a button on each, turning on a little red light. Steps back as all the lights turn green in unison. A purple lightning crackles and flashes between them, lighting up the area around the fire. She waits. He frowns. What is she doing?

The video shakes and glitches. Coloured pixels flicker across the screen. The audio distorts over a low bass throb that is too loud for the camera's little microphone.

There's one more lightning flash and suddenly something like molten plastic bubbles out of the surface of the tree. He leans closer to the screen, but the resolution isn't very high in the dark. It looks like hundreds of little blobs have grown out of the bark. They give off some sort of bioluminescent, purple glow, like hundreds of tiny fairy lights.

He stares at the screen, frozen in confusion.

She has her back to the camera so he can't see her expression, but she pauses a moment before walking straight into the fresh growth on the trunk and disappearing altogether.

What?

He pushes himself up from his chair and runs to the tree. The metal things are still there, stabbed into the bark, but their lights are off. They hadn't been there earlier that evening, but now between the things stabbed into the tree in the shape of a door grow hundreds of tiny fungus-like tubes.

What?

He knocks. "Terra, are you in there?"

No reply. Stupid. He circles the tree. Did she come out of the other side? He looks up. It'd be a tough tree to climb.

He must have missed something. He runs back to the shed and resumes searching through the video until he sees himself enter the security room.

Where was she? And somewhat more pressing, where were The Guardians? Bobby had seemed quite sure they were on their way. He flicks between a few other camera views, scanning through each. Taps a finger to his lips. They hadn't come. Why hadn't they come?

Something crashes outside.

A tile falling and smashing on concrete.

Oh.

He leans forward and turns off the computer monitor, leaving himself in complete darkness save the almost unnoticeable moonlight outside. He holds his breath.

Something creaks. Movement on the roof of the hotel.

Oh.

He lowers himself from the wheelie chair down to the ground as a shadow drops from the roof into the courtyard.

An engine roars nearby, the sound of vehicles coming up the gravel track towards the hotel. At least three.

Oh.

Oh no.

Splinters bite at his fingertips as he shuffles backwards further into the shed on hands and feet, through dust and dry leaves. A dark shape floats up to the doorway.

"I know you're in here," it hisses.

He holds his breath. Surely, the crazed banging of his heart will give him away.

It ducks to enter as he inches backwards through another door and into a greenhouse of about ten by ten metres. Three rows of trestles covered in various plants divide the room.

He looks around for another way out, but there isn't one. He scurries behind the second trestle, finding himself in the middle of the room as The Guardian stalks in.

From his position on the floor, Mac can see those long skeletal legs just standing there.

Light from the nearing vehicles shines and reflects through the glass. He hears them stop. Hears the crunch of footsteps as those inside exit and either head inside the hotel or towards him.

Coming back for Terra had been a mistake. Who did he think he was? Mr White Knight galloping in on his idiot horse to save the princess who he'd known for four days max, and who wasn't even bloody here.

Thank you Macadamia, but your princess is in another castle.

"Is it just you left or are the rest hiding somewhere?" The Guardian waits by the door. Draws a knife. "If they are, I'll make you talk. Why don't you save me some time and yourself some discomfort and just tell me?"

Mac stands. Raises his hands. Adopts a west country vocal disguise. "'Fraid I know nothin' 'bout that. I'm but a simple gardener. Just gettin' these tomatoes watered and I'll be out of your hair."

The Guardian doesn't look convinced.

Mac hops over the trestle behind him. Falls to the ground, landing on something chunky in his pocket.

Bobby Feta's bracelet. He clicks the bracelet shut. A little red light comes on. He stands and launches it across the room, and drops back down. The bracelet rises and falls in slow motion before clunking The Guardian in the face and falling to the ground. Mac covers his head.

"What was that?" The Guardian looks down.

"Um... How big would you say this room was?" Mac asks from his crouched position. "I was thinking about ten metres by ten."

Two men appear at The Guardian's side.

Mac wrinkles his nose. "Now I'm thinking a bit less."

"Get him."

They start forward.

"Wait," Mac says, holding up the receiver with a thumb poised as if over a button. "Come any closer and I'll detonate it."

The two men hesitate.

"He's bluffing," says The Guardian, bending and picking up the bracelet. "It's a bounty bracelet." He leans his head to one side. "I know who you a—"

"I am not bluffing." Mac looks up. Tries to remember something from a year nine maths lesson. The ceiling of the greenhouse is about a metre taller than the Guardian. It could work.

"You're Trent Macadamia. You won't esca—"

Mac holds up a finger. "Just one second please, I'm trying to do some quite tricky trigonometry."

He pauses for a moment.

Shrugs. “Oh, what the heck?” With a little jump, he throws the receiver up into the air as hard as he can. It smashes through the glass above, showering him in shards.

He ducks, and as the receiver reaches precisely the right height, whatever that might be, the bracelet in The Guardian’s hand detonates firing the two men either side of him out through the greenhouse walls and dissolving the eight-foot tall ninja into a spattering of red goop.

“Yes Pythagoras,” shouts Mac, clapping his hands together in triumph as he stands.

He sprints out through the smashed up greenhouse wall furthest from the hotel. Jumps over the fallen soldier that lies tangled in a thorny bush. Then stops. Returns and strips him of his armoured jacket, helmet, and pistol holster. He gags a little when he realises the right sleeve is wet with blood. Hoping his own dark trousers will pass, he pulls the jacket on over his own clothes, and slots the man’s helmet on his head. A visor covers his face.

Disguised, he runs perpendicular to the hotel to put some distance between him and the soldiers running towards the site of the explosion. Then sprints as fast as he can into the long grass towards the forest on the far side.

He looks back. The driveway is clear save one guard standing outside the front door. He guesses the others are searching the hotel. As far as he can see, no one is following, so he shrinks away into the woods, and towards the car he left at the opening of the driveway.

Slowing to catch his breath, and shaking his right arm to remove some of the warm, but rapidly cooling, crimson slime from his sleeve, he sneaks through the forest.

He stops as the car comes into view. From the darkness of the wood, he spots two armed guards hovering near the entrance to the driveway.

This is going to take some drama. He removes the pistol from its holster. It’s not his first time handling a firearm. The first time had been last year back at television centre. And he’d been acting then too.

He takes a deep breath, then lurches out of the bushes before falling to his knees. With the second greatest acting performance of his life, he says, “There was... an explosion... help... me," and face plants to the ground on the gravel driveway.

The two guards rush towards him. He hears one speaking into his radio as they approach. Reminds himself that these guys are super bad and that he should have no remorse in popping caps in both of their asses. As they come close enough so that he can't miss, he springs up to seated and fires as fast as his trigger finger can pull, moving between them until they both lie dead on the path, and the pistol clicks empty.

His hand vibrates with the aftershock of the shots. His helmet has eliminated some of the noise but his ears still ring. He stands and holsters the weapon. Jogs to the car without looking back at the two men lying on the drive, bleeding out.

He pulls the car around and heads towards the only place he can think of.

Terra's building.

Doll

Finn cries. Lily gives him cuddles. It makes her feel a bit better, too. He keeps asking when they are going to see their new Mummies and Daddies, but Lily thinks it was all a fib Mr Godfrey told. She thinks maybe this is where all the other children from the home have been taken. But she hasn't seen Noah or Ethan. Maybe they are here somewhere.

The next time the lady comes to bring food, she brings enough for all of the remaining children.

Lily has taken time to think about her question. Although all of the other children are scared of her, Lily stands closer to the bars this time to accept her bowl.

"Are you going to take us to our forever home?" she asks. "Mr Godfrey said that's why we were here."

"I'm sorry," says the lady. Her shoulders droop. "I can't help you, little one." She swallows, then searches in the folds of her cloak with shaking hands. She takes Lily's hand in her own. Her skin is cool and rough, but not bad. She places something in Lily's palm. A small doll. It glows purple.

"It's a gem dolly," Lily says, delighted.

The lizard lady nods with a smile. "It's called a star stone. My name is Aspid. And yours is Lily?"

Lily nods.

She turns the doll over. It's beautiful. She doesn't think it's a people doll. It's more like Aspid, and carved from a glowing purple gem. She waves it around. It lights up the dark cell around her. The other children gather around to look and she passes it to Finn when he holds his hand out.

"Wow," he says, passing it back.

"Is it mine?" she asks Astrid. She hopes so.

"I'd made it for my daughter." Astrid takes a deep breath. "It's a light in the dark. I thought you might like it, but if The Overseer comes make sure you hide it otherwise I'll be in trouble." Aspid moves her trolley towards the door. She glances back, her eyes move over the other children in Lily's cage. Her lips tighten into a sad smile. "Don't be scared. Try to have some fun together if you can."

If Your Name's Not Down...

Mac pulls up next to the little booth outside of Terra's building and climbs out of the car. The valet from the other day is still there.

"Sorry, I don't have the keys, but if you keep it running, you'll be fine." He pats the valet on the shoulder. "Good man."

"Can I help you?" the valet says, as if they've never met. He moves to stand between Mac and the building.

Mac points to the door. The bagman approaches, looking none too happy. "I was here with Terra the other day. I need to see her."

"Miss Terra isn't here." The valet steps back as the bagman arrives. Together, they form a formidable meat wall between Mac and the building. "Even if she was, we have instructions not to let you anywhere near her."

Mac looks down at them. "Can you just call up to her room? Ask her to come. I have to talk to her."

The valet looks at him with a straight face. "If you don't leave right now, the police will be called. This is your only warning. Leave and don't come back."

"But..."

Mac looks at the bagman, whose face is equally solemn. There's no way he's getting in.

"I'll call her." Mac takes out his phone. It goes straight to answer phone. Presumably blocked.

How can he reach her?

He feels like screaming up to her room. Getting a boom box and holding it above his head. But this isn't some American teenage romcom. And he's not twenty-storeys tall.

For a mad instant, he contemplates running past.

"I'll be back," he says. "I'll find Terry and I'll bring him here."

The valet and the bagman look at each other, but say nothing.

Mac climbs back into the car.

Defeated, he heads for home.

Play

Each day, when Aspid brings the bowls for the children's third meal, she always places one less than is needed in the cage opposite. She then takes one child. On these occasions she doesn't talk to Lily.

Lily wonders where she takes the children, because they don't come back.

There aren't many games you can play in a space as small as their cage, but Finn has invented a good one. One person is a catcher and they close their eyes. The others have to try and get away. If you get caught you have to stand on the back wall and can help the catcher.

Pip and Michael, the last two boys in the other cage, are allowed to help too. It's fun, but she feels sorry for them not being able to join in properly, and they don't join in every time.

They stop playing when food is brought. The other children are happy to take the bowls straight from Aspid now.

"Is there anything else?" says Lily. "Like fish fingers?" She's a bit tired of mushrooms.

Aspid smiles. "I don't know what they are." Her voice is gentle and warm.

"Fish come from the water," says Lily, pointing at the black pool that runs through the centre of the room. But she wouldn't want to eat anything from that water.

"We have fish down here, but they don't have fingers. I will see if I can find you something different."

"That would be nice."

Homeward Bound

Mum is both delighted and disappointed to have Mac home with a depressing ratio of about 20:80 respectively. He convinces her it was a mutual separation. Shrugs it off when she asks if he and Terra will see each other again. Tries to look unbothered.

"But she seemed so nice."

And saying things like that is going to make him feel better, how?

Thinking about it, it wasn't like they were even together. But then why is he so down? Something about a lifestyle missed. Potential, once more, wasted.

He has no idea how he's going to find Terry. Doesn't know where to start.

Vikram offers to give him his job back despite the fact that he has hired no one else to fill it, and doesn't look particularly fazed by the extra workload he's had to take on.

So he plugs back into small village life. Two things are different. He doesn't feel the need to drink anymore, and now he knows what it's like to be interested in someone and lose them. To have liked and lost, as it were.

It sucks.

It's a strange feeling. He was ok before - before he knew what it was like to want someone. But his whole being has expanded a little around the hope for a lifestyle that he'd never even knew could exist, and, now that hope is gone, he's left distended and flabby like an overstretched elastic band or a deflated balloon. Though he might shrink back into his previous life, who he was before is irretrievable.

As he performs his rounds once more, something niggles in the back of his mind. Something he's missed that scratches at him while he walks from house to house. He doesn't chase it. What's the point? He hopes it'll just disappear with time.

He knows it's time to put the PI part of himself to bed. Let it die. Embrace his new life of loss. Which is exactly what he intends to do until the following day. Valentine's day.

He arrives home from his shift to find a stack of laundry at the end of his bed. Freshly ironed, and topped with a card written in his mother's handwriting, with a question mark instead of her name. He groans. He'd forgotten to get her anything.

"Happy Valentine's, Mum," he shouts down.

She giggles below.

Beneath the card, positioned atop a pair of clean pants somewhat undermining its importance, is a USB stick that at first he doesn't recognise.

"I found a thing in your pocket. You're lucky, I nearly washed it," she shouts up. "It looks important."

"It is." He grips it between finger and thumb and rushes to his laptop so fast that he almost trips over his office chair.

He spends the afternoon and into the evening flicking through video footage of Terry sitting with The Guardian back at the hotel. Takes dinner upstairs when his mum cooks it for him like she's always done.

"Ooo, is this for a case?" she says, her voice lowering with excited interest as she places a plate of his favourites next to him at his desk.

He removes his headphones for the briefest of moments. "Thanks Mum," he says, too engrossed, or obsessed, with his task to give her the time. She squeezes his shoulder, then leaves the room without another word.

In the video, Terry often sits facing The Guardian. Sometimes he paces. Sometimes they talk. Sometimes they sit in silence. A lot of what they say is too difficult to hear due to the camera's poor microphone. He hopes he's not missing crucial information.

He does notice one thing. More often than not, whenever Terry is sitting in silence, he fiddles with something glittery in his hands.

In one of the later videos, the barn door is left open and there's good enough sunlight on Terry for Mac to zoom in without the image becoming too pixilated.

Mac stuffs a forkful of mash lovingly prepared by his mother into his mouth and pauses the video. For a second, he just stares. Puts an eye right up close to the screen. Everything comes to him at once. The answer hitting him like a cricket bat to the face.

In the frozen zoomed-in image, Terry holds a torn piece of the foil lid from a pot noodle. And in the corner, balanced on the arm of his chair, stands a small model of a person just like the one Mac had found in the underground room in the catacombs near the church. How had he forgotten it?

The room must have been Terry's.

Bingo. Mac explodes up, fists in the air, triumphant, ripping the headphones from his ears by the cable still stuck in his laptop. The computer jumps from his desk and lands on the floor.

He hears his mum let out a shocked gasp from downstairs.

"It's ok, Mum, I just dropped my laptop."

She doesn't answer. He waits for a moment.

"Mum?" He moves to his bedroom door. Calls down. "Mum, I just dropped my laptop."

He listens to the quiet house. Despite it being Valentine's night, Vikram is out. Second Thursday of every month is poker night with the guys. He'd spoil her absolutely rotten tomorrow. He always did. He was good like that.

A tingle of nerves develops in the pit of his stomach and he takes the first few steps down. "Mum, are you ok?"

The front door is open. A chilly wind blows through. He checks outside. She's not there so he closes it and proceeds to the kitchen.

"Oh, there you are," he says, spotting her sitting at the dining table in the dark. "Why are you in here with the light off?"

He flicks it on. Someone else is there.

"I tried to tell him you weren't in, Trent," she says.

"Mac," says Bobby Feta. He aims a gun at her. "You really should have come with me. We could have avoided this."

"Stop pointing a gun at my mum." He's not scared. He's furious. How dare anyone put her in danger?

"No." Bobby's hand shakes. He looks pale, gaunt, like he hasn't eaten or slept in days. There's an ugly, purple bruise over his right eye. It's almost swollen shut. "Tell me what I want to know, and maybe one of you can get out of this."

Mum takes a sharp intake of breath. Covers her mouth with her hands. The gun twitches.

"I told you I don't know where Nige is. I told you he hasn't contacted me."

"They don't believe you." Bobby flexes the hand holding the gun. His good eye rolls unsteadily. He looks at Mum.

Mac holds a hand out. "Please Bobby, please, I don't know. He went down to Cornwall, and that's the last I heard of him." The anger at his abandonment bubbles over and his voice rises, "he left me. They all left me."

"And where exactly did they find his father's boat?"

Mac shakes his head. "I don't know. He said Port Isaac. Probably sailed it around that bit between Cornwall and Wales."

"The Bristol Channel?" says Bobby. He angles his mouth down, and Mac realises he's talking into a phone headset. Someone's listening.

"Look Bobby. We can talk about this. Whatever they are offering you—"

"You'll what?" He tightens his lips. "They are offering not to kill me. How are you going to protect me, Mac?" His voice breaks as he shouts.

"I—I don't know. But just let my mum go—"

"I can't," says Bobby. He takes a shuddering breath. "I have to... I'm sorry."

He clears his throat and fires. Mac doesn't even hear the gun go off. He's already halfway across the kitchen. Bent low. Expecting the bullet to pound in to him as he flies forward. But it doesn't. His shoulder connects with Bobby's stomach. The butt of the gun comes crashing down on his back. But he doesn't feel it. He drives Bobby into the mantel piece sending decorative plates and little mugs collected over the years smashing to the ground around them.

Bobby groans, and Mac reaches for a piece of broken plate. His fingers moving like spiders. Arachnid automatons attached to him by flesh alone. Grabs a shard, and without thinking, buries it up to his fist in Bobby's neck. Screams as he does so. The blood pours out around his hand, splashing him on the face.

Bobby splutters, and Mac takes the gun. Stands. Aims. But Bobby is dead before his vision clears. Not that hard to kill then.

Mum sits still in her chair. Her eyes aimed at him, though her face remains straight ahead.

He drops the gun and rushes to her. Kneels at her feet. "Mum, are you ok?" He throws his arms around her. Breathes in her perfume. "I'm so sorry."

She touches his back. Her hands light. "Don't worry Trent. It's not your fault." Her voice is low. Strained.

He sits up. Looks her over. "You're ok, right?"

There's a dark spot on her white blouse, and for one moment he thinks maybe it's Bobby's blood coming off his hands. But then it suddenly grows.

"Mum...?" His heart stops. He stands and grabs her phone, which sits next to her dinner for one on the dining table.

"Trent."

"I have to call an ambulance."

She leans her head against the wall behind her. Closes her eyes as he dials. "Trent. This isn't your fault." She smiles and reaches out a hand as the operator picks up. "Listen. If they are willing to hurt you for what you know, then you have to make sure what you know gets out."

"I need an ambulance," he says to the operator. Gives them the address.

When they confirm they are on their way, he drops the phone and kneels once more at her feet. Takes her hands. "You'll be ok. You'll be ok." His whole body is shaking, vibrating.

She touches his cheek. "This will be hard, but you can't give up."

"No, but..."

"You are capable of so much more, Trent. It's time you showed them all." She closes her eyes. Lets out her last breath.

"Mum?" His fingers spasm. He squeezes her hand. "Mum. No." He can't breathe. Can't see through the tears. All of his muscles tense at once. He shakes her gently. She has to wake up.

Blue lights flash through the house. The blip of a siren. Not an ambulance. Too quick for the ambulance. A police siren. He stands and opens the hatch between kitchen and living room. Through the window out front, he can see the police car parked on the road. Two men get out.

Either they were nearby and drawn by the shot, or they were on their way before the shooting started. Which would mean they aren't really police, and they aren't here to help. He returns to his mother. Kisses her hand. "I'll show them."

And escapes through the patio doors.

He grabs his bike from next to Vikram's shed. Free wheels it down the garden, then throws it, followed by himself, over the back fence and into the wood that stands the other side. He comes down in a bramble bush, almost loosing a slipper.

How is he going to tell his sister? What will happen when Vikram comes home? What are those fake cops doing inside right now? Mum. He almost breaks down in the dark and damp of the forest, but the thorns digging into his legs bring him back.

He rubs at his face. Closes the pain off. Builds a wall in front of it. Squashes it down. Something Nige taught him. Something he's never had nor wanted to do before. Something he has to do now just so he can keep moving, keep breathing.

With brute force and no thought, he wrestles his bike out of the thorns. He needs to move now otherwise he'll stop for good. Needs to get a vehicle. Needs to get back into London to investigate Terry's room in the church. But the car Bobby stole from the hotel is out front of Mum's house with whoever it was in that police car.

He clambers out of the bushes and hits the dirt track through the wood back towards the centre of town. Down past the line of oaks by the river that he'd passed every morning on the way to work. He pushes his legs as hard as he can.

Trying not to think. Hurting himself with the exertion so he doesn't have to feel anything else.

His legs don't stop pumping until he gets to the sorting office. He jumps off his bike letting it career off on it's own in to the middle of the road, and takes the spare key from the lockbox hidden near the back door. He unlocks the door and heads inside.

His face is cool with sweat or tears and he wipes it with the bottom of his T-shirt. It comes away red. He removes the shirt and wipes it over his face. Throws it to the side. There'll be clothes here somewhere.

Visions of Mum sat motionless at the dining table creep into his head like black tentacles, probing, prying, trying to make him feel something.

He grits his teeth, and growls deep in his throat, pushing that feeling down again. It's easier if he keeps moving. He heads to the hooks with the keys for the vans. Takes one. Grabs a spare shirt and shoes from an open locker. A coat too.

It occurs to him that Terry may not be at the church anymore. But finding him, and getting him to Terra is all he has. She's hiding something important. She knows about The Guardians, and now they've taken as much from him as they have from her, maybe he can use whatever she is hiding to strike back.

He strides outside. Unlocks the van and heads for London.

He'll show them.

Going Under

It's gone eleven by the time he arrives at the church. Traffic into London is always terrible and the wait gives him time to think the worst, most excruciating thoughts.

It is all his fault. Everything is his fault.

He leaves the post van on the street outside and heads straight in.

En route, he'd bought a head torch from a petrol station. He straps it on and turns the powerful beam up to its fullest.

He's also bought a bottle of vodka. With a practiced flick of his palm, he whizzes the lid off, sending it clattering to the ground with all the other detritus. Won't be needing that again. He takes a long draw.

Goes straight down to the lower level. Across the burnt basketball court and into the catacombs.

He moves through the dark, retracing his steps until he finds the underground room. By that time, half the bottle has already gone.

Looking at the room with fresh eyes, it's so obvious. Someone grew up here. Some poor little kid abandoned and forced to make his own way. And that little kid was Terry.

How had he not seen the clues? The cook books on the bookshelf. Had Terry not been a chef?

On first inspection, nothing has changed. But there's something in the air. A draft. The musty smell has gone, replaced by a fresher odour of newly dug earth, like someone somewhere has broken a seal.

He shines his torch towards the archway that he'd started to investigate last time. The opening descends into darkness. How far does it go? What does it lead to? He shrugs. A reaction. There's only one way to find out. And this time, it's not like he's got anywhere else to be.

He steps over the threshold and looks back the way he came. It feels different being here at night. Almost safer. Or maybe it's just the vodka.

He runs his fingers along the rough wall as he steps into the corridor beneath the arch once more. The brick is older here than the catacombs outside of Terry's room. A slightly different colour. A shiver runs through him.

The ground descends gradually as he walks. It's not long before his shoulders become constricted once more. He turns sideways. Scrapes along the wall sending powdered dirt to the ground. Dry mud crunches beneath his feet. It looks as though someone has dug through a blockage in the corridor.

Looking back, there is no difference between what's ahead and what's behind.

He sidles along and soon the corridor widens again, allowing him to walk as normally as is possible in his increasing state of inebriation. He comes to a corner. Around it are steps leading down, and in the wall is a rusted cobweb-ridden sconce. He reaches out to touch it. What is this place? Who would ever need to come here and why?

He climbs down the five steps to another corner. The pattern repeats. A spiral staircase beneath the ground. Empty sconces on every other level.

He's pretty sure he's never been down so many steps in his life. He must be far below the London underground by now. It's unclear how long he descends, the steps all seem to blur, but as his thighs begin to burn, a large underground room opens up around him and he climbs down the final flight.

He looks left and right. His torch illuminates shadowed walls twenty feet to either side. The ceiling is just over an arm's reach above his head, and in front is another wall of carved stone.

The floor is a dust covered mosaic of tiles. He kneels and wipes some of the dirt away. Beneath the brown, bright reds, blues and yellows shine in his torchlight. What is this place? Who built it, and why?

He steps towards the wall in front of him. The torch picks out the shape of an arch carved into the rock. No, not carved exactly. The arch has a frame, about his height, made up of intricate winding carvings of long-stemmed mushrooms, but the interior looks like something he's seen before. Thousands of tiny little tubes like the ones he'd seen on the tree back at the hotel. Dead here. Browned and desiccated with age.

It looks a little like a door. Though there are no handles. No hinges.

Just to the right is a mosaic buried beneath decades of dirt. He pulls his shirt over his mouth so as not to inhale the dust, and scrubs at it with his sleeve.

The tiles of the mosaic come up in bright colours. A picture. On the left side, three men. The lead holds something. A box. Perhaps a gift. He holds it out to another set of figures on the right. But that's not all. What catches Mac's attention about the leader of the men is the fact that he has a large pair of impressive wings.

The three figures on the right are strange. The two standing at the back have triangular-shaped heads. Their skin is red. He rubs more of the dirt away. Frowns. Their leader is blue. Each of them has strange, dog-like legs. The blue leader reaches out to accept the gift from the men on the left.

He's not seen anything like them before.

He steps back and looks at the archway once more. Might it open? Might something lie beyond? Terry? There's a shape just to the left made from a different material to the stone wall. Some sort of crystal. Dust covers it like everything else. He spits on it, and polishes the gem with his cuff.

As he does, a faint crackling comes from the interior of the archway. He leans back to observe. The sound continues for the briefest of moments, then stops, but he doesn't pick up on any movement.

He tries again. Grips another piece of his jumper and puts some elbow grease into it like he's rubbing a genie's lamp. The sound doesn't return.

In the white light of his torch, he can now see it's some sort of button. A gemstone of a purple so deep it's almost black.

He glances back to the stairs, checking to see that no one else has crept in. Not that anyone would hundreds of metres below the city of London in some weird, forgotten room. Nevertheless, the hairs twitch on the back of his neck. He has the creeping, instinctual sensation of being watched.

His focus returns to the button. Leans closer. Tries pushing it, but it doesn't budge.

It reminds him of the ring-pops his mum used to buy him from the newsagents as a kid. Great coloured gems of sugar attached to a plastic ring. Absolute tooth rotters that he could never imagine eating as an adult, not without experiencing a severe ache in the molars. He can remember them being almost juicy in their sweetness. With constantly rising sugar taxes, they were practically illegal now.

He'd been happy back then. Nothing had mattered. His mother had been a force, a shield between him and everything that wanted to hurt him.

And now she was dead.

He closes his eyes. Presses the feeling down again. Deeper this time. Takes another swig from the bottle. He'll deal with that later.

The lollipopiness of the stone makes him want to lick it. It makes his mouth water.

And he's not sure why, but he leans in, holds his wet tongue out. It touches the smooth stone. There is no nostalgic sweet taste of sugar, only the mustiness of something ancient and untouched.

He takes another swig to take the taste away. Looks at the bottle in disgust. "What am I doing?" he shouts and launches it across the room. It shatters on the far wall.

This was hardly showing anyone. Climbing down dark holes to drink booze and lick rocks.

He sticks his fingers down his throat. Retches. The vodka burns coming up, just as it had going down. He drops to the ground by the wall and pushes his hands against his eyes, hard enough to hurt. Squeezes his face in his hands and just tries to breathe. Tries to force that crushing emptiness, the loss, the despair, back down.

"What am I doing?" He shouts, kicking out at nothing.

It was all his fault. If only he'd... If only he'd...

"If only I'd what?" The shout rips his throat hoarse.

What could he have done differently? Bobby was there for one reason. To kill him.

If only he'd not gone home.

He glimpses movement in the dark of the stairway that he'd just come down. Small. Gentle. A face seemingly made for fading into the background.

"Mac?"

He wipes his eyes with his sleeve.

Terry wears a funny grey suit and a large, over-stuffed backpack. Both the suit and bag look homemade. Pieced together from a small amount of old cloth. Mac frowns at the flared trousers. The Adler's taste in clothes must be genetic. A glimpse of sandals over socks beneath. Terry has tiny feet.

"I thought it was you," he says stepping out of the shadow.

Behind the glasses fixed with tape, behind the mop of brown hair that grows down in shabby spikes around his ears, Mac can see the family resemblance. Something in the nose, the colour of the skin. A strange glow in his eyes.

This is definitely Terra's brother.

"Terry?" He didn't expect to find him so quickly. "What are you doing here?"

"I moved in to the flat across the road. I've been watching the church. I was hoping to see someone come out." Terry tiptoes across the room like a little scared mouse. "I didn't expect to see you go in."

"Who did you think you'd see?"

Terry's eyes drop to the floor and he shrugs.

"Your family is trying to find you."

He freezes. "My family?"

"Your sister specifically, Terra." Mac glances at the vodka dripping from the wall on the other side of the room. Heat blooms in his cheeks.

"Terra?" Terry's lips part. "She's alive." He takes several hitching breaths. "And my mother? My father? Gaspar?"

"Gaspar is with her, but..." Mac doesn't know how to tell him about his mother and father.

Terry looks down. "Ah, ok, I understand." Then he screws up his face. For a moment Mac thinks he might get angry, but then he sighs sadly. "But why are you here? I don't get it. How do you know my sister?"

"She hired me to come and find you. It's why I'm here."

"She sent you? Why now? Where have they been?"

"They thought you'd died. But then they saw you on the show last year. It took them this long to find me."

"And how did you know I'd be here?"

"I've been to see Dave and Pete at the hotel. I saw you making tin foil figurines in a video, and I'd found the ones here before. I should have put two and two together sooner." Mac pushes himself to stand. "You need to come with me."

Terry begins pacing back and forth, rubbing his temples. "I want to. I want to." He lets out a frustrated sigh, then stops and turns his attention to the engraving beside Mac. "But I... I need to check something first. I need to be sure. I have to find my way through this door."

For a second Mac has the impulsion to grab Terry and shake him. He doesn't want to be here. He wants to find Terra.

"What do you need to check?" He grits his teeth.

Terry continues to look past him. Mac follows his gaze.

"Before I found The Church of The Fallen Angels, I'd spent years trying to figure this door out. It drove me a bit loopy. I could have sworn I'd come through there," he says, nodding towards the arch on the wall. "Thought I'd made it up until The Guardian told me I hadn't. Thought I was the only one, that I was just a bit of a freak, but..." he trails off with eyes focussed on the arch.

"What do you mean?" Mac frowns. "Is that why you left the hotel?" He steps closer to the wall. Inspects the tiny desiccated tubes of fungus.

Terry nods. "I can't go and see Terra until I know I'm not crazy. And to prove that to myself, I have to go through this door."

"OK. Fine," says Mac, reluctantly. He needs Terry on side "But how do you open it?"

"I think it has something to do with that gem. I thought I'd tried everything, but," his eyes meet Mac's, "it sparkled when you licked it."

"Sparkled?"

"Like a purple fire. I've not seen it do that before. I've pushed and prodded it. Even shouted at it." Terry looks down.

"How can this be a door? It's just a wall of dead mushrooms."

Terry reaches forward to touch the gem. Gives it a little push. Nothing.

"Lick it again."

"I'm not bloody licking it again."

Terry gives the gem a little buff, then bends over and sticks his tongue on it.

The wall of tubes snaps and crackles once more. Mac listens. It sounds like rice krispies.

"Water?" says Mac. "Maybe we need water."

Terry rifles in his pack and pulls out some sort of weird looking flask. Douses the button. The tubes. Everything.

The crackling sound intensifies and the button pops outwards as if on a spring.

Terry hits it.

Silken purple light pours from the archway, blinding him. Mac stumbles back, rubbing his eyes with balled fists. The whole doorway erupts in purple flame. A waterfall of lilac and white light shimmers as the tubes pulse and glow and soften.

The colour of the mushrooms settle like pixels on a screen to show another room. A space similar to the one he and Terry stand in now, given a purple hue by the colour of the fungus.

"We did it," says Terry, punching a fist in the air.

"We did? Are you sure we haven't just turned on some sort of organic TV?" He inspects it further. Hands on hips. Steps a little closer so that he's only an arm's length away from the wall. The tubes seem to move towards him like questing little mouths. "How do we actually open it, then?"

"I'll show you."

Terry grabs him by the arm and tugs him forward. He's strong and in his inebriated state Mac can't stop him.

Every single bit of him prickles as if stabbed by pins as he crashes face first into the wall of tubes. It hurts, but only for a moment.

And then he's standing on the other side, in that second room, identical to the first, but with less brown dust covering everything.

He also appears to be naked from the waist down.

Last Meal

Lily spends most of her time looking at her dolly. She likes the way its glow makes her fingers purple.

The longer they stay here the more tired and blurry she becomes. It's like the air is heavy when she breathes. They are all sleepy. Too sleepy to play their game most of the time.

"Wake up, Lily"

The words bring her to consciousness. She opens her eyes. Aspid is there with her trolley.

She passes bowls through the gaps and the other children accept them. "Eat quickly children. You'll need your energy."

Lily's is last. Several fried pink tentacles rest on top of the normal brown stew. She wants to say 'yuk', but doesn't.

"Fish fingers," says Aspid.

Lily shakes her head letting her hair whip back and forth. These are not fish fingers.

"Try them," says Aspid speaking quickly. She seems different. "You might like them." She glances back towards the door.

Lily takes one between her first finger and thumb. It wobbles a little, like jelly. She takes a bite. It's warm and the outside is crunchy. The inside is soft. It does taste a bit like a fish finger. She smiles then looks past Aspid at the empty cage on the other side of the water.

Aspid notices and follows her gaze. "I'm sorry," she says. "But..." She swallows. Her eyes flick nervously between them, watching them all eat.

She moves closer to the bars and lowers her voice while the others finish their bowls.

"Listen to me, little ones," she says. "I need you to listen and to know. Some friends are coming. They will help you. I'm going to take you to meet them, but we have to be quiet." Her wide yellow eyes stare into Lily's. "Do you understand me?"

Lily nods, still chewing. "I can help. I'm the oldest."

"Good girl."

Something clicks outside, Aspid turns her head to listen. When there are no other sounds, she removes the key from her pocket and unlocks the door of the cage.

She beckons. "Come. Come, children."

Lily steps out of the cage, then points to the one on the opposite side of the room. "Are we going where the other children go? To where Pip and Michael went?"

Aspid shakes her head. "No." Her voice wavers. She presses her lips together and takes a steadying breath. "No, you are not."

She manoeuvres her trolley so that it's in front of the cage door. Lily notices for the first time that it is bigger than is necessary for twenty bowls. She thinks perhaps there are other children who need feeding.

"I want the littlest ones to climb underneath." Aspid points at the three smallest children. "You, you and you."

The trio climb under, curling into little balls on the bottom level of the trolley.

Aspid removes her cloak and lies it over the top hiding them. Beneath she wears a grey, all-in-one tunic. Lily thinks her legs are strange - like a doggy's.

"The rest of you will need to stay as close to me as you can." She takes Lily's hand in her own and gives it a little squeeze. "Come on, we don't have much time."

The Underworld

Mac pulls his T-shirt down over his groin, and finds it, and himself, coated in a sticky residue. His legs feel a little wobbly, like he's never used them before, but the sensation quickly fades. Terry keeps a hold of his arm to steady him.

"Where the hell have my trousers gone? And what am I covered in?"

Except for his socks, which hang loosely around his feet as if the elastic has gone on them, he wears nothing on his bottom half.

"Oh," says Terry, averting his eyes. He lets go with an unusual sticky click between the skin of his hand and Mac's arm.

Strangely, Mac feels quite sober. Renewed. In fact, despite having all his bits on show, physically he feels bloody fantastic.

Terry is still fully clothed. Still fully kitted out. He removes his backpack and beckons Mac closer. "Your clothes should still be back on the other side. Forgot to mention the no plastic rule."

He whips a cotton towel from inside his bag and hands it over. Mac wraps it around his waist and looks back at the doorway. On this side, the walls are coated in moisture. The tubes all look healthy, though there are two pixels about midway up the image that seem dead or gone.

The fungus shows an image of the room they were just in. Terry is right. Mac's shoes and trousers lie in a little heap on the floor on the other side. Also, some squiggly white lines that he presumes are the elastics from his socks.

"Can't I just go get them?"

Terry shakes his head. "No plastics." He walks a little way across the room, beaming. "We're really through. Look," he gasps, "there's steps going down."

"Where are we?"

"Nearly home." He's shaking.

Mac follows Terry's gaze. Home? Could he really have come from down here? He tries to remember what Terra had said about the moment her family had lost him.

"Have you seen enough?"

"Not yet. Um..." Terry moves across the room. "I want to go down. Do you want to come with me?" he says.

It's uninviting at best. "Not particularly, but—"

"Oh, go on. It'll be an adventure." Terry puts his hands together.

"*Buuut*," continues Mac. "I'll do it if you help me get back in your sister's good books."

"Yesss." Terry pumps a fist. "I've been up and down those stairs in the other room countless times, but I've never made it through the door." He returns to Mac, and acting a little too overfamiliar, wraps his arms around his torso. "I'm glad you're here." He squeezes, then releases. "With Trent Macadamia PI by my side, I can face anything."

Mac wants to laugh. "Yes. Quite."

"Then we shall go." Terry turns, and with pack rattling on his back, skips and hops towards the steps.

"What exactly are you expecting to find down here?" says Mac, as he follows Terry towards the stairs. Together, they hurry under a lip of stone and descend beyond the limits of the room they'd just left behind.

"I don't know. But look..." Terry points ahead.

His backpack almost fully blocks the slim stone stairway, so Mac leans to the side to glance over his shoulder. They descend into darkness, but ahead he can see something. A pale glow. A purple rectangle of faint light below them.

"Something's down there," says Mac.

"And you can hear that, right?" Terry turns his head. In the near pitch blackness, Mac can see a joyful little smile on his face.

Mac listens, but it's difficult to hear anything over his and Terry's unsure and scraping footsteps. "What is it?"

"Sounds like life." He sniffs. "Smells like life, and fire, and maybe people, but not people people."

Mac sniffs. All he can smell is the musty odour of the dirty, damp stone that surrounds them. "Not people people? Can you clarify?"

"People like me."

"People like you?"

Terry pauses and looks back. There's a twinkle in his eye. "Yeah, not people like you."

Mac rubs his eyes with rigid fingers, lighting up sparks of colour behind his lids. Best not to ask any more stupid questions. Best just to wait and see what's down there.

It takes a minute to descend, and they exit the stairway into a huge cavern. An enormous geode hollowed from the earth. Huge purple crystals hang from the ceiling high above. They look like amethyst but cast their own lilac glow, which lights up the whole space. Motes of yellow and orange flicker and sparkle in gentle currents. Hundreds of fireflies high above where he and Terry now stand.

Mac can't help but stare. It's awesome.

Terry points. "Wow! Star stones," he says, looking up, mouth agape. He gives Mac the biggest grin. "Look, star stones."

Mac does a double take. The shining gems reflect as dots of light in Terry's upturned eyes.

He reaches for his wits, to gather them safely around him, but they fucked off ages ago. "I think I've been pushed a little over my limit today," he says. "The cup of what I'm going to question is overflowing. Those are star stones, and I'm deep under London in some sort of cave system. And..." he trails off. Looks down as the slow, clutching darkness inside him rears up. Batters it back down again. "So are you crazy or not?"

"Turns out I'm not," says Terry.

The flat enclave of stone that opens out at the foot of the stairs would struggle to fit a car, but looking up, he can see the roof of the cavern covers hundreds of metres. A maze of stalagmites and outcroppings has portioned the floor into small enclosures. Towering columns of grey stone stretch up to the ceiling.

He can't see further than a few metres ahead, but looking up, it's like he can see forever.

To the right, a pool of fluorescent water skitters with small fish and other aquatic creatures. The air is thick with moisture and a humid, earthy warmth that he can almost taste.

Thousands of small, donut capped mushrooms cover the nearest column. They twist around it like light-brown tinsel reaching all the way to the ceiling. Their slender noodle-like stems sway as if caught in a gentle ocean current.

"Oo, oo, oo," says Terry like an excited little chimp. He jumps forward, flapping his hands in front of himself in delight. He rips a fistful of mushrooms from the wall...

"Wait, they—"

... and stuffs them into his mouth.

"—might be poisonous."

Terry pinches his thumb and first two fingers together on both hands and looks to the ceiling in pro-chef-like appreciation. He says something that sounds almost French, but misses what could be described as one of the most beautiful languages in the world by a few choice consonants.

"This... this is it." He plucks a few more rubbery stalks from the wall and spreads them out in his hands in front of Mac. "Try one."

Mac holds up a palm. "I think I'll wait to see if your liver comes crawling out of your butt first." He looks up at the surrounding cavern. "Is this what you meant by home?"

Terry shakes his head. "Not yet. Wait until you see the city."

"The city? There's a city?"

Terry nods. "There's a city. Come on." He grins and disappears around a pillar.

"Wait." Mac hitches up his towel and hurries after, splashing through a pool of disgruntled, fist-sized frogs.

The space opens out a little around the corner. Rock moguls cover the ground, worn smooth over hundreds of years by the steady drip drip of drops. Although he seems to have sobered up completely from his earlier drinking session, the shallow valleys and hills make it difficult to walk without slipping.

Each valley is home to a puddle. Each puddle, home to a vibrant community of flora and fauna coloured with bioluminescent pinks, blues, and purples that are bright enough to see by. Each puddle is a whole new world to the last. All so close, but divided. He wonders if the creatures of each know their neighbours exist.

Squiggly blue little tentacled things slip and slide in the water. Some occasionally leave the surface and bobble upwards only to splash back down again. There are more mushrooms, of brown and yellow and red, growing in clumps under the light of the huge gems that cover the ceiling. Small anemones and fish and frogs. There's a sound to it all. A white noise of clicking and buzzing, of swaying and rustling. An entire ecosystem.

Terry is already some way ahead, gazing up and around in awe with both hands gripping the straps of his pack tightly. His mouth hangs open. He looks like a seasoned tourist in an exotic new city.

"Hold up," says Mac, trying not to slip and die on the smooth wet stone. He knows they should go up, but wants to see more.

Terry doesn't seem to have anywhere near as much trouble traversing the treacherous ground. And now Mac is seeing him from a distance moving with nimble ease across the slippery rock for the first time, he can see there's something unusual about Terry's legs below the knee. They have a strange bend. As if he has another joint somewhere around his shin hidden beneath his trousers.

"Hey," Mac calls after him.

His shout echoes around the chamber, and with a swish and flurry of wings, a large swarm of something dislodges itself from a shadowy area of the ceiling and flutters around for a few moments before reattaching itself in another darkened corner. It sends a shiver up his spine.

"Wait," he whispers again and scampers to catch up. "Where are you going?"

"I want to see the city." He points further into the cavern. "It's this way. Can't you smell it?"

Mac sniffs the air. A real nostril opener. "Does it smell like damp and mud?"

Terry crinkles up his nose. "No, on the other side of the damp and mud. It doesn't smell quite as I remember, a bit more chemically maybe, but I guess it's been a while. Do you think my mother is here?"

Mac sniffs again. It smells a bit like his old office. Fusty.

He looks back. Can no longer see the hole they'd come through. Hidden in the grey rock upon grey rock.

The city of London is so far above—

His breath catches as a thought comes leaping uninvited into his brain.

Or is it?

When he'd climbed through that door, where had it taken him? Had he travelled centimetres? Or miles?

Was he even in England anymore?

Nah! There was no such thing as teleportation. He'd watched too many sci-fi mov—

Was he even on Earth anymore?

Nah! There was no such thing as not being on Earth... right?

Terry has moved on again.

What *had* he meant when he'd said, "people people"?

"We should set up camp," says Terry, as Mac catches up once more. "This place is a good spot. Flatter. Drier. Sheltered."

Mac turns his nose up. Stamps his bare foot on the cold, hard stone beneath. "We're not sleeping. We should go back up." As if his brain would let him sleep anyway. "It's late, and I didn't come prepared for um..." he looks about him, "... adventures in drippy underground caverns lit purely by giant purple gems and inhabited by thousands of weird little creatures?"

Terry sighs. "OK. I guess I've seen enough." He places his bag down and pulls out a fistful of dried sticks. "Maybe a snack first?"

"Alright, but then we're going to see Terra."

"I'm a bit nervous, you know?"

"Yeah, I'd be too. She's actually very nice though."

Terry begins rubbing one of the sticks over another to create fire. It lights surprisingly quickly.

"How are you doing that?" says Mac.

"It's not wood anymore. This lights quicker." He points past Mac's shoulder at another clump of the donut capped mushrooms clinging to a huge stone pillar. "Grab me some of those bad boys, would you?"

"You're sure they're safe?"

"Yeah. Definitely. I think. The way you can tell is that I'm not dead."

"Suppose." Mac grabs a handful and moves to crouch next to Terry's makeshift kitchen, while Terry is busy collecting a pot of water from the nearest pool.

"I'm not drinking that."

"It'll be fine. I'll boil it. That kills anything." Terry bends low and blows a faint wisp of smoke. Flames flicker.

"That water is so filled with those weird little octo-jellyfish, you boil it, you're just making gross soup."

Terry holds up a hand, coupled with an appeasing twist of the head. "Yes, delicious mushroomy noodley soup. It's the flavour sensation I've been searching for my whole life."

Mac's stomach rumbles at the thought. Delicious mushroomy noodley soup does sound good right now.

"Imagine a pot noodle..." Terry pauses, allowing Mac time. Then, in the style of an all-knowing super being, closes his eyes and pinches thumb and forefinger on both hands as if the following words are set to contain unparalleled wisdom. "... times ten!"

"Not times ten?"

With eyes still closed Terry nods. "Times ten."

Mac hands over the mushrooms. "I'm a vegan though, so please save anything that's moving."

Terry rolls his eyes, then agrees by flicking out a few tiny creatures. He rolls out a stretch of cloth revealing several very sharp looking black knives and chops the mushrooms. He slides them into the water along with a few other herby green bits.

Mac sits next to him.

Terry wafts the vapour from the pot up to his nose. Smiles and places a lid on top. "It's good to see you again, Mac."

"And you."

Terry watches him for a moment. He leans his head to one side as his eyes flick across Mac's face. "Did something happen to you?"

Mac shakes his head. "No."

Vikram will be home by now. Mum will have just popped one of her cartoon plasters over the bullet hole and warmed up his dinner. No fuss. No bother. Mopped up the mess Mac had left of Bobby Feta. Swept up the broken plates. Perhaps asked Vikram to bag the body and chuck it straight into the outside bin. *Don't want it stinking up the kitchen.*

She's fine until he says she's not.

Terry gives him a subdued smile. "Is this one of those times when I'm supposed to ask again and you say yes, or do you really not want to talk about whatever is causing you pain?"

Mac considers this. "I don't know. Try it."

"Do you want to talk about it?"

He breathes deeply. Sucks the moisture from his lips. "My mum died. It was them." Just saying it hurts.

"I'm sorry." Terry looks down. His lips press together. "I know what I said before, about why I wanted to come down here, but I think they got my mum, too." He lifts a spoon and stirs his pot for a moment in silence. "If I think about it logically. She would have followed me through if she'd been ok. She would have found me. She..." He swallows, but doesn't say any more.

"What happened to you? How did they lose you?" he asks.

"It's all just little flashes. I was at home with Mum. Dad, was away at the time, with Terra and Gaspar. And suddenly Dad's friends came in." Terry slurps from the spoon. Purses his lips with satisfaction. "I don't really remember what they said," he continues, "but we had to go. It wasn't like our usual trips to the surface. Mum didn't even pack a bag. But we were going to see Dad, so I knew it was ok. They sent me through that door." He jabs a thumb over his shoulder. "But no one met me on the other side."

Mac doesn't want to say it, but Terry must be mistaken. Terra couldn't have come from down here, from a hole in the ground.

But Terry had grown up in that room. He tries to imagine what that must have been like. A young boy on his own in the catacombs.

"I waited and waited. Mum and the others had been right behind me. But no one came. I got so hungry. So I went up. I stole food. No one ever came to find me." Terry looks down.

Mac feels himself wavering. Other people have it far worse than him. He couldn't imagine being so young and feeling the absolute loss he feels now. The confusion.

"How did you survive?"

"By hiding mostly. Blending in. By becoming the people I saw up there. I was able to get a lot of handouts by going to the church. For the most part the people there were nice. And the catacombs came right out near Camden market so food was easy to come by."

"You must have been a tough kid."

Terry smiles.

"I'm sorry about your mum," says Mac.

"I'm sorry about yours." Terry has kind eyes. They have an unusual shape to them. Something Mac hadn't noticed before. The pupil is not quite round. They are Terra's eyes.

"You look like her, you know, like Terra."

Terry leans his head to one side. Eyes dance as if he's trying to remember something. "Tell me about her."

"She's lovely." A smile tries to cross Mac's face as he remembers their dancing. "Good fun. She said your name is Enki."

A light comes on in Terry's eyes. "Enki. I remember." His head shifts to one side. "I would like to meet her. I wanted to see the city, but that can wait. I know how to open the door now. I've seen enough down here to show me I wasn't mad all along."

"That's if we can find our way back" Mac stands. Pokes his head around the nearest column to see if he can see the stairs they'd come down. Rocks and fungi camouflage the way back. He hopes Terry can find the exit because it all looks the same. Grey glistening stone in purple light.

Something moves roughly twenty feet away. A small head-sized shape ducks down behind a rock.

Then, in his periphery, across the other side of the open space, something skitters behind a tall thin stalagmite. His heart pounds as he backs into their camp.

"Er, Terry," he whispers, keeping his eye on the entrance to the clearing. "I think we're being followed. Or watched. Or watched and followed."

"You are."

Mac chances a look back. Terry stands upright with his hands above his head. Behind him, shorter than Mac, covered in a dark cloak that leaves most of its face hidden in shadow, and holding a spear with a sharpened glowing gem on the end, is a creature. It edges the spear forward to give Terry a little poke. As it does, the light of the gem illuminates its face.

Though very nearly human, there's something wrong. Its mouth is too wide. Its eyes, too dark. Brown diamond pupils surrounded by yellow. In the faint light, its skin looks almost scaled. And definitely green.

Terry smiles when he sees them. "Ah, people like me." Then something happens to his skin. It goes blue.

Mac presses his lips together while he tries to compute. But not even the human brain has enough RAM to survive this apparent error in the matrix. Especially not with the amount of denial programmes he's currently running.

His vision turns grey, and he succumbs to unconsciousness, the fortnight's mental pummelling having finally caught up with him.

Escape

Purple gems glow brightly at regular intervals along the long and thin corridor that runs outside of the cage room. The space is just big enough to fit Aspid's trolley. She presses it along with one hand, gripping Lily's with the other. Finn and the rest of the children follow closely behind.

Lily's heart beats quickly in her chest, like a little bird. She likes being out of the cage and she likes holding Aspid's hand, but something about Aspid's hurry makes her nervous.

Finn bumps into her when Aspid stops just before the door at the end of the corridor.

"Wait here a moment," she says, letting go of Lily's hand. Lily doesn't want to let go. Aspid presses the door open and disappears through it.

"Where are we going?" asks Finn.

The light in the corridor is better than the cage room — almost as bright as the lights at the home — and in it she can see how dirty the children's faces are. Little clean lines trace their cheeks where they have been crying.

"Somewhere nicer," says Lily.

The door opens. Aspid.

"Come on," she says. She takes the trolley and pulls it backwards through the door, then holds it so the kids can come through.

They are back in the cathedral-like room they'd entered when they'd first arrived here.

"Are we going back through the purple door?" says Lily in a hushed whisper.

"No," says Aspid, "that only goes to one place. Now, try to be quiet, and stay close."

Aspid sniffs the air then darts the trolley across the hall to a side door. She holds it open allowing the children to move through and into a well-lit dining hall. A long wooden table sits in the centre surrounded by tall chairs. One wall is made up of long open windows. Although she is too short to properly look through them, Lily can see that this building is definitely not in London, but instead in some sort of giant cave. The ceiling of the cave extends for hundreds and hundreds of metres and is covered in huge, shining, purple crystals like the one her doll is cut from.

Huge columns of stone rise up to support the ceiling. Small square buildings cling to the columns like barnacles with bridges and stairways branching between them.

She hasn't time to look long before Aspid grips her hand and tugs her across the hall with the others in tow.

"We don't have much time," she says.

The spongey carpet deadens their footsteps as they move towards a low archway on the far side. Aspid quickens her stride as they enter into a tunnel beneath the archway and head towards what looks like a dead end of rock.

They stop next to an open doorway. The sizzling sound of cooking and warm smell of mushroom stew comes from within. Lily can also hear the low mumble of others talking.

Aspid lets the three children out from beneath her trolley.

"Wait here," she says, then pushes it through the doorway.

Lily hugs close to the wall and peeks around the corner after her. Inside she can see two more people like Aspid. One stirs a huge, steaming pot. His skin is scaled and a dark red, his head is an unusual shape. The other chops vegetables with a large knife and has a colouration more like Aspid.

When Aspid enters, the red one shakes his head and turns away. The one more like Aspid places her knife down, and says something to her that Lily doesn't hear. She then pulls her into a hug. Her eyes flick to the doorway over Aspid's shoulder. Lily darts back knowing she's been seen.

Aspid returns moment's later. "Come on, children."

When Lily passes the open doorway, she sees the red one now stands close to the one that had hugged Aspid. He puts his arm around her as the children continue past the kitchen.

As they near the end the soft flooring gives way to slippery grey rock. Lily wants to ask so many questions. Where are they? Where are they going? Where did the other children go? But she keeps them all in.

Finn takes her hand and together they try their best not to fall as they reach the end of the corridor. Lily realises it's not a wall of rock they are heading towards, but a corner which turns sharply into a darkened tunnel.

Her eyes follow Aspid when she moves to the back to herd the children on.

"Lily," she says. "Take out your doll. Soon we will come to a place where the tunnel splits. Take the left route."

Lily removes the doll from her pocket and holds it up. The wet rock around them gleams purple with its light, and here and there, growing up from the rough cracks and crevices, are bunches of tiny, capped mushrooms. The mushrooms react to the light of the doll and begin to tingle with a faint but building glow. The effect catches from clump to clump and suddenly the whole tunnel is lit with an arctic blue just bright enough to guide their way.

"It's not far," says Aspid, holding up a fist-sized gem of her own.

Lily leads the way.

New Friends

For the second time in two weeks, Mac wakes with no recollection of having gone to bed. But this time he is not lying on his bed back in his room at home with the sound of his mother making breakfast downstairs. This time he's lying wrapped in a towel on solid but uncannily warm rock, surrounded by the ceaseless fizz of tiny creatures and the delicate drip of condensation.

And somewhere nearby, hushed voices speak. A strange chuckle. Low in timbre. Quiet. Restrained.

He opens his eyes. A fire burns just two arm lengths away. Seated around it are three figures. Two have their backs to him. The other sits opposite.

Where's Terry?

From his position on the floor, he can't see him. Can't see anything past the enclosure of grey rock. High above, the star stones still shine as he expects they always have.

He eases one hand out. Picks up a fist sized rock. Feels its weight in his palm.

He'll need to be quick.

He takes a deep breath. Counts down.

Three. Two. One.

Explodes to his feet.

Raises the rock, ready to crunch one of the creatures over the back of the head and leg it.

"Oh, Mac, you're up," says Terry from behind.

Mac swivels around, his rock remaining raised. Terry rests on his haunches stirring the pot of soup. His skin is a deep ultramarine blue and there's something wrong with the shape of his face. More angular. Sharper. He takes a sip of the murky liquid from his wooden spoon.

"Just in time." He points at the soup as a hip-hop star might at his crotch. "This bad boy is done."

Mac swivels back. His head is a pendulum swung around by his feet. He can't catch his breath. The three around the fire remain seated, but each of their eyes are upon him.

In the amber light, he can see they aren't like him. Though their faces are so close to being human, their skin is scaly, their noses are flat, and they don't have visible ears.

The one sitting across the fire, the one he'd first seen with Terry, stands and clutches its spear. It is about four-feet tall but looks strong, agile. He would not like to fight it. Its green features can almost be described as feminine. Its yellow eyes stare at him with threatening intensity. Sharp hair-like spines cover its head. It wears slim fitting grey clothing of a style Mac has not seen before. Trousers. Boots. Some sort of close-cut tunic. A belt with several pouches and packs and three glinting blades at its hip.

The other two, the ones sat closer, are an orangey-red. A little bigger than the green one. Their lower jaws jut with several fang-like teeth. They wear similar dark grey clothing with a looser cut to allow for broader shoulders beneath.

One seems older. More wrinkled around the eyes. More yellow around certain contours of his face. The lips. The nostrils. It has a beard of tendril like mushrooms growing down from its nose and from the corners of its mouth. A single scar runs the length of its face from forehead to lip. The scar, though healed, seems bound with more fungal extrusions.

Mac looks back at Terry, who has moved a little closer. "Huh?" is all he can think to say. Even 'what' has escaped him. His head hurts.

"I can probably explain." Terry holds up his palms. "Maybe have a sit down." He puts a hand out to suggest a flat rock next to the fire.

"Yeah?" Mac staggers around the flames, seeing now that a pyramid of dried fungus burns rather than wood. It releases a sweet smoke that smells of molasses.

He gives the red creatures a wide berth, without taking his eyes from them. The nearest seems to smile, so he reciprocates with absolutely no confidence. Once again, he feels faint, like each breath has less oxygen in it than it should. "Is it me or is it getting a bit hot?" He fans his towel a little.

"Don't worry, Mac," says Terry. "They won't hurt you. These guys are friends."

The nearest red one gives a friendly thumbs up. Or rather, as he's now seeing their hands properly for the first time, a claw up.

"Friends." He clears his throat. "Friends?" Terry smiles a blue smile and passes him a mug of soup. Mac swirls it around. Looking at the contents doesn't do much for his nervous, churning stomach. "I..." he begins, but doesn't know where he's going with it.

"How about I start with names?" Terry points at the green one, who still holds her spear pointed at him. "She's Gila. And these two are Ig—"

The nearest red one raises a hand and smiles. "Welcome."

"—and Agamo."

The mushrooms on the face of the older one quiver as he smiles, too. The tips of sharp teeth poke up over his lips. "Welcome," he says.

"They are who we have come looking for," says Terry, presenting them with both hands. "My people."

"And who exactly are you, Terry?" Mac studies him. His blue skin. His strange eyes.

Terry raises a brow. "I'm still Terry, or Enki, I suppose."

Out of the corner of his eye, Mac notices a slight movement from the trio. A meaningful look passes from the older red one, Agamo, towards Gila. A slight widening of his yellow eyes.

Mac scratches his forehead. "No, um... I mean, whooo um... what are you?" He tries to smile. But knows he probably looks a lot like the joker without the make-up.

"We are lacerta," says Agamo, straightening his back by pushing up on his bent knees. "Gila, show our guest some hospitality. He is welcome. Put the spear away."

Gila remains silent, but lowers her weapon. She sits again by the fire and lifts a bowl to her lips.

"We're freedom fighters," says Ig with an amicable grin.

"Mm." Mac nods as if all has become clear. Truthfully, all has not become clear. All is murky as balls.

"Who's freedom are you fighting for?" he asks. He relaxes his shoulders, but doesn't approach them, or sit on his designated stone.

"Everyone's," says Agamo. He taps himself on the chest, then points at Mac and says, "Our people. Your people."

"We've not done much fighting, though. Not really," adds Ig, with a rhythmical bob of his head. "You see, there's not many of us. But we're building up to it."

"Who haven't you done much fighting with?"

"The winged ones." Ig's nostrils flare, and for a moment, his friendly demeanour becomes buried beneath a deep frown. "Those who enslave our people and yours."

"They *are* his people," says Gila, putting her bowl down and spitting something into the fire. The flames hiss. "He's just a baby. Give him long enough and he'll grow up to be just like them. He'll sprout a pair of wings and call himself a God. He's a man. A hateful, despicable man." She glares at Mac over the fire.

"Gila." Agamo frowns.

Mac looks at Terry. His voice shakes. "Do they mean The Guardians?"

Gila laughs. But there is no humour in it. Despite the way the lacerta look, their voices, their language, everything about them is very human. "The Guardians? And who exactly are they supposed to be guarding us from?" she says.

"We know they took on the moniker long ago. When it meant something else," says Agamo. "We had trust with them once. Then they abused that trust."

"That was a long time ago," Gila says. "Before Ig and I were born. He and I have witnessed nothing but evil from *his* sort." She nods towards Mac.

He spots that at some point she's removed one of the three blades from her belt and clutches it in her hand. He takes a step back.

"Put that away," hisses Agamo. "Not all humans are alike."

Gila stands and moves away towards the edge of the stone enclosure. She looks back. "Maybe not, but if there was a chance he could grow into one of them, it'd be better to kill him now." She disappears out of sight.

"Sorry, that wasn't very welcoming," says Agamo, looking a little embarrassed. He looks at Terry as if expecting some sort of reaction. "So, Enki, was it?"

Terry grins. "Apparently so."

"What brings you and this human down to the caverns?" He leans his head to one side.

"I was looking for home. The city. Can you take us?"

Agamo's uneasy eyes shift to Ig. "We can't take you in. It's not what it once was, and we daren't go back lest we are caught."

"Why?" asks Terry.

"Racken is no longer ours. It is a slave camp," says Agamo. Mac senses a deep sadness in his low voice. "The Guardians run it now. Along with every major lacerta city on the planet."

"The planet? Earth, right?" says Mac, with a little hesitancy, looking to quell his earlier fears. "We *are* still on Earth?"

A wrinkle appears on Agamo's brow.

"We're roughly two miles below the city you call London," he says. "I guess you found and opened a hidden portal."

Mac flicks a finger between himself and Terry like a flopping fish. "Pretend we don't know what's going on here and hit us with the lowdown. Pretend you're explaining your entire history to a child." He jabs a thumb at Terry. "For Te—Enki's sake."

"Oh, don't worry about me, I think I understand," says Terry, taking a slurp of his soup from a wooden spoon.

Mac gives him a look of betrayal. "Really?"

Agamo chuckles. "There are two types of dominant bipeds on this earth. Human and lacerta. You and us. Long ago, you ruled above and we ruled below. We had a symbiotic partnership. We traded. We worked together. And sometimes," he sighs. The fire gleams a little brighter in his eyes, "we loved one another. It was a beautiful thing. We were united." He grimaces, showing sharp fangs. "Until they came. The dark ones. The Guardians. They wanted to control everything. Not just above, but below also. We were not expecting it. They used the very portals we set up to trade with to attack us. Abused our trust and whispered their subversions into our towns and our minds. They used our fungus against us, creating slave camps of our once great cities. Processing plants for their abhorrent appetites. Factories for the poisons they pump out above to keep you humans controlled and docile. Racken was the first to fall, but it wasn't the last." His body sags. "Sometimes, when the critters of the caverns are quiet, you can hear the lamentations of our brothers and sisters. Of your children."

Mac's chest aches and a tingling itch starts in the corners of his eyes.

He folds his arms across his chest protectively. "Children? Down here, in this place? When was this? How long?" He turns away to hide a sudden rush of grief he can't control. A wave of abject misery that tries to press him down and hold him there.

"They took Racken when Ig and Gila were young. Some of us managed to get away." He looks to Terry. "Your father was supposed to help them. They baited him into betraying us by threatening his family, but as any good lacerta would, he refused, so they took the city from us a different way, by pretending they were allies."

"You're talking about Saurian Adler?"

Agamo nods, then looks to Terry with hope in his eyes. "Are you here as part of some sort of reclamation? Is he finally coming back to save us?"

Terry frowns. "A reclamation?"

"I know you. I know your family." Agamo hesitates, unsure a moment, then carries on regardless. "Your sister, your brother. You're blue skins that can blend in above. How many more of you are up there?"

Terry opens his mouth to speak, but doesn't say anything.

"It's been long enough. You must be ready for something. I always knew he'd come back." A fire burns in his old eyes. "Others called me crazy. Said he was a coward for leaving, but I told them Saurian wouldn't go unless he had a plan to come back. That no matter how long it took, he wouldn't abandon us."

Mac taps a finger to his lips. "I don't know how best to put this, but I'm afraid Saurian Adler is dead. The Guardians killed him long ago."

Terry makes a small noise in the back of this throat. Agamo appears to shrink.

"I'm sorry, Terry." Mac pats him on the shoulder, then turns back to Agamo. "I'm sure they would have come back if they could. But I don't think anyone's coming to help."

Agamo closes his eyes.

Mac scratches his head. A queasy realisation finally punching through everything he's learnt. "Wait, are you telling me Terra is a um... a lizard person?"

"Lacerta," says Ig, lifting his chin. "Lizard person suggests we are a subset of people." He leans his head to one side with a little nervous laugh that suggests he's deadly serious but doesn't want to offend guests. "We don't call you ape people."

"Sorry." Maybe he doesn't care if she's different. Maybe it doesn't matter.

The fire in Agamo's eyes has gone. "Yes. Skin-changers. Not all of us can do that. They are the only ones who can walk above undetected. That's why they could operate above the surface. Are you really telling me you aren't here to help us? We need you now, more than ever."

Mac shakes his head. "I'm here to find Terry, to take him back to his family. And he's here to see his old home."

"Racken? You won't recognise it. It's changed." Agamo pauses. Stands. Retrieves the spear from by his side. Now he's up, Mac notices how broad the old lacerta is. His posture is strong. He could give Nige a run for his money. "But I can show you. We were on our way to the overlook when we heard you."

"After what you've said, I don't think we should go anywhere near that place," says Mac.

Ig stands as well. Drains his bowl in one hungry swallow. Tucks it into a pouch in his pack. "It will be good for you to see what your kind are capable of."

"I'm very aware of it."

"And you, Enki, to remind those above that we need their help," adds Agamo. He throws a powder on the fire, choking it into a small amount of black smoke that quickly dies away.

"Gila," he calls, and she reappears from around the corner. "We take them to the Racken overlook."

Tunnels

Following Aspid's instructions, Lily leads the group along the left route and then, when they come to a place where the tunnel splits into three, Aspid moves to the front and leads them along a rising path. As they walk they pass several dark passages. It would be very easy to get lost here.

Her legs are tired. She doesn't think she's walked this far in her life.

"Next right and up and we're there," says Aspid.

Ahead the path splits in two and Aspid takes them along a tunnel which rises steeply into the purple glow from the gems that cover the ceiling of the large cavern she'd seen through the window. They climb out into a small clearing of rock. To their left, through a jagged gap in the stone, Lily can see a sliver of the city below them.

"George," says Aspid, rushing forward towards a small group of tall figures sat in a group on the other side of the clearing.

They wear similar grey suits to Aspid, and each carry a long spear. She throws her arms around the biggest of the four as he stands to meet her.

He hugs her tight, and smiles, revealing several sharp teeth. Aspid doesn't look afraid of him so Lily isn't either. His face is red like the other in the kitchen.

"What are they doing here?" says one of the others. He nods towards the children.

George's eyes widen when he sees them and he looks between them and Aspid.

"Don't get cross," she says moving back towards the children. She takes Lily's hand and leads them forward. "I've don't care what they might do to me. I want you to take them with you."

"Then you have to come too." George shakes his head. His lips hang slightly open. "Aspid, they'll know it was you."

"You know I can't." Aspid rolls her sleeve to her elbow and holds up a bracelet attached tightly to her forearm. "I might have a chance back there, but not if I run. Please take them. I can't bear it any more. Knowing they are safe will help me to atone for what I've done."

George groans softly, then puts an arm gently around her shoulders. "You've only done what you needed to survive. If not you, then someone else would have..."

"Would they?" Aspid brushes his arm from her shoulder, and leans away.

"We can't stay here arguing," says the other that had spoken. He picks up George's spear and passes it to him. "Agamo will be waiting for us. He won't like this."

"I don't care what Agamo likes and doesn't." Aspid turns angry eyes on him. "He hasn't seen what I have seen."

"Well, we can't take them all. How are we supposed to get them back?"

George looks into Aspid's eyes then stiffens. "We will take them. All of them."

"Then we must go now otherwise we won't make it past the guards."

"Aspid." George moves close to her once more. "Are you sure?"

She nods, then kneels next to Lily and puts a hand on her shoulder. "You have to be brave, little one. George will look after you."

As she talks, George and the other reds usher the children towards a dark tunnel on the far side of the clearing. Lily is the last.

"Why don't you come?"

Aspid's lips tighten into a smile. "I can't. You have to be brave and look after the others."

Aspid puts her arms around her. She doesn't think she's ever been hugged by someone big, not since Grandad. It makes her happy and sad. She tries not to cry, tries to be brave for Aspid.

"I will."

Something bangs. She's never heard such a noise. It hurts her head, and everything goes quiet around her. Dull like she has her hands over her ears.

Aspid's eyes stare behind her, and she turns. George is shouting but she doesn't know what he's saying. Can't hear him over the sudden ringing. She feels another thump, the sound vibrates in her chest. Another bang, followed by another. The red one next to George is struck in the shoulder. George throws his spear then pulls the injured one back.

She tracks the spear towards that long crack through which she could see the city. Clinging to the edges of the rock are two tall thin black figures. The spear strikes one and it falls away. The other clambers forward landing between Lily and Aspid, and George and the other children. She sees Finn being dragged back by the other reds, his frightened eyes on her, staring. His lips screaming her name.

Aspid shouts.

Motion from the way they'd just come. Soldiers in masks. Flashing guns. More thumps felt in her heart and her stomach. A pair of black gloves grip Aspid by the shoulders and pull her back.

"Go!"

Lily reads the words on her lips, but when she turns to run George and the other children are already gone. The tall black figure standing between her and their exit turns and grabs her. She fights, but it's no use.

Many men rush past her following the children and the reds, but Lily is dragged back towards Aspid. Another man hits Aspid over the head with the butt of his rifle and she goes limp.

Lily screams her name, but Aspid doesn't wake. They drag her away across the rocky ground and pull Lily back into the dark tunnel after her.

Racken Ruined

They lead Terry and Mac to the edge of the cavern, where a tunnel carved into the rock ascends. The slippery ground and steep climb is hard going even for Mac's well-honed postman's legs.

The underground is like a steam room, so warm and humid. It makes it difficult to breathe. Water drips almost constantly from the ceiling, running by in little streams on the sharp incline. He grips the rocky walls for support as he trudges after Terry and the three lacerta. He can see now that their legs are closer to a dog's hind legs than a man's. The two red lacerta more so. It appears to make the climb very easy for them.

He gets it now. The reason why Terra and Gaspar wore such flared trousers was to hide their legs. And he realises now that Terry had always worn his robe when he'd been at the church, even when the others had donned their basketball gear. Mac had just thought him very devout back then, but turns out he was a shape-shifting lizard person all along. Who could see that coming?

He lets out a sigh, which comes out as a groan.

"Nearly there now," says Agamo, without looking back. "We'll rest at the top."

A circle of lilac light ahead marks the tunnel's end. As they near, the smell of burnt fuel and burnt meat taints the air. It fills his lungs with a sickening thickness.

The others speed up, and step onto a plateau, as he slows. Agamo and Ig look back, waiting for him, but Terry and Gila move ahead, out of sight. Ig returns and offers him an arm, which he gladly takes. The younger red lacerta pulls him up to the plateau. A short platform high up in the side of a cliff. They creep to the edge where Terry, Agamo, and Gila crouch.

Beyond is a cavern far larger than the previous. Its expanse takes his breath away.

Immense columns rise from the ground covered in clusters of squat, square buildings that appear to have sprouted like fungus from the rock, defying everything he knows about the law of physics and biology, which, if he's being honest, is minimal. Once brightly coloured facades and roofs – now left to ruin – are covered in tar and soot from fires that burn unchecked. Long rope bridges track at different levels between the columns. Many broken and hanging limp, like fractured limbs.

Bundles of ugly cable run all over the city, linking up every home and every building.

A black tar-like river oozes through the centre. Bridges cross it every hundred metres or so, and at the far end sits a huge factory. Blackened chimneys belch out noxious smoke filling the air above. Electric lights flicker and wink as filth gushes from pipes straight into the water. The cables running from every building all lead to it.

Racken looks like it might once have been beautiful, a marvel of engineering, but instead it is a smoking, dirt covered vision of hell.

Small figures, hunched and broken, wander the streets. Armed Guardian soldiers corral them onward, as do the odd red lacerta sentry. Snippets of their orders carry from megaphones.

In the centre of the city is a large circular stone object. It is about the height of five men.

For a city, it is smaller than he expected. Closer to the size of Ripley overall. "It's...?"

"You expected it to be bigger?" says Agamo.

Mac nods.

"We control ourselves," says Gila, with a scowl. "Unlike you, we only have children when we need them."

"This is a confined space," Agamo adds, batting a placating hand at Gila. "To overpopulate would be impractical. When we were flourishing, the population of Racken was around a hundred thousand. There's less than half of that now."

"I can't stand to be here," says Gila to herself. She gives Mac an accusatory glare.

Agamo places a reassuring hand on her shoulder.

Huge billboards flicker near the ceiling, blinking slogans and images. One shows an angry looking blue lacerta. It reads. "We'd never abandon you. Together we can make Racken great again."

"What's that about?" says Mac, nodding to it.

"That's Saurian Adler," says Agamo. "He led the blue council's human relations. Our liaison to the overworld. He was working on once more reuniting our people with yours. The Guardians use him as a scapegoat for everything that's wrong in Racken. The lacerta believe it was his forces that attacked the city vying for control, that The Guardians defended it, when in fact the opposite is true."

"What happened?" asks Terry.

"Human and brainwashed lacerta soldiers attacked. Eased in through the portal while the city slept." He points at the circle of stone. "Assassinated the council, attacked key infrastructure across the city. Occupied Racken for nearly two months. Then The Guardians swooped in to save the day." His scaled lip curls. "Called themselves the heroes of Racken and the people listened. Stepped in to help lead when there was no one else. All was well for a long time, but they never left, and slowly, over the years, they've brought the city to its knees." He sighs. "Our people have forgotten who they were. Once where there was only peace and prosperity through science, there is only death and suffering."

"Why? The Guardians say they do what they do to save the planet. Save it from us." Though Mac had never really believed them. "How can hurting you be helping?"

Agamo grunts. A humourless laugh. "That may have been their goal once. The greater good, they called it. But some of these men are over two hundred years old. Their minds are warped, broken over time. They are hateful sons, given everything they want, taught to look down on those they see as different and worthless by senile, old fathers who think themselves gods. As everything degrades over time, so does morality. Is it any wonder they do what they do?"

The five of them stare out over the city in silence. It's horrible.

"Dark beginnings make sick and twisted endings," says Ig, breaking the moment's quiet.

"What happens in there?" Mac nods towards the factory.

"It used to be our university, but now..." Agamo looks to Gila. "Gila's the only one of us who's been in."

"They call it the factory. And only two things happen inside." She points down to ground level. "That blur you see in the air down there."

Mac looks to the bottom of the cliff. To the narrow streets that cut through the buildings and columns of rock. A hazy yellow fog covers the ground.

"It's a genetically engineered spore brewed in the factory. Makes our people docile, obedient. It's pumped directly into every home, out of every grate in every street. Added little by little over time. The people don't even know they are breathing it." Gila glances at Mac. "They also export it to the surface. I expect they use it on you, too."

"I wouldn't be surprised." Mac glances from her to Agamo. "And what's the other thing that happens there?"

Gila presses her lips together. She looks away.

Agamo speaks, low. "It's a farm."

Mac feels like someone has punched him in the gut. He almost can't get the words out, but has to ask to be sure. "Children?" He stares at the building, shaking all over at the thought of what might be going on inside right now.

Agamo nods, eyes downcast. "I expect they have them all over the underworld," he says in a low voice. "Other cities fell just like Racken."

A klaxon sounds, echoing across the cavern. An ugly, pale face appears on each billboard.

Agamo puts a hand to his bowed forehead in disgust. "The Overseer."

"Good day to you, lacerta," says the face on screen. "A reminder that in three days we will make the cuts. The tables are very close." He holds his thumb and index finger a centimetre apart. "So those of you inside still have time to drag your way out." The flesh of his cheeks wobbles. "Believe me when I tell you this is a measure that we'd hoped to avoid, but it has become inevitable due to *your* lack of progress. If this isn't done, none of us will survive down here." His large bottom lip blubbers out in a mockery of sadness. "You know this is for the greater good."

Agamo growls and glares at the empty screen. Gila's face twitches with rage. Ig just stares.

"What's that?" asks Mac.

Agamo sighs. Covers his eyes with one hand and squeezes his temples. "They are going to kill five percent of the lacerta adults in three days," he says. His hand drops to his side. "The ones who have had the lowest output in the last year."

"They can't do that."

"They say resources are low. Population is too high." The old lacerta's face drains of colour. He looks exhausted.

"Why don't you rebel? Why don't they fight?" He looks back over the city. "There's got to be more of them than guards down there."

"The people think this is as good as it can be," says Agamo. "Racken has gradually gotten worse. So slowly that they don't even realise how bad it's become. And of course, The Guardians enforce the belief that it would have been worse if they hadn't been in charge. The announcement came years ago that something had to be done soon about the lack of resources. Small at first. Rumours. And softly, bit by bit, rumours were confirmed and announced officially. Last year they told the lacerta it would be ten percent, so now The Overseer praises himself on the fact that it is only five."

"Rebellions only happen when people get angry enough," adds Ig. "The spore and the propaganda keep them docile." He shakes his head. "Some here are even happy with the nothing The Guardians have allowed them to have."

"The population is so segregated, so divided that over half of them won't even know someone affected. And those who aren't capable of working hard enough to live are looked down upon as something other, something lesser." Agamo shakes his head. "I'm disappointed in my people that they let this happen, but I am not surprised. If you're in the stronger majority, why risk dropping your productivity to help someone you don't know, someone you've been taught to blame for your society's ills? It's mainly the old, the disabled who are affected. The only way anyone can help someone is by singling themselves out, by taking their place."

Gila snarls, as much at Agamo as everything else. "I still can't believe we're not at least willing to try to help them. We could do something, anything..."

"You know there's nothing we can do." He speaks as if he's said the same thing a hundred times. "We are too few. Ill-equipped."

"If we could just use the portal." She points at the huge circle of rock, then jabs a closed hand forward like a spear. "Come from inside. A small team could get to The Overseer. I know the way. We cut off the head."

"You know the portal doesn't work."

"Well, maybe if I'd had a better teacher, I could fix it." She gives him a look that could kill a lesser lacerta.

He looks down, clears his throat. Her face drops too. She opens her mouth as if to say more. She hesitates.

"I'm sorry," she says.

A different klaxon sounds. A warning, not an announcement.

"Look," shouts Ig. He points to the base of the cliff. "Who's that with them?"

Mac follows his gaze. Down below, a number of dark shapes sprint out from a field of dwellings next to the river, heading towards the rock wall.

Behind them, a handful of guardsmen follow. Shots are fired. He can hear the small pops even from up here.

"They're not going to make it." Agamo points back down the tunnel. "We need to set up a portal for them, quick."

He and the others break into a run.

Mac and Terry share a look, then give chase.

"What's going on?" he calls after them, running as fast as his legs can carry him.

"Reconnaissance," calls back Agamo. "George has taken a few into the city to get intel — see if there's anything we can do about the cull. We have to prepare their escape."

Mac struggles to keep upright as he stumbles down the steep incline behind the others. Small stones slip beneath his bare feet.

Gila and Ig are the first to disappear out of sight at the bottom of the tunnel. By the time he's caught up, they've created an archway in the soft earth of one wall, made up of those knife-things Terra had stabbed into the tree back at the hotel.

"What is this?" he asks, as he reaches them. "Do you guys live in this wall?" He looks it up and down then scratches his head. It's definitely solid.

"No, you bonehead," says Gila. She doesn't look at him.

"So it *is* a teleport?" He leans closer to one of the knives — he'd only glimpsed one briefly in the dark before. It looks more primitive to the ones Terra had used, but still impressive. "Wow."

Gila's exasperated expression is reminiscent of one Mac had received from a year eight music teacher when in class she'd asked him to give her a sentence with the word 'beat' in it, and, after a moment's careful deliberation, he'd replied seriously with the sentence, "Tap".

"This is a fungal network input," she says.

Mac wrinkles his nose.

"The way I understand it is this," says Ig, helpfully, "these mushrooms gobble you all up, copy you, and send you along the fungal network to your destination." He stretches his arm out, wiggling his fingers. "And then, at the destination, they grow you a nice new body." He punches a fist through his open hand and blows a wet raspberry to demonstrate.

"Um... I'm pretty sure that's not how it works," says Mac with a splutter of nervous laughter and a cocky wink.

"Sounds like what I remember," says Terry, with a nod. "It happened to you when you went through that door before. You're basically a mushroom now."

"You're kidding, right?" He looks between them, then back at the wall. "This thing doesn't just eat you and grow you again." He laughs. They're messing with him. "I think I'd know if I'd been eaten. I'd know if I was a mushroom." He pats himself down. Stops at his missing trousers. *No plastics.* Would he know?

"Whatever you say," says Gila, with a nonchalant shrug. "If it doesn't work like that, then I guess you can just stay here and fight those guardian soldiers when they come, but I'm getting eaten and grown again someplace safe." She looks towards a shadowy corner of the cavern in the direction Mac guesses the lacerta should come from. Her body tenses. "They should be here by now."

"Look." Terry points.

Several small children appear out of the shadow. Running for their lives. Their faces are dirty and terrified. A large red lacerta leads them dragging one by the hand and carrying another.

"Children?" Agamo takes a deep agitated breath through his nose. "Where's Flax? Where's Ardent?" He turns to Gila, "get the input operational," then starts forward.

As he does, the final three lacerta appear behind the group of children. Two carry another between them, but the going is slow.

"Flax is hurt," says Ig. His yellow eyes widen. "They're not going to make it." He runs too.

Gila presses the buttons on each of the knives, turning them red. After a short delay they snap to green. Purple lightning jags across the soil of the wall and, with a miniature thunderous crackle, hundreds of tiny fungal tubes punch out of the earth between them.

"Ready," says Gila. "You two should go."

"Let me help," says Mac. "Those kids are scared. They'll want to see a human face. Please."

He looks back. Can't stand to see those children down here. They must be so scared. He waves a hand. Tries to shout something reassuring as he counts them. Six in total. "Hey kiddos. I'm a human." He gives Gila a meaningful look that he hopes screams, *and definitely not a mushroom.*

Agamo and Ig pass the children and meet with the others. The four of them throw the wounded lacerta up on to their broad shoulders and sprint.

Shots sound from behind. Muzzle flashes as guards give chase.

"What weapons do you have?" shouts Mac over the noise. Luckily, the ground is so uneven it gives the lacerta some cover as they run. He stands on tip-toes to see better. Nervous, bubbling energy fills him.

"Just spears," says Gila, giving hers a shake.

The kids reach them, led by the eldest boy and the red lacerta. He's a unit. Scaled muscle bulges out from beneath his tight grey tunic. He greets Gila.

"What's happening?" She looks surprised to see the children. "What did you do?"

"Aspid, brought them." He glances back. Grits his teeth. "I couldn't carry them all." He rubs a hand over his eyes. His voice comes out constricted and low. "I couldn't get them out." He growls low.

"Aspid?" Gila looks nervous. "Is Flax hurt?"

"If we can get him into the portal, he'll recover." George looks back. Agamo, Ig, and the others stand huddled behind a thick column of rock. It's not far, but the guards have them pinned. "Get these kids through." He grabs Gila's spear from her hand. "I'm going back."

"Wait!" she calls.

George turns away. He launches Gila's spear as he does. It flies so far and strong embedding itself in the chest of one guard as they creep up to the column where Agamo and the others hide. The guards take cover, separating and ducking behind the moguls and outcroppings of grey rock. George sprints forward, ripping two blades from scabbards on his back before merging with the shadows.

Mac kneels and gathers the frightened children around him, turning them away from the battle. He doesn't know what to do with kids.

"Hi, I'm Mac." He tries to look them each in the eye. They don't meet his gaze. "You've all been so brave. If you follow me, we'll get you away from all these nasty people and home."

It's not his best look, leading a gaggle of small children through a mushroom portal, dressed only in a towel, but he's all they've got. And part of him feels responsible. He knew the truth about what went on and he'd wasted his time drinking when he could have done something more to help. His inaction has caused this to continue.

"I want you to all join hands in a line," he says, "and then we'll just run through this magic door, like a fun little conga. You first, Terry." He glances up to Gila to see if that's the right sort of thing. She doesn't say no.

Terry has changed his blue face back to its human appearance. He smiles and helps Mac get the kids into a line while, using the distraction created by George, the other lacerta arrive.

Terry holds his hand out to the eldest at the front. A boy of about five. "Hi, I'm Terry," he says. "We'll be safer through this door."

The boy looks unsure as he studies the wall of tubes. Terry gives him a reassuring smile.

Mac looks back to the advancing guards. With the flashing of guns, and the occasional scream, something moving swiftly in the shadows appears to be taking them out one at a time.

He sings what he thinks is a conga beat with exaggerated loudness, and slaps his hand on his thigh in time to drown out the sound of fighting and murder and death. "Come on, Terry. Choo, choo, choo!"

Terry, stood just next to the door at the front of the line, joins in with a percussive beat boxing and a rhythmical wiggle of his shoulders. "Come on kids, follow me!"

One at a time Terry and the children are sucked away into those tiny tubes, as if they were crumbling sand sculptures attacked by a hundred tiny vacuums. Mac closes his eyes and follows the final child through. His body prickles all over as, almost instantly, he opens his eyes in a different place, covered once again in a sticky residue.

His legs wobble and he remembers what he'd thought last time — *as if he'd never used them*... Before taking in the room where he now stands, he turns to look at the archway he's just appeared through. It looks similar to the one in the room where he'd found Terry.

His mouth falls open as Agamo sprouts from the entrance, followed by Ig and the others. Gila is last.

The wounded lacerta, Flax, pushes himself up to stand. The gun-shot wound in his shoulder now closed off. Grown over by hundreds of white, finger-like fungal strands.

He staggers to one side.

From within the nearby shadows, more lacerta emerge and surround them. There must be five or six. All red. Mac tries to keep his head for the children.

"It's ok," he says, ushering them to the side and away from the sudden noise of frantic voices. He crouches down and holds his arms out to bring them into a huddle.

"Where's George?" shouts Agamo. "And where did these children come from?"

"He was coming," says Gila. "They were following him."

"He'll know to destroy the gate, if he can't get through." Agamo stands ready with his spear. Ig is with him.

"He'll get through."

The crowd hush.

A faint crackling begins behind the wall of fungal tubes.

"Get ready," calls Agamo. "If it's not him. We'll need to fight."

Mac moves the children back.

With a wet blip, a huge red shape bulges out of the wall, but something's wrong. George falls to his knees. Cradled in his arms are the fungal network knives. His face is open, scared. His yellow eyes stare inward.

The others hold worried breaths as the light from the door dims behind him.

Silence.

"George?" Gila hurries forward. Pulls his arms away from his chest letting the knives tumble to the ground to reveal a large indentation in his breast covered in fungal strands.

He takes a deep, shuddering breath. Grimaces. His eyes look into Gila's and he nods. "That… was close."

A collective sigh of relief. A few laughs. Even Mac, who it appears is now a mushroom, smiles.

Camp

"We've been here almost twenty years, now" says Agamo, gesturing at the small hollowed out cavern where he, Mac, the children, and a couple of their rescuers now sit, eating another of Terry's delicious mushroom stews.

The kids huddle together nearby, each with a bowl, each quiet and content to be scoffing. The youngest must be three or four. What horrors have they seen? He feels he should give them a hug or something, but the idea makes him feel awkward.

The children each wear a grey suit that appears made from the fungal cloth that the lacerta use in their own clothing.

Mac has also traded his towel for a set of the lacerta trousers. The cut didn't quite work with his human anatomy so the lacerta in charge of finding him clothes had just chopped the legs off from the knee down.

"This used to be the red training camp," Agamo continues. "We'd bring the apprentices here to test their survival skills. When we escaped Racken, we made it our home."

The cavern rises high above them. Huge chunks of star stone glitter down, filling the space with spectacular purple light. Something about the quality of the strange, dark illumination relaxes him. Warms him. Reminds him of his mother. He presses his tongue against the back of his teeth and takes a slow breath to quell the deep sadness that now lives with that thought.

Around where they sit, the lacerta get on with their lives. Laughing, conversing, working. Trying to get by despite the bleak situation that they all know affects their brothers and sisters in Racken.

Agamo places his unfinished bowl down next to his feet, leans both hands on his knees and arches his back to stretch it.

"Look," he says. Nodding towards a couple of lacerta children who have come a little closer to the human ones. The two groups regard each other from a distance.

One of the braver lacerta children steps forward. "Welcome," she says. "Do you want to play with us?"

The eldest of the human boys looks to the others, then nods, and the two groups move away together at a joyful run. Even the littlest ones are included.

"Not too far," calls Agamo after them.

"Yes, Agamo," chorus the high voices of the young lacerta.

He chuckles as he watches them go. "Warms your heart, doesn't it? All any of us wants is good cheer, good friends, and love. And that connects us more than any difference. Shouldn't matter that we don't look the same." He sighs, then his eyes flick up to Mac's. "This isn't our cavern, it's theirs. The star stones, the fungus, the creatures. Everyone uses them, but nobody owns them. They belong to the next generation. We are stewards of it for them, so that they can become better stewards for the next. This is how our society once thrived, not by constant growth, but by constant improvement. We gift to our children rather than take. Lift them up on to strong, stable shoulders, even if it means we ourselves have less."

Mac nods as he watches after the children. "Where will you take the children? Do you get them back to their families?"

"We have a few contacts on the surface who can look into it, but I expect they might stay here for a while. We don't rescue many children, the odd one here and there. This is the most we've helped. The old university is deep inside the city so it's almost impossible to get there." He glances towards George who sits nearby. "This wasn't planned." He shakes his head. "I guess George saw an opportunity and took it. I'll have to have words. We risk everything if The Guardians find us."

At the sound of his name George shuffles closer. "It was Aspid. She helped them escape."

"Aspid?"

George lowers his voice and leans away from the children. His lip curls in disgust. "They will certainly kill her."

Agamo looks down. "What can we do? We are few and they are many."

"We have to do something," says Mac. "What about what The Overseer said?"

"I'm afraid with only the twenty of us here, there's not a lot we can do to help Racken."

"What about Gila's plan?" says George. "It could work."

"The portal?" says Mac, he doesn't know what he can do to help but seeing the children here makes him want to try.

"We've been over this..." Agamo closes his eyes and takes a tired breath, then turns to Mac. "The Guardians killed the fungus that grows inside it. They used the previous attack on Racken as justification, and the lacerta didn't question it because they thought it would keep them safe. But it was just to limit freedom of movement between cities. To limit communication. No one can repair it. The only one that might, was Saurian, but now..." He lifts a hand, and lets it slap down on his thigh.

"If we could get it working, we can get to The Overseer," says George. "Kill him."

"And what will that change? Another dictator will just take his place." Agamo's eyes sparkle a little. "The idea of using the portal has some merit," he says to Mac. "There's an armoury offshore, our greatest technologies hidden away so that The Guardians could never find them. If we can reclaim the portal, we can get to the armoury, and then we can arm ourselves properly. We can use the portals and the weapons to take back lacerta cities across the globe. Lacerta cities used as farms and headquarters for The Guardians. If we do that, they'll have nowhere to go, nowhere to hide."

"What do you need to make that happen?" Mac leans forward.

Agamo chuckles. "Only the capability to fix a portal that no one knows how to fix and that we can't even get access to. And that's only useful if we can find enough trained lacerta warriors to help take back the city. And they'd need arming with something better than what we have here." He touches the spear that leans against his seat, then looks over at the children, running back and forth. “But three days just isn’t enough time for all that.”

“Terry might be able to help with one of those things. I’ll take him to his family, see what they’ve been doing these past twenty years.”

“We can’t come with you, it’s too dangerous, but if there’s anything the Adler’s can do, I am eager to hear it.”

The Overseer

Lily finds herself back in her cage. Quite quickly three of the other children, Sam, Perry, and Thomas, are returned also. Not Finn. She hopes he's safe somewhere. She's supposed to be looking after him.

Aspid lies unconscious in the cage on the far side of the room. There's a large bloody bruise on her head where the gun had hit her. Lily calls to her but she does not wake.

She starts as the door to the prison clanks open. The Nightmare Bat enters wearing a long flowing robe that splits down the centre showing the pale ball of his pronounced stomach. He glances towards Aspid in her cage, curls his lip, but doesn't keep his gaze on her for long.

"Children, children, children," he says. His toad-like face splits into a grin as he takes the bars in his huge fists. "What a thrilling afternoon you've had. I can't imagine the cocktail of emotions you must be feeling. The hope. The disappointment. The fear." He takes a deep, delighted breath. "I can smell it on you from here. We have a special event coming up soon. Once you've had a few days to stew, to think about the denied possibility of your escape, then you should be ready to help us celebrate." He clears his throat as his eyes travel from child to child. "I look forward to it."

Cross Town Traffic

Mac and Terry arrive together in the room beneath the Camden catacombs. The faint stink of vodka and vomit lingers with the stench of age. This time Mac arrives fully clothed. They climb the stairs, through Terry's old room, and back out through the church. The post van is clamped out front and plastered in wads of parking tickets.

"Jeez, I've only been gone a day or so." He gives the clamp a good solid kick, possibly breaking a number of important toes, then hops about for a bit, clutching his foot.

"We could take Alan's old bike. I hid it in the church."

Terry leads him back inside, all the way to the sheet with the painting of the angel.

Mac tuts when he spots the massive graffiti cock on its head. "Some people."

Terry looks at him a moment, and Mac can see the question forming on his lips.

"How do human females cope?" he says.

"With what?"

He nods at the graffiti. "With the shape. Are they all triangular like that?"

Mac shakes his head. "I think having a pointy end is limited to the sort of person who finds it necessary to draw nobs everywhere." He taps his lips with a finger. "Or maybe there's just one poor, unfortunate soul who draws them all?"

Terry considers this. "I'd always wondered."

He pulls down the sheet, revealing a hidden vestibule. Inside is the bike with sidecar that Mac had first seen the cultists ride up to Nige's warehouse in.

"Jump in," says Terry, sitting astride and pulling on his helmet.

Mac does as Terry lifts a hidden flap beneath the handlebars and removes a key. It starts first time with a guttural growl that shakes Mac to his bones.

"Where we going?"

Mac takes out his phone and taps in Terra's address. Passes it to Terry who secures it in a holder between the handlebars.

"Helmet," says Terry.

Mac fishes the smooth green helmet from the footwell and pulls it tight over his head. Terry twists the throttle and cruises the bike out through the front door, along the garden path, and on to the road.

"Step on it," says Mac, with instant cheek ripping regret for Terry does indeed step on it.

Mac covers his eyes. Not because he fears hitting something and doesn't want to see, but because the speed the bike rockets along at is sure to suck them from their sockets. Although he has faced lethal ninjas who would stop at nothing to kill him at least four times in the last year, Mac has never feared for his life with such certainty than he does with Terry behind the handlebars.

Terry swings them from left to right, dodging cars and buses, honking at pedestrians with aplomb, and stuffing the bike into gaps an e-scooter would struggle to fit through.

At first Mac shrieks at him every time there's a hazard, but in no time at all it dawns on him the hazards are so frequent he might as well just scream the entire journey, only stopping to fill back up on air with which to let rip.

"Are you ok?" shouts Terry over the competitive din of Mac's face and the engine.

"No, I am not ok."

"What?"

"No!"

Under his helmet Terry looks heart broken. "Oh, that's a shame. I want to look nice. I'm a bit nervous meeting my family after all this time."

"Wait, what did you say?"

"I said do I look ok?"

"Ooooh. Yeah. You look great." Mac unclamps one hand from the rim of the sidecar and gives Terry a lacklustre thumbs up. "Do you think you can slow down?"

"Well, you said step on it."

"That's right I did."

It doesn't take long to arrive outside Terra's building. About half the time it should. Mac is sure more than double the time saved has been scraped from the end of his life.

So all in all, a net loss.

They pull up next to the valet booth. Mac catches his reflection in the bike's mirror as he removes his helmet. Hair dishevelled. Eyes red. It's not how he'd imagined rocking up to Terra's and presenting himself as her hero, but he guesses it will have to do.

The valet steps out from behind the booth. "I thought I told you..." Then he spots Terry removing his helmet and swishing his hair away from his face like a sloth in a l'oriel commercial. The valet's eyes widen, and his mouth works with no sound. He touches a radio on his lapel. "Um... It's—"

"Yeah." Mac tosses his helmet into the sidecar, then shoots the valet with finger guns. "Look who ol' Trent Macadamia found. Where's Terra?"

The bagman sprints across the pavement towards them with what looks like vicious intent to cause Mac harm. He slows as he nears, and his hand goes to his brow as he spots Terry. "Is that—?"

"The one and only," says Terry. "I expect."

"Take us to see Terra, now," says Mac, prodding a finger into his open palm for emphasis.

"You're not welcome," says the valet. He holds out a hand to beckon Terry towards him, but Terry doesn't move from Mac's side.

"I'm not going anywhere without my best friend," he says, giving Mac a wink and a tongue click.

Mac eyes him. Best friend? Bit of a stretch. "Yeah, he's not going anywhere without um..." He pokes himself in the chest, "me... you're talking about me, right?"

"Oh yeah. You helped me find my family. You're the best friend I ever had."

"Yeah." Mac whips a hand out to point at the bagman. "You better not even think about whatever it is you were thinking about." He tries a sort of walking backwards Michael Jackson dance. It feels good. Truth be told, he's a little excited about seeing Terra again. His body feels like it's full of bees, but in a nice way.

Terry joins in with a robotic arm wave. "Enki Adler and Trent Macadamia in the place to be."

"Coming in hot, running the show."

The bagman rolls his eyes. "Follow me." He turns and marches back towards the building.

"You ready?" says Mac, extending a hand to touch Terry's shoulder.

"I think so." Terry straightens his top, flicks something that could be mashed up underworld puddle octopus from his sleeve, and lets out a shaky breath. "Do you think they'll like me?"

Mac tightens his lips into a smile and gives the best advice he's ever received. "Make them see who you really are inside. They'll be hard pressed not to like you."

The bagman leads them to the same elevator that they'd used to get to Terra's room before. But instead of pressing a button, the bagman pulls out a keycard from a retractable chord on his belt and swipes it over a reader. The lift descends.

Mac's stomach sinks with the lift. "Why are we going down?"

"Miss Terra isn't upstairs, and neither is Gaspar. They are in the lower levels."

"The lower levels?"

"The lower levels."

"Sounds ominous."

The lift doors open on a corridor that curves off to the left and right. The hall is circular, clean, clinical, as if the walls and ceiling have been cut from the inside of an enormous piece of white stone. Every few metres, an entrance sealed with a gun-metal grey door splits the illusion. Light grey carpet covers the floor. Mac feels as though he's in a spaceship.

"Come with me," says the bagman, and leads them to the right.

There's a dull hum ongoing. A background noise that suggests an excessive amount of power is being used around them.

Ahead, a door slides open. Someone emerges in a hurry. Attention on a tablet in their hand. For a moment Mac doesn't recognise her. Her skin is a stunning azure blue, much like Terry's had been, but more... vibrant. Her face is a slightly different shape also. Her eyes appear larger. Her nose blunter. She spots them and stops. Her lips part, and for a second the three just stare at each other. Then her face starts to change back to how he remembers.

Mac waves a hand. "It's ok. I know." He smiles. Tries to show her he doesn't mind. He doesn't, does he? He blinks and holds both palms towards Terry. "Ta dah! Look who I found?"

She's already looking, transfixed. The arm holding the tablet falls to her side. "Enki?" she whispers. She wipes her eyes. "Is it really you?"

Terry glances to Mac. Mac nods his head towards her to say, go on. As Terry steps forward, his skin changes to match hers.

She gasps at the sight of it. "Where have you been?" she says, lifting a hand to his cheek. Her eyes move from side to side, looking into his.

"I've—"

She wraps her arms around him, presses her face to one side tight against his chest, and for a moment he stands there, arms out like a scarecrow, as if he doesn't know where to put them. Then he relaxes and hugs her back.

"I've been lost," he says.

"But now you're found." She lets him go and holds him at arm's length. "I've missed you. You have to tell me everything. We have so much to catch up on. And Gaspar, he's here, too."

She looks past her brother and for a moment her eyes lock on Mac's. At first she fixes him with a hard glare that he can't stand, but soon the look softens. "How did you find him?"

He steps forward. Words come tumbling out of him. "Look, Terra, I'm sorry. Bobby Feta tricked me. He—" He feels suddenly vulnerable. Crushed, as if the weight of everything has been dropped on him from a great height. "He killed my mum."

Her face falls. “Oh, Trent.” She hugs him.

He squeezes back. Closes his eyes. Turns inwards, into the darkness inside of himself, surrounded by her warmth. Thinks the loving arms of someone might be the only place he could ever heal. And without his Mum, there’s no one left.

“I’m so sorry,” she says. She takes his hands and looks him in the eyes.

He composes himself. “I’ve seen Racken. They need our help. And soon.”

It catches her off guard. “You’ve been underground?” She looks at the bagman, who shifts his stance uneasily. “How?”

“I found a portal. Why haven’t you gone back?”

She turns back to the room she’d just left. “I’ll show you.”

“Miss Terra?” says the bagman, standing forward. “We shouldn’t—”

“Trent knows enough. It is time we admitted we need help.”

He nods and takes a step back.

She strides up to the door, and it opens, revealing some sort of laboratory come storage area beyond. Inside, several green faced lacerta work around complex machines. “Follow me. I’ll show you what’s really going on here.”

The room is roughly the size of three double-decker buses placed nose to end and perhaps the length of one wide. It stretches to either side of the doors.

He feels a little like a newcomer in a western saloon as everyone there turns to stare at him. He raises a hand in nervous greeting as he studies the room.

To the left, at the far end, a circle of stone stretches from floor to ceiling. It is much like the disused portal in Racken. The stone glistens, covered in small mushrooms and fungal growths, as well as pieces of technology he couldn’t ever hope to understand. Unlike the portal in Racken, this one hums and glows and crackles with a purple light around its circumference. It stands on a wide platform three steps above the floor beneath a black panel covered in what looks like thousands of brightly coloured flickering LEDs.

In front of the portal, two lacerta in lab coats watch him from a control desk.

Through a set of glass doors on the other side of the room is another area. Racks of equipment cover the walls inside. Spears and other weapons to the left, and to the right, helmets and armour in a light matt grey.

Between the different racks is some sort of robot. Long slender legs, hocked like the lacerta. Its front hangs open like the petals of a flower, revealing a seat big enough for one. Slim arms end in sharp scimitar blades.

It's about the coolest thing he's ever seen. Every teenage boy, and potentially most teenage girls, must have dreamt about owning such a thing. Or at least he had after staying up lost in comics with a torch beneath the bedcovers.

"What's he doing here?" comes a voice snapping Mac back from drooling fantasy to an amazing sci-fi reality.

It's bloody Gaspar. Blue too.

"Gazza," Mac says, lifting his head and chest in caveman-like greeting, asserting some manly dominance. I'm a man. A human man. Don't mess with me, he says with a twitch of the lip and a wrinkle of the nose.

"Are you ok?" says Gaspar. "You appear to be having a stroke."

Mac rolls his shoulders. "Yeah, of genius, when I went deep into the bowels of the earth and found your brother." He points at Terry, who stands next to Terra.

Gaspar's cocky sneer slips from his face. Then his eyes glisten in the lights of the laboratory. His whole body softens. "Enki?" He looks at Terra, not believing. "It's… it's…?"

"It's," says Terry with a slow blink and knowing nod. "This place is cool. Is that a robot?"

Gaspar hurries forward and scoops Terry up in his arms, lifting him into the air. He lets out a laugh. "Enki, my brother." He places him down, leans back, and studies him. The pair look so alike. They all do. "Where have you been?"

Terry jabs a lazy thumb over his shoulder. "I was just over in Camden."

Mac watches Terra. Tears spill down her cheeks. "Mac did it, Gaspar. And he's been underground. He's seen Racken. He knows."

Gaspar's eyes remain on her for a moment, before he steps towards Mac and holds out a hand. Mac flinches as if about to be struck. "I don't know how you did it, but you found him. We are forever in your debt and you are forever welcome, Mr Macadamia," he says.

Mac takes the hand and shakes. "It's Mac." He folds his arms. A warmth churns inside him that makes him want to laugh. But he has to ask, "How *did* you lose each other all those years ago?"

"Dad knew what was going to happen to the city," says Gaspar. "Knew he would get the blame. He tried to warn them, but The Guardians had already sewn seeds of distrust against him. Enki and Mum were the last of us to come up. We don't really know what happened, but they didn't come to the meeting place." He glances to Terra and his lips press together. "And when we went back through to the room they were supposed to teleport from, Mum and her guards were dead. Terry was nowhere."

"There are gates all over London," says Terra. "We think Mum must have sent Enki through at random. Somewhere no one could follow."

"So why haven't you gone back to save the city? To tell them they were wrong about your father. It's rough down there."

Gaspar's shoulders drop in resignation. "There's not enough of us. And most of those that fled the city were scientists. It's how we've come as far as we have. How we survived up here. We've developed some of the overworld's greatest technologies, and it's meant we've been able to get by, but, despite that, despite the weapons we have created," he gestures to the armoury across the hall, "there are too few of us to take back Racken."

"So what you're saying is you need an army?"

"We have the equipment, we even have a fast working antidote against their spore, just not enough warriors to get us in and free the city."

Mac taps a finger on his lips, looks at the portal, at the scientists, at the armoury, then points a finger at Terry. "Terry's got an army."

"I do?" Terry looks inwards for a moment, then his face brightens. "I do!"

"And we know an old lacerta with a plan. A plan that might just be crazy enough to work."

The Army Of The Fallen Angels

It's the first time Mac has been back to Mikey's bar since that fateful night when he'd met Mikey's cousin.

It is no different. Though the skyline of London seems to change daily, the little places, the dirt-poor ground level that no developer would want to touch, remains.

The same slouching husks of men leaning in to their pints and watching football on the big screen on the wall. Same smoky smell of Mikey's cheese smoker out back. Same scratch of metal guitars through tinny speakers that have seen better days.

"Trent Macadamia," booms Mikey as he steps in out of the cold with Terra and Terry. "When you promised you wouldn't bother my regulars again, I thought that was too good to be true, but then it's been six months and you've kept your word." He grabs a pair of menus then passes them over the bar. "You eating?"

Mac nods. "And three more coming. We ok to grab a booth?" He points.

"Sure, I'll send Bess over to take your order when they get here."

Terry moves over to have a glance at the football. He and Mikey both stare up at the television.

"Oh mate, this is an absolute travesty," Mikey says with an angry thrust of an upturned palm. "Bloody Schnozmichael keeps diving and ref can't see it for shit." He folds his arms.

Terry mimics his posture exactly, then scoffs with a shake of his head. "Football, hey?"

Mac leads Terra to a booth. Wants to take the first private moment they've had to talk about where they stand.

"I used to come here all the time," he says, as she sits across from him. He's nervous. "On my own, just to drink next to someone. I watched Dave and Pete announce their little cult on that TV." He points. "It's funny, it's sort of the last place I felt normal. Before I knew... you know?"

Get to the point, Macadamia!

Her lips tighten, and she fiddles with her fingers on the table. "Trent, I—"

"Yes," he says, leaning forward.

"I'm sorry about the night that we danced."

"That's... um... you're sorry?" His stomach takes a Schnozmichael. As often as he's gone over this moment in his head, he hadn't anticipated 'sorry'. This can't be good.

She continues. "Sorry if I was being a little forward. I'd had a drink and what that Guardian said kind of went to my head. I don't get out much. Sorry if I made you think I meant it as anything more than friendly."

The words knock him flat. It's not what he expected.

"Pfft! No, yeah, absolutely." He points at himself, then at her. "Me and you? No." He waves a hand and scoffs. "That'd be weird... wouldn't it?" He laughs. He's an idiot. What could someone like her ever see in someone like him?

She laughs, but it's somewhat muted. "Yeah. Can you imagine?"

"Ha. Don't worry, I felt nothing."

Her laugh dwindles. "Oh."

He waves a hand, then folds his arms. "Let's forget about it. It was just a dance. People dance all the time."

"Yeah." She laughs again. "So what now?"

"£500 a day, wasn't it?" He wants to throw up and then die.

"No, I mean, what are you going to tell Phil, and the others?"

"I expect the truth. That we need them."

She nods. And looks at her brother, still watching the football with Mikey.

Saving what promises to be a very awkward silence, the front door of the bar opens and a wall-like figure dressed in a moleskin coat enters flanked by two slimmer characters in cagoules.

"Spoony," Mac waves. "Yoohoo. Over here." Beckoning over an angry east end nutcase whose months of hard work you ruined is preferential to sitting alone with the woman who just told you she doesn't like you like you like her.

The three of them cross the room. Phil stands at the end of the table, looking tough, somewhat annoyed, but mostly unreadable. Dave tries to mimic him, missing the tough part by quite a distance.

"Alright Mac," says Pete cheerfully. "This place is nice."

"Peter," hisses Dave. "We're supposed to be being annoyed at him. It's his fault our Guardian got out. He brought Bobby to the hotel."

"Sorry," says Pete. He leans one hand on the table and shakes a fist at Mac. "Oh, you've really gotten on our nerves, Mac, you ruddy idiot..." He looks at his brother. "How was that?"

"Better," says Dave.

"Alright lads," says Terry, joining them.

Dave's pseudo-tough guy demeanour evaporates.

"Terry!" he and Pete both shout, garnering a few ticked off looks from some of the more aware drunks at the bar. They move in for a group hug and jump around in a circle for a bit.

"You really fucked us, Mac," says Spoony Phil, flattening the celebratory mood like a steam roller through a children's birthday party. His eyes are big and staring. Two angry cue balls. He folds his arms. "Why we here? You better have something good to say."

"You better sit. This is big."

Terry squeezes in next to Terra. Dave and Pete fill Mac's side of the booth. Phil remains standing.

Mac lays it all out.

Phil eyes Terra for a while before saying, "she don't look no different to a normal woman."

She smiles. “Blues like me and Terry can camouflage ourselves, and we’re the closest to humans in body shape and bone structure.”

“Fair enough. But what does this change?” Phil says. “We ain’t gonna take a whole city.”

“The lacerta have built weapons and armour that far exceeds anything The Guardians could hope to have,” says Mac. “And there’s another ace up our sleeve. The portal. As soon as we’re all through, we start transporting lacerta back, curing them, and sending them into the city armed and dangerous.”

Terra draws a circle on the table with her finger. “If we can get the portal in Racken working, then we can transport our force directly into the heart of the city. As long as they don’t see us fix it, they won’t expect anyone to come through.”

Phil rubs his nose with thick, hairy fingers and looks at Dave and Pete. “What d’you boys think?”

“We can have everyone back together in a day or two,” says Pete.

“Another couple of days to train up with whatever equipment you have,” adds Dave.

“You think you can get down there and get this portal going by then?” Phil clears his throat. His face serious. “If that factory is what you think it is, if you think they got kids in there, we can’t hang about. We have to strike hard now.”

“The attack is in two days,” says Mac. “No other time will work.”

Spoony Phil leans back and whistles in disbelief. “Two days?! We better get cracking, then.”

“You get your army back together. Leave the rest to us.” Mac pushes a card across the table. It has the address of Terra’s building on it. “Tell them to meet here.”

Phil nods. “Sure. Two days. We’ll be ready.”

Snap

The day after recruiting the army of the fallen angels, Mac sits in the equipment room beneath Terra's building. He wears a strange figure hugging suit. It has the feel of lycra, but he has been assured it is not. It stretches to fit his body, and when he'd pulled it on, it had constricted and tightened around him. For a moment it had been difficult to breathe, but then the suit had relaxed and now he's quite comfortable.

Nearby, Pete and Terry practice removing bracelets from each other. The lacerta trapped in Racken wear them on their arms. Mac isn't quite sure what they do, but part of Agamo's plan for getting into Racken includes removing a number from lacerta in the city, and both Pete and Terry, with their experience in removing bounty bracelets, are perfect for the job.

Somewhere in a different part of the building, Dave and Spoony Phil are making calls to draw the army back together.

The green scientist working with Mac on his suit is called Marzle. Together they have spent all morning recalibrating the lacerta armour for human wearers. He feels a bit like a model being prepped for the catwalk.

"That's cool," he says.

At his statement, she looks up from the bracer attached to his ankle. She has bugging eyes and spiked black hair. Her left arm is a strange fungal appendage culminating in several malleable tentacles. Each holds a different tool. It looks like a cross between a squid and a swiss army knife.

"What's cool?"

Mac nods at the robot that stands open between the racks of weapons and armour. "That."

He's even more impressed up close. It looks brutal. Strong, dextrous legs. Killer blades for arms. Designed by someone with an eye for beauty, flare, and, quite possibly, murder. Mac wants to be inside it... in like a cool, mech-warrior sort of way.

"A prototype. I'm still tinkering. It's not ready." Marzle shakes her head. "I wish it was, but it's just not reliable enough to take into battle."

"Why?"

"I've only just finished the build. It uses a neurological connection to control. It's borrowed tech. Not something designed for lacerta. Our brains are slightly different to yours so it doesn't respond quite right. We'll get there though." She resumes her concentration on the bracer.

"Shame," says Mac. "It's one of the most amazing things I've ever seen."

"It's bulletproof. Flamers on the end of each blade arm. Can jump over ten feet in the air. I'm very proud of it, despite..." she holds up her strange arm, suggesting the robot may have something to do with it.

He raises an eyebrow. "How did it do that?"

"Sometimes if someone goes through a portal with a lost limb, the fungal network does it's best to fill the gap. I lost my arm to the robot's blade."

"Oh, right, probably best not to play with it then."

"Actually..." Marzle stands and considers the robot for a moment. "Do you mind if we try something?"

"Is it putting me in the robot?"

"No." For a moment she looks horrified. "No, definitely not. It's built for a lacerta, specifically red. If you got in and shut it up, it would splinter your shins and invert your knees." She clicks her fingers -snap-.

Mac shivers. "You can't just change the legs out."

Marzle laughs. "It took me three months to build those ones."

"So no?"

"Mm?" The scientist looks at the robot a moment and wrinkles her brow, then shakes her head. "Doesn't mean we can't try it out though."

She inches around behind it and pulls a length of wire attached to a band towards Mac. She wraps the band around the top of his head.

"Stay as still as you can for a moment."

Marzle returns to the robot and closes the front with a heavy hydraulic thunk. It stands to attention, bobbing slightly like a character awaiting selection in a fighting game. She then scurries across to the other side of the room, putting a table between herself and the robot.

He spots both Pete and Terry having stopped what they are doing to watch.

"Now," she says, "raise your arm."

Mac does as he's told and the robot mimics him instantly.

"Coooool," says Pete, giving Terry a friendly elbow.

"Yeah, cool," Terry confirms.

"Indeed." Marzle vibrates with excitement. "Now, move your lower leg backwards and forwards from the knee."

Mac does and the robot kicks.

"It works." She claps her hands together. "Ok, don't move a muscle."

She scuttles back to Mac and removes the headband. Then presses a switch on the robot, which opens it up once more. It sags on its joints.

"After everything, I never thought we'd have humans on our side again, otherwise I would have made it a little less form fitting. This thing is my answer to our limited numbers, but I just can't get it right with lacerta thought patters. With the right pilots, a couple of these could possibly win us the war for Racken." She looks sad for a moment, as if she wants to say something more, then squats back down to the bracer attached to Mac's ankle. "Let's try this out, shall we?"

Mac shifts his leg closer to her.

"I think I've got it," she continues from below. "It wasn't a big change. You humans are taller but slimmer. I made the armour to suit different builds. With a little recalibration, the armour spore will fit to your human shape rigidly, hopefully without breaking any bones." Her lips jump into a brief smile.

"What do you mean broken bones?" he asks nervously.

She winks then presses a button on the bracer. It lights with a faint blue glow and a small compartment opens. With an almost inaudible high frequency buzz, a cloud of glittering silver dust puffs out and attaches itself to Mac's body. Little rigid scales of white fungus pop up all over the lycra-like suit, joining to form thin plates of armour that build all the way to his chin.

"Who said anything about broken bones?" She smiles.

He raises a hand and moves it in the white light of the room. From certain angles the armour looks matt and white, but as he moves, he can just make out thousands of tiny scales glimmering with a pearlescent, fish-like sheen.

"And this can stop bullets?"

Marzle nods enthusiastically. "We haven't shared this technology with anyone. I've not found a bullet that can pierce it yet."

Terra enters the room. "Looking good," she says. She smiles at him. She wears a full suit of armour like his. It fits tight to her frame. "You ready?"

"Am I?" Mac says to Marzle.

"I've analysed all the changes and will recalibrate the rest of our suits with your human DNA," she says. She stands back to admire her handy work. "So you're good to go."

Mac thanks her and follows Terra out of the armoury and back into the main room, leaving Terry and Pete to continue their practice.

The portal in the lab is powered on. The tiny fungal tubes in its centre show a pixilated view of Agamo's cavern. That is the rally point for the big day.

Terra climbs the steps on to the portal platform. Butterflies wriggle in his stomach as he watches her approach the circle. There's no going back after this.

She notices him loitering at the foot of the steps and holds a hand out.

He takes it gladly, moving to stand beside her.

"Are you sure you still want to help us with this?" she says. "You've already done so much."

He thinks of his mum, and any worry he has subsides. Sure there might be people better suited to the job he's been given, better fighters, but he wants this, he can do it. He owes it to his Mum to make The Guardians pay. "There's nothing that could turn me away."

"I'm glad you're with me," she says, and steps forward. With her confidence filling him, he doesn't hesitate. Just steps into the wall.

He feels a shiver run through him. An electrical impulse from head to toe. And then he's there. Standing, once more, miles below London, and once more an entirely new person.

Distraction Is Good

One more night until the big day and things are going according to plan. Mac feels the tingle of anticipation in his stomach. A dwelling nausea that makes him want to stretch and yawn and run and hide. He must have been to the toilet more times in the last twenty-four hours than he has in the last month.

The army of the fallen angels have dripped through the portal from Terra's building in duos and trios over the last few days. Mac recognises most from the hotel. Hollywood Johnson has rallied a few additional bounty hunters, and Mac finds he's strangely happy to see Red and Blue are with him. They give him a smile and a wave when he spots them before heading off to get fitted for armour and weapons. He hasn't seen the sisters since his altercation with them and Bobby last year.

Almost all forty of the army of the fallen angels have been through armour fitting. They are enthusiastic, assiduous, but how far can that get them?

Now, he and Terra sit side by side near a smouldering fire on a discarded flight case that had come through the portal filled with spears, but is now empty. They watch Agamo, along with the red warriors he raised, lead a training session for the humans with the lacerta weapons. It all looks very impressive. Spoony Phil and the bounty hunters have trained them well. Pooling their street smarts and group knowledge to create a savage fighting force.

The twenty lacerta that live here have been together for the last two decades, training and readying themselves for this day. Hiding from Guardian patrols. Surviving off the land.

"Apparently, he is the greatest lacerta spear-wielder to have ever lived," Terra says, nodding towards Agamo as he circles his trainees, occasionally correcting form.

"He does seem to know his stuff."

"My teacher learnt from him. We had no idea he'd escaped Racken. Many of the red guards that remain in Racken trained with him. If we can free them, they will follow him into battle."

"We're going to need every able body we can get," says Mac, watching the troops perform their drills. He hopes what they learn in the next twenty-four hours will stick. Wonders if they know exactly what they've signed themselves up for. Wonders if they care, or if they are just propelled by vengeance, anger, or duty to their fellow man.

He knows why he's here. Her name is Alyssa Jane Macadamia. She died valentine's night 2036 aged fifty-five. He's slowly coming to terms with it.

The distraction is good. It helps. His anger has settled in the recesses of his brain, like a fine silt at the bottom of a rocky river. Soon, he fears, it will be disturbed, and he doesn't know what he might do.

He hopes he can play his part in making The Guardians pay, in showing them.

Death To The Guardians

The morning of the assault and the expectation is palpable. The feeling is near to excitement, but not quite. It's close to the one he'd had that time when he'd stepped in front of a lens down which a billion eyes were staring, preparing to inform everyone on the planet that they'd been lied to since birth.

The big players, which he's happy to find includes him, stand around a large table. A scroll of fungal paper lies flat on the table illuminated a faint purple by the light of the star stones above. Someone's drawn a map of Racken and part of the nearby cavern. Heavy hands hold scuffed and bent corners down. The map is detailed with arrows and markings that represent different plans and operations that Agamo and his lacerta have tried over the years to win back the city or at least free its prisoners.

Nearby, he can hear the chatter and clink of the army of the fallen angels and Agamo's warriors breaking bread together ready for the fight.

"I can't believe we're finally doing this," says Agamo, casting his eyes around the group. They fall on Mac, accompanied by a warm smile. "It's all thanks to you."

"Um... don't mention it." He suddenly feels a lot of weight on his shoulders. No... all of the weight on his shoulders.

Gaspar places both hands on the table. "There's a lot to think about, but between us," he looks to Agamo, "we think we've covered everything. Gila here has given us as much as she can. Her knowledge of the ever-changing city layout has been invaluable."

Gaspar holds a hand forward, inviting Agamo to step up and explain.

"It's brazen, but we're going through the front door." The old red lacerta points to the intersection between the two caverns. "This is where everything comes in and out of Racken. Every day several hunting and foraging parties are sent into the cavern to gather some of the food for the city. We're going to commandeer a forager group and use them to walk straight in." He points to two boxes on either side of the entrance. "Foragers are checked in and out here. Ten foragers to a group led by two human guards, usually armed."

He looks up. Catching eyes with Mac for a moment.

"But there's one problem," Agamo taps his wrist. "Every lacerta in the city has an ID bracelet." Gila scoffs, and Agamo hums in agreement before continuing. "It tracks location, records hours worked, and output. It's what The Guardians are using to track the tables for the cull. Guards can also use it to remotely incapacitate those committing undesirable behaviour." He looks to George who stands silently arms folded across the scar on his chest. "It's what they used to follow Aspid and the children."

Mac shakes his head. "How did the lacerta ever agree to those bracelets?"

"A few years ago there were riots. The Overseer sold it as protection against them ever happening again. 'If you weren't breaking the law, then what did you have to worry about?'"

"Shit," chuckles Spoony Phil. "These fuckers bent you right over, didn't they? How gullible can you be?"

"We're not gullible, we're honest. Trusting," says Gila, with a glare. Her voice rises. "We're not used to the lies your kind spit with such ease."

Agamo waves his hands to restore focus on the map. "We only need to replace three bracelets in the foraging party, and Pete and Terry assure me they can do that."

Pete gives Agamo a thumbs up.

"We just need three. Terra can fix the portal." Agamo looks to her and she nods. "Gila to show them the way, and Enki, to get more bracelets off once you're all inside. Mac and Pete are going with them to take the place of the guards."

"But don't you think they'll just use the bracelets as soon as you lot come charging through the portal? Shock every lacerta walking?" says Mac. "Maybe we could cut the power or something?"

Agamo looks to Gila, who moves up to the end of the table towards the factory. She points at a short building within the fence that runs around it. "This is the main power station for the entire city. It runs off star stones. The route there is heavily guarded. If you try to force your way through, the element of surprise is lost."

"And as outnumbered as we are, surprise is our best asset," says George.

"This is the only way," says Agamo. "You just need to make sure you aren't spotted."

"And once the portal is going," says Gila, pointing to the circle in the centre of the city, "the army comes through with the Adler's anti-spore cannons, and breaks our people out of their stupor. Then we can hit them with everything we've got."

"It's risky," says Spoony Phil. "There's only forty of us and twenty of you. Even with all your lovely shiny armour, they'll outnumber us ten to one. And they'll have guns, and we'll have spears."

"Yes," says Gaspar. "So once inside, Enki and Pete are going to free as many lacerta from their bracelets as they can. Once they are cured of the spore, they'll want to fight. We'll have crates of weapons and armour brought through the portal ready for them."

"This all depends on us getting the portal to work." Mac looks around at the faces gathered. The tension in the room is butter thick. "First things, though, how are we supposed to commandeer a forager group without sending a big warning back to the city?"

"My reds will help you," says Agamo. "They'll take out the two guards without being spotted. You and Pete will dress in their uniforms. Enki and Pete will remove the bracelets from three foragers and then Terra, Gila, and Enki will wear them." He moves his finger through the tunnel that connects the caverns. "The foragers will show you where to go. There's two check points. One where they deliver their tools. And another where they deliver their payload for the day."

"And what if we're found out?" says Mac, pointing between himself and Pete. "They'll string us up."

Phil chuckles. "If anyone can bullshit their way past a couple of guards it's you Mac."

Mac lets out a nervous laugh. "Ok, we're in the city, what next?"

"Mac, Terra, and Gila get to the portal. Gila knows the way." Agamo looks to Terra. "You're happy you can fix it?"

She closes her eyes slowly and nods. A slight movement that oozes confidence.

"And meanwhile, Enki and Pete will head into the residential camp to free as many lacerta of their bracelets as possible. Those they do are to come to the portal where we will supply them with armour and weapons." Agamo looks to Phil, who stands impassive with his arms folded across his chest. "Then, once the square is secure, we strike for the power station. Shut it down. Free the rest of our brothers and sisters."

"So in short..." Mac takes a deep breath. "Sneak in pretending to be Guardian soldiers using a group of farmers as cover, fix the portal, reinforce our army, arm our reinforcements, shut down the power station, free everyone else, save the day... party?"

"I like a party," says Agamo with a twerk of the hairless hump over his eye.

"We all like a fuckin' party," adds Spoony.

"Hm," says Mac, loud enough so all eyes turn to him. He thumps a fist on the centre of the map. "It's ballsy, god damnit, but it might just work."

Spoony Phil rolls his eyes. Gaspar groans.

Terra laughs. "You couldn't help yourself could you, you cheese face."

"I'll never get a better opportunity to do a 'pre-heist just finished going over the plan,' one liner."

He leans over the table and puts his hand out in the centre.

Pete is the first one to catch on. Slapping his palm down on top of Mac's. Dave follows. Then Terra, Spoony Phil, Agamo, Gaspar and finally Gila.

The chorus of mixed messages that follows is disjointed but enthusiastic.

"Goooooooo, the army of the fallen angels," say Mac, Dave and Pete together.

"Let's fahck 'em up," booms Spoony.

"Death to The Guardians," adds Gila.

"Death to The Guardians." They all agree.

The Dog On The Nail

Pete, Terry, Gila, Mac, and Terra take the portal one at a time, returning to the spot where Mac and Terry had first entered the caverns. Accompanying them are three red lacerta, Ig, George, and another from the raid, Ardent. The red trio slink, as quiet and as elegant as water snakes, over the rocky ground, leading the humans and the blues deep into the cavern towards the foraging grounds.

Gila, Terry, and Terra wear civilian lacerta clothing over their armour. Both Terra and Terry have made their skin green like Gila.

He and Pete, and the three red lacerta, wear suits of fungal armour too. As they enter the cavern, the purple glow of the star stones reflects from the armour's surface, making it almost invisible.

George signals for them to wait as he crosses one of the more open parts of the cavern. In the middle distance, underneath the constant hum of life, comes the shuffle and scrape of digging.

An order given over a megaphone. "Thirty more minutes. Get your crates filled."

George stops behind a tall rock formation. Peers around it. Looks back to their group and nods. Ig and Ardent sprint across the space, drawing blades from their belts. They make no sound as they cross the slippery, rock strewn ground as if it were flat tarmac. They wait another moment, communicating with their hands, then the trio dart around the rock formation.

Mac holds his breath. Listens. There is neither the sound of blows being struck, nor gasps or shouts of surprise.

He and the others watch the rock with bated breath.

Moments later George's head appears from behind it. He beckons them closer.

The five of them sprint across. Mac almost loses his footing twice on the slippery ground. On the other side of the rock formation stand ten green lacerta in a clearing. They stare in wide-eyed shock between the dead soldiers on the ground and the newcomers. Dense growths of mushrooms rise high up the walls. Tall ladders stand nearby, allowing for easier pickings. In the centre of the clearing are ten crates half-filled with produce.

Terra speaks first. "Don't worry, we're here to free you."

The nearest lacerta fall to their knees, and several cries go up amongst the group. They don't look happy about it.

One steps forward, shaking. "You can't. You can't," she sobs with her hands out in front of her in supplication. "If they find out what you've done, they'll blame us. They'll add us to the cull. Not today. Not today, of all days." She covers her face with her hands and sobs.

More cries go up. One even moves to one of the dead soldiers and checks for a pulse. Shakes him by the shoulders. "Wake up."

Terra holds up a hand. "Please, listen, all of you." Her tone is commanding, and, while they still look desperate, they stop and gaze at her. "We have an army waiting on the other side of the portal. We need your help to get it working again. Today is the day we liberate the city of Racken."

"But the bracelets?" says the forager's leader. She pulls the cloak away from her arm to reveal a thick black bangle. "They won't let you back in unless you're wearing one."

"We need three volunteers. One male and two females." says Terra holding up three fingers. "The strongest of you. Those who are most up for a fight tonight. You will have your bracelets removed. The rest of you will help us enter Racken."

A worried hush descends on the group.

"Anyone?" says Terra.

How could they have anticipated this? How could they have anticipated that the lacerta of Racken would be so downtrodden, so beaten, that they were too scared to be saved for fear of angering the tyrants that ruled over them?[maybe use the anti-spore here]

A strong female lacerta steps forward. She holds her head up high. "I will volunteer."

"You can't. This is madness," another forager pleads.

Mac steps past Terra and raises a hand at the crowd who step back in fear from the human, the oppressor.

"Hello, my name's Mac." He's got a story in his head. Doesn't know if he's got it quite right, but he'll tell it anyway. Exactly as he heard it. "I want you to listen to me. A great man once told me a story... So there's this dog on a nail, ri—"

"What's a dog?" says one of the lacerta.

"Uh..." not a good start. "It's like a um..." he looks towards the three red lacerta. "What do you guys have for... for pets?"

They give him a look of incomprehension. He notices Terra observing him.

"Companion animals?" He tries.

"Squid-pig," says Ig, giving him a supportive thumbs up.

Mac nods and takes a breath to begin his story anew, then looks back. Did he hear that right? "Squid pig?"

"Uh huh, oh yeah, squid-pig."

"Sounds terrifying." He addresses the group once more. "So there's this squid-pig on a nail, right? But he's lying by a fire. He's all lovely and warm and relaxed by the fire, but there's this nail digging into his guts." He pokes a finger into his stomach and purses his lips in pain for a little added drama. "It's not that ba—"

"What's a nail?"

"Um... like a sharp thing?" he says.

"He means like a pointy bit of rock," says Ig helpfully, addressing the crowd.

"Oh, we've all heard the one about the squid-pig on the pointy bit of rock," shouts a male lacerta at the back.

"You have?"

"Yeah," says another. "All he has to do is get up off the pointy bit of rock, wriggle to another bit that's not so pointy, and then he can lie down again."

Another chips in. "But he's too snug by the fire to do it, and the pointy bit of rock doesn't hurt that much. But it is annoying..."

"It's a metaphor," says the first male, who shouted from the back. "It tells us to put comfort off for a moment now, so that we can really enjoy the future."

"I guess," says Mac, very glad that they understand, but ultimately confused as to how they all know a version of the story a sixty-five-year-old bouncer told him just last year. He tries to recover his moment. Straightens his back and lifts his chin. "A great lacerta told me that you were stewards for the next generation. That it is your duty to face some pain today to make your children's lives better. Isn't that the lacerta way?"

A discussion starts amongst the group.

"I volunteer," the male at the back says, raising a hand, and with it, other hands shoot up throughout the group.

Terra gives Mac a look that strips away all the nerves in his body, leaving him on a floaty warm high. "Well done," she mouths.

He grins as she picks out the first three that volunteered. "The rest of you, please keep foraging," she says. "We need to make the trip look as successful as possible, so there are no hitches at the border."

Pete and Terry start work on the bracelets as Mac undresses the dead guards. Not the most glamorous of jobs, but one that fits his skill level.

Whilst removing blood spattered trousers and trying not to throw up, he senses someone approach from behind.

"Where did you hear that story?" says Terra.

"From a friend," says Mac.

"It's a story we were all told as children. Gaspar used to tell it to me when it was just me and him in London. It gave me hope that the pain I was experiencing then might give us a better life later."

Mac pulls on the guard's black trousers. They are a little big for him.

"I guess it's just one of those things."

"Maybe," she says, but she doesn't look convinced.

Pete approaches with the first bracelet. "Here you go," he says, helping Terra click it around her wrist. He adjusts it with his screwdriver.

As Mac dresses, the small clearing is a hive of activity. Everyone chips in to fill the crates to make up for lost time.

Before long, Pete and Mac are both dressed as guards, Terra, Gila, and Terry wear the bracelets, and the three freed lacerta are on their way back with Ig, George, and Ardent to Agamo's cave.

With the food crates full, the lacerta lead them back towards the city. They enter a huge tunnel cut from the rock, flanked by ornate statues of lacerta warriors and thinkers. Shards of glowing star stone embedded in sconces light the way. Carvings of unusual technologies and what Mac expects are great deeds, are cut into the rock through the tunnel. A story of the history and hopes of the city.

One catches his eye. A great pyramid of lacerta, each standing on the shoulders of the ones before. Gifts are passed up the pyramid to the smallest at the top. He thinks of his forefathers and mothers. Of a great ancestry building towards him, the pinnacle of the Macadamia pyramid. He remembers his grandparents. Remembers his mother. Are they together? Would they be proud if they could see him? Has everything they've ever done, each action, each deed, each word, built to this moment, now?

Once more, he feels the pressure. A hundred eyes turned towards him. Billions more turned away, not even knowing what transpires below the surface of their own world.

The helmet he wears is wet with perspiration. His or the previous owner's. The caverns are warm and sweat pours off him, partly due to the dual insulation of the guard's suit and his armour, but mainly the nerves. How will this day end? Victory? Or failure? There will be no middle ground.

How has it come to this? Just the other day in Terra's spare room he'd been marvelling at how quickly things could change, and now here he is storming an enslaved city with a rebel group of shape-shifting reptiles. There are probably easier ways to live up to your potential.

The tunnel widens, and over the heads of the lacerta in front, he can see the first checkpoint. Three guards stand by. One of the lacerta turns and looks at him. Beckons him towards the front. He steps forward through the small group and raises a hand to the guards standing by the small wooden building.

Should he raise a hand? Are these guys friends? Or do they just work together?

He drops it by his side.

"How d'you get on?" says the nearest guard. "These fuckers give you any gyp?"

He shakes his head.

Another guard addresses the lacerta. "Come on, you know we haven't got all day. Got the cuts tonight."

The group, tired and worn after their day's work, enter a small hut one at a time to drop off shears and ladders used to collect the mushrooms. They then line-up by a raisable barricade and wait to be let through.

"Kline," says one guard as they wait for the last lacerta to drop off their equipment. "Did you see the game the other night?"

Though he can't see the guard's face, Mac has a sneaking suspicion the question is aimed at him. His mind races. What game?

"Kline?"

The sweat runs rivers down his back. He glances to Terry, who watches him with a worried look from within the group.

He mouths the word 'football'.

I bloody know he's talking about football, Terry, Mac yells internally. Tries to get his point across with a very angry look from inside his visored helmet.

"Oh mate," Mac says, almost on autopilot. He can't help it, but both of his following phrases come out as questions. "It was an absolute travesty? Bloody Schnozmichael kept diving and ref couldn't see it for, um, shit?" He winces as if that will help should everything be about to go tits up.

"Don't get me started on Schnozmichael," says the guard, opening the barrier. He laughs. "You better get on. Overseer'll be pissed if anyone's late today. Catch up later for a beer?"

Mac nods. Lets his mind wonder a moment. No, you won't, because this guy is dead. I mean Kline, not me. And you'll probably be dead, or I'll be dead. Or everyone will be dead. So, you know, no beers for you.

"Kline?" The guard clicks his fingers. "What you doing, mate?"

Mac, realising he's stood motionless for a moment too long, says "Yeah, beer sounds good," then continues under the barrier, leading the lacerta onward.

The first thing he notices on the other side is the filth. The road into Racken has fallen to ruin. Dirt covers the stone ground and garbage fills the gutters. The carvings continue here, but they are chipped and worn. Etchings and tiny pieces of graffiti cover them.

There's a smell he can't quite describe, burnt meat, and sewage, and underneath it something so rotten it's almost sweet. He's blessed that his helmet covers some of it.

They traipse up a slippery incline to the next building. Two more guards weigh each of the forager's crates as they bring them in. Then the lacerta tip their haul onto a conveyor belt that carries the produce inside for processing.

The quality of control is so calculated. It's diabolical in its detail. He'd often wondered how a small group of overlords could take over and manage the ten billion people in the world. But, if the level of conniving that they use to control lacerta is anything to go by, keeping the humans above in check can't be too difficult. They mostly do it to themselves.

With the mushrooms counted and the crates collected, the lacerta trudge up towards the city. He and the others walk with them. When they reach the top of the short hill into Racken, his breath is stolen.

Before, from up there on the overwatch, the city had looked bad. But you needed all of your senses to take in the severity of it. Flanking the road as they enter are lacerta heads skewered on pikes. Some hold three or four. Terra gasps. Gila steps closer to her and whispers something in her ear, and her resolve hardens once more.

The smell of rot and the buzz of insects intensifies. On the left side of the road is some sort of camp. A long muddy field of temporary homes made permanent. Homes built from battered canvas tents and tarpaulins pulled taut across crates and wood-like fungal supports. Small fires smoke, topped with cooking pots. Lacerta children run and play as best they can with what little they have. Elders sit and watch them, thin and tired, and worn. He expects what little food there is here goes to the children first, to the future.

"There was a fire," says Gila, pointing up to one of the immense columns that dominates the cavern. Blackened, crumbling buildings cover it. "With no one to put it out, it burned for days. Some say it was intentional, set by The Guardians. Another culling. The survivors made their homes here in the open." She stands and lets her gaze travel across the hundreds of little homes. "This field was once a training ground where children were sent to become apprentices. Somewhere to learn their trades. That doesn't happen anymore."

To their right, the river burbles past, black and broad. Its surface oozes as if covered in a thick layer of viscous oil.

"What do you usually do now?" says Terra to one of the foraging party.

The female lacerta points along the river up to where the portal stands at the edge of the courtyard. There's already a crowd gathering in front of a large platform flanked by two columns of speakers. Soldiers coral them, pushing and moving them into the centre of the square.

"Usually we get to go home, but tonight we are to meet in the courtyard," she says, not meeting Terra's eye. "They announce the cull this evening. Whatever you do, make sure you're in the square by then." She takes hold of Terra's arm to hold up the bracelet there. "Otherwise they'll know something's up and send someone looking for you."

Terra thanks her, then beckons the foragers to come closer. "Spread the word," she tells them. "As soon as we have the portal open, the army will be coming through. I expect when they do, The Overseer will use the bracelets to incapacitate everyone, but anything you can do in the fight before he does will improve our chances. We only have one shot." She turns to Pete and Terry. "You two go with them now into the camp. Remove as many bracelets as you can. Make sure they know to keep them close."

Terry nods, and he and Pete follow the group into the camp.

Mac, Terra, and Gila follow the path between the river and the encampment towards the square. Other lacerta flock with them, heads down. Step slow. It pains him to see people like this. Their defeat is absolute. They are prisoners in their own city.

A tall metal gantry manned with dozens of guards surrounds the square. Blinding white search lights point into the gathering crowd. There must be ten thousand of them already there.

"What happens when The Overseer flicks the switch?" says Mac to Gila. "Electric shock?"

"For most," she says. She points to a line of red LEDs that runs around the bracelet. "For a random selection of unlucky ones, this lights up. It could be anyone. Males, females. Children. It's all done by computer, so there's no room for mercy and the guards are too sick in the head, too brainwashed to question it. Anyone with these alight is hunted down and imprisoned by the guards. Doesn't sound so bad, but prisoners don't get food, don't get to see anyone for days. And there's no hiding." She grimaces.

"How can they do this?" says Terra.

"They see us as tools only. But, if that wasn't bad enough, that's not all. In twenty years, The Overseer has only ever had to stop two rebellions using the mass incapacitation switch, because for every lacerta that still has these LEDs lit at the end of every hour, another two are added. The lacerta end up policing themselves." She clicks her fingers. "It goes from rebellion to civil war like that."

Mac shakes his head in disbelief.

"Most lacerta here are guilty of hurting another," says Gila. "It breeds contempt. People don't really make friends anymore. They can't afford to get attached."

"We're running a massive risk here. Are we sure we should do this?" he says.

Terra pushes ahead towards the portal. "We're the only ones who can."

To The Portal

Gila leads them off the main path between two tall abandoned buildings carved from the walls of the caverns, down a darkened tunnel into a network of rooms and corridors. Torches line the walls, but they aren't lit.

Bioluminescent green mushrooms growing here and there cast some illumination, but not enough to see by.

Gila takes a torch from the pack on her back and lights their way. "This used to be the old market," she says. "They tried to keep it going for a long time after the takeover, but the power was diverted to the factory as it grew, then The Overseer stopped all trades and introduced rationing. We're pretty sure they put something in the food. All eyes are on the square tonight, but we can get closer to the portal without being spotted through here."

She leads them through old stores and restaurants. Past knocked over chairs and overturned tables, empty shelving and produce bins. Despite the pieces of abandoned tech that he doesn't recognise, it all seems very familiar. This could be any city on earth. Each room could be any family run business owned by any group of humans, friends, loved ones just trying to get by as best they can.

It makes him sick. It makes him furious. It pushes back any particle of fear that he might be feeling.

At the end of a final corridor is the familiar glow of the star stones in the cavern, and Gila leads them out into a shadowy corner at the portal end of the square.

"We used the portals to trade between cities. The square was the market. Lacerta from elsewhere brought goods back and forth. They'd trade knowledge, tech, food, everything."

The portal here is almost double the size of the one back in Agamo's cave and beneath Terra's building. The space in the centre is bigger than a house and the ring around reaches roughly three or four metres higher than that.

It has been forgotten. Left disused and unguarded. Large metal hardware crates stand stacked around it. Stiff fronds of dead fungus extend down from it in buttresses of white and brown. Beyond it the square is filling up. Every lacerta in the city must be coming.

They hurry across to the portal and duck down behind it. The throng of lacerta and the thin band of guards that surround them stand only metres away. All eyes point to the opposite end of the square to where the platform sits.

Terra scans the back of the portal a moment, then removes a set of tools and a vile of purple liquid from a wrap in her bag. She brushes away the dirt and dust to clear a space behind the base of one of the portal's legs, then places them in a specific order on the floor.

"Do you know what the problem is?" says Gila, studying the things from Terra's bag.

"I've practiced killing and fixing ours," says Terra. She places her bag down and removes a panel from the back of the portal. "The fungus is pretty hardy. The only way to kill it is with— ah," Her fingers work quickly inside the panel and she removes a dark plastic container. Inside, Mac can see clear tubes filled with gunk. "This is it."

She throws the container aside, then picks up two prongs joined with lengths of wire to a piece of diagnostic equipment. She stabs the prongs into the earth in the centre of the back of the portal.

"As expected, they've contaminated the soil. I can neutralise it, but we'll need a huge surge of power to grow it again quickly."

Or at least that's what he thinks she said. Between staring at the bullied lacerta out front, fighting the urge to throw up, and his lack of scientific know how, he's admittedly a little lost.

She disconnects one tube and is spattered with brown filth. With a long, thin brush, she cleans the interior of the pipe, and holding it up so that it doesn't spill out, empties the vile of purple liquid inside the pipe before reattaching it. She flicks a switch and a little light comes on inside the panel. Clear liquid pumps through the tube, taking with it the purple stuff she'd poured inside.

A telltale crackle starts from inside the earth in the centre of the portal.

"Trent, call Gaspar. Tell him to be ready."

A burst of shrieking feedback fills the square and the lacerta fall quiet.

A huge screen above the stage at the far end activates with a close up of the jowls of the overseer. When he speaks, he sounds like he has a mouthful of frogs.

"Good evening lacerta," he says, and Mac's urge to throw up intensifies. The voice reminds him of rancid chip fat. "You have all done so well over the last few days. Production has been up twelve percent. You deserve a round of applause." He claps his chubby white hands slowly. "I'm afraid I do have some bad news. Because some of you can't be trusted to behave yourselves, the population has risen significantly over the last five years, and despite my best accounting efforts, we are forced to increase the cull back from five to ten percent."

A woeful but sedate sort of panic grips the crowd. Muted moans and lethargic wails. Worried looks are exchanged. Wide eyes stare at the guards that surround them. Many fall to their knees, weeping. The noise threatens to overspill until on the screen The Overseer raises his hand over a switch. The crowd noise quietens to a low whimper like a child who's regularly beaten threatened with the belt.

"Now, now," he snaps. "It could just as easily have been fifteen percent, but I thought it best to stick with ten... for morale. Those of you who remain should be grateful. The weakest, the least productive, will be destroyed, so that the rest of you may live better lives. There'll be better sanitation, housing, more food. Their sacrifice is for you." He smiles. "Those of you who are chosen will have those little red LEDs light up within a few minutes. You know the drill. Line-up ready to be taken to the factory. Make it easy or we'll just add more."

Mac looks to Gila. She breathes fast and shallow. Her lips tight against her teeth. "I'll kill him. I'll kill him myself." She looks at Terra. "How much longer?"

"Almost done," she says. "Trent, call Gaspar."

Mac does.

"How is it going?"

"We're nearly there." Mac takes a deep breath. "We really have to make this work. They've increased the cull from five to ten percent."

There's a pause on the line. "That doesn't change our plan. In fact, it might help. The lacerta have more incentive to fight."

Terra holds out a hand and Mac passes the phone. "Everything's in place, Gaspar. I'm going to power it up. As soon as you detect us, start coming through."

A huge control desk sits on the right side of the portal. It's covered in dust and grime. She wipes the screen over to clear some of it away. Then flicks a switch.

Lights flicker on across the desk. The screen illuminates. "It's on," Terra says into the phone.

"Got you," says Gaspar. "Dialling in now."

A low hum rises. It vibrates deep inside his bones.

The space in the centre of the circle of stone vibrates as sparks of purple lightning arc in from the edges. It ripples and bulges like a viscous liquid before millions of tubes bubble to the surface like writhing worms in a rainstorm. She takes his hand. He squeezes it as they watch the portal open.

The low note falters, then dies, and the vibration stops rising.

"Terra," says Gaspar on the phone. "Something is wrong. The portal won't connect."

Terra's fingers fly over the control desk. She puts a hand to her brow. "There's not enough power going to the portal. Can you boost it from your side?"

"It's not possible."

Mac glances past the portal at the mass of lacerta standing in the square. Some notice the portal's activity, as do the guards.

"How many can you send?" she asks.

"Marzle says there's only enough residual power for one, maybe two," says Gaspar.

Mac can hear worried voices in the background over the phone.

"Can you get us more power there?" says Gaspar.

"We'd have to divert it from the factory," says Terra.

"And the only place we can do that from is the power station." Gila peeks her head out from behind the portal.

"How do we get there?" says Terra.

Gila shakes her head. For the first time since he's met her, she looks worried. "There's a way through one of the old residential districts." She points towards a collection of short buildings to the left of the square. "But we'd have to cross the square to get there. Then we'd have to fight our way through the factory gates before we head to the power station."

While Terra and Gila discuss options, Mac looks out towards the square. Guards are moving this way, drawn by the portal's activation. The crowd of lacerta are being ordered back.

"We can't stop. Everything is in motion," says Terra. "We have to do this now."

Sneaking across without being spotted is impossible. They'd need to power through.

He racks his brain. Goes over every possibility he can think of. Comes up with one option. He hates it, but it's all they have.

"Can you send me back?" he says.

"I think so." Terra's brow furrows. "What do you have in mind?"

"And is there enough power for me to return?"

She nods. "Just you, and maybe one other, yeah."

He takes her hand, and for the second time in his life choses himself to be the one that jumps in harm's way. "Something amazingly, and possibly stupidly, heroic."

Gila glares at him. "He's going to abandon us."

"I promise. I'll be back. I have a plan."

Could it work? It's the only shot they have.

Terra studies his eyes for a moment. He holds his breath.

"You come back and find me, and we'll finish this together," she says, moving to the control console and firing the portal up.

"I will."

He steps around her towards the front of the portal. Holds both hands up as he side-steps into the open space between the platform and the huge crowd of lacerta and guards. More guards rush over to form a line roughly twenty feet away.

As he arrives at the centre of the portal, he gives them a little wave. He counts at least twenty automatic rifles pointing at him.

The Overseer's voice cuts in over the PA system. "What's going on down there?"

"Hi," says Mac, inching back a step at a time. "I'm Trent Macadamia. You may remember me from such shows as Kenneth Bailey's 135th Birthday Party. I'm not about to disappear through this portal, so you might as well all just look the other way and get back to what you were doing."

He hops backwards up the last two steps.

"Actually, what you were doing was awful. Don't get back to that." He twirls a hand around to indicate his audience. "Maybe just chat amongst yourselves for a bit. Be right back."

He steps backwards through the centre of the portal.

Licking Frogs

"Where the hell do you think you're going?" Gaspar shouts as Mac emerges through the portal. "Where's Terra?"

The army of the fallen angels stands behind him, led by Spoony Phil. They look formidable with their spears and plated armour.

"There's not enough power to the portal. You lot won't be able to come through unless we can get to the power station and divert it. But I have an idea." He runs over to the technician manning the control desk in front of the shiny new portal setup in Agamo's cave. "How quickly can you get me back to the lab?"

"It'll take me a moment to recalibrate." She looks at Gaspar.

"Do it," says Mac. "Quick."

"Wait," says Gaspar. "If you recalibrate, they'll be trapped in Racken."

"They're trapped now. There was only enough power to send me back. Don't worry, I have a plan."

Gaspar meets his eye for a moment. "Fine." He turns to the technician. "Do it."

The technician's deft fingers fly over the interface and the light in the portal dies for a moment before reigniting.

"And I need Marzle. Is she here?" Mac looks around. "Marzle?"

The scientist appears. "What can I do?"

"I'll tell you on the way," says Mac, grabbing her arm and dragging her back through the portal, leaving the cave and the army behind.

They arrive on the portal platform in the lab beneath Terra's building.

"When you lost your arm the portal grew it back, right?" he says.

Marzle holds her tentacled arm up and touches it gently with the other hand. She looks confused.

"Well, sort of grew it back. I mean, you got something, right?" he says, feeling a little queasy just looking at it.

"Yes."

He takes a deep breath. "Terra's in trouble and I can't think of any other solutions. Do you think you could... um, make me fit into the robot?"

She studies Mac's face for a moment with a look of lizard horror.

He takes her elbow in his hand. "You said it could win the battle. Tell me you weren't tooting your own horn."

"It's a bullet-proof, blade wielding, flame throwing killing machine. With an expert pilot, it can do just about anything."

"And with an average to poor pilot, it can probably get me and Terra and Gila to the power station in Racken, right?"

She wobbles her head. "Probably."

"So, can you make me fit?" He winces and holds out two fingers. Showing more confidence than he feels, he makes a little snip-snip motion. His stomach lurches.

Marzle grimaces. "If it's what you want, I can do it, but—"

"Don't get me wrong, it's definitely not what I want, and if I could think of any other way, I would not be here asking you to bust my kneecaps, but if it can get me to the power station, then I have to do it." He wants to throw up, but he ain't got time to vom'. "Can you make it so it doesn't hurt so much?"

"I have drugs." Marzle doesn't look convinced. "But—"

"Don't try and talk me out of it. I've made up my mind." His thoughts travel inward. *It's time you showed them all.* "OK. Better hurry up before I think about it too much. Where do you want me?"

Marzle starts towards the armoury. "In here."

Mac follows.

"Remove your armour."

Butterflies dance inside his stomach as he peels the suit of armour from his body and sits up on the table next to the robot.

Marzle moves around the room collecting up tools while Mac rocks back and forth on the table. Last of all, she grabs something wet and bulbous from inside a large vat, then slaps the assortment of bits onto the table.

He hazards a look. An electric drill, something that looks like a large flat branding iron, a sharp looking industrial saw, and a rather fat frog covered in slime. The torturer's starter pack.

Maybe he does have time to vom' after all. "I feel a little bit faint." His stomach holds up its hands, threatens to vacate, but can't decide which end to use. He lies back on the table.

"I'll make sure you don't feel a thing." Marzle moves quickly around at the extent of his vision.

"It's a good robot, right?" He does not raise his head.

"You'll be able to do what needs to be done, if that's what you mean." She holds something over his chest. "I need you to lick this. A good lick. The more you get, the longer it'll last."

"It's the frog, isn't it?"

"It's the frog."

Mac turns his head to the side and projectile vomits off the table and on to the armoury floor. "I do not like this idea."

"Well, it was your idea."

He takes a deep breath. "OK." He holds his tongue out and closes his eyes. "Jutht thlap it on der."

His tongue is accosted by wet, squirming coldness, coating it in buttery slime.

"—gaah."

It doesn't taste of anything, which for some reason makes it all the more revolting. She splats the frog next to his head on the table. He turns to look it in the eye. It regards him for a moment with cold, slimy indifference. *Could have bought me dinner first,* those eyes say.

A snuggly feeling of pleasant numbness descends from his mouth down his body, filling him up with warm relaxation.

"Oh woooow," he says. "I've become a hot water bottle."

"Can you feel this?" says Marzle.

"Feel what?" He giggles. What a lovely time he's having! All the niggles and fliggles have melted away.

"Good."

He can feel her hands move up and down his right leg. Then his left. For a second, he considers raising his head to see what she's doing, then he remembers why he's here.

Then begins the grinding of the saw. It doesn't sound like he expected.

"Nooooooo..." he says, the word coming out as a never ending reverb saturated drone. "I'vvvvve doooonnnne aaaa baaaad iiidea."

"Well, it's too late now," says Marzle, holding up the saw. "I've decluttered the robot's legs as best I can. You've got such puny little thighs I think it might just work."

"I do a lot of walk— What?" He raises his head. His legs are still attached to his body. "I thought..."

"I was trying to tell you. I didn't need to—" she holds two fingers out like he had and gives the same snip-snip gesture, "anything."

"Then why the frog?"

"It's still going to hurt. Your shins are probably going to take most of the weight. They might shatter, and your knees will be under a lot of pressure."

He sits up feeling a bit of a fool — a lucky one. He'd been quite prepared to do whatever it took.

"How long does this painkiller last?" he asks as she helps him climb across into the torso of the robot.

"A good half an hour or so, which should cover you until you've gone through the portal. When you're done, you're going to want to seek some proper medical attention. I estimate the portal is going to guess what your lower legs are supposed to look like based on your DNA and with the robot in the way I have no idea what it's going to do. I expect it'll improvise..." Her lips part in a sort of rictus grin. "After the painkiller runs out, it might start hurting... a lot!"

"Plenty of time," he says, giving Marzle a wobbly thumbs up. His arm begins to wave around in front of his face like a belly dancer. "Who's arm is this? Is it mine?"

"The euphoria should wear off in a moment," says Marzle, pressing Mac's arms into the robot's sleeves where his hands find gloves. "You should find a heightened sense of focus once it does." She fixes the band around his head. "Good luck." Then presses the button to close the front.

It slides shut. A low groan is forced from his throat as the pressure crushes his shins. He senses an unnatural movement in his knees felt more as a nauseating clunk than pain. It's possibly the most unpleasant sensation he could imagine, but it doesn't hurt.

While he waits in darkness for something to happen, he tries to focus on the less distressing effects of the robot's closing. His ears are pinned down, crumpled against his scalp. He remembers a warning his mother had given him as a boy. 'If you sleep with your ear folded over, it'll get stuck that way forever.' As some of the fog clears, he realises surviving this with ears like over-frazzled bacon as his only permanent disfigurement would be a dream outcome.

"Are you ok in there?" He hears Marzle say.

"I've been better," he says. "Should it be doing something?"

There's a click and a hum and suddenly his vision fills with a near perfect digital display of what he would see if he was not wearing the suit. Diagnostics appear on the right. Little numbers and gauges that he does not understand.

"The flamers are fully fuelled, and you have at least nine hours of air," says Marzle.

"Air?"

"Yep, completely airtight. You could go to space in this thing." Marzle clutches her hand to her chest like a proud mother. "Magnificent. Can you move?"

Mac tries and the robot staggers forward, applying, if possible, more pressure to his abused lower limbs.

It's strange. He expects it to be difficult to control, so he thinks about moving differently. But he needn't. The robot mimics his movements exactly. He just needs to think about putting one foot in front of the other and it does the rest. He feels light, buoyant.

"How do I fi—" A burst of flame shoots out of his left arm, engulfing a table. "—re the flamer..."

The frog dives to safety and Marzle ducks away. She comes back, eyes wide, beaming with the look of Frankenstein noticing movement in his monster… it's alive!!

His mouth drops open. "Ah, sorry."

"Pssh." She waves a hand. "For the flamer, you just need to think about firing it and it does it." She then grips her own bicep and holds her arm out as if shooting a gun mounted on her wrist. She vibrates with excitement. "Trust the system."

He strides forward and out of the armoury, obliterating one of the glass doors as he tries to push it open. Green faces watch as he crosses the lab, heading for the portal. He stands head and shoulders above them. Marzle jogs to keep up as Mac passes through.

All eyes stare as he strides out of the wall. He waves a hand, nearly decapitating three people.

"Oops, sorry." He looks at Gaspar. "Get me back to Racken, now!"

He hopes he's not too late.

Mech Mac, Mac Mech, Or Mechadamia

A line of guardian soldiers greets him as he steps through the portal. The lamenting lacerta beyond are being corralled to the far end of the square. Their frightened faces watch. He'd be frightened too, if he were them. And being him, a former PI, current small town postman, he should be frightened. But he's not.

Maybe a side effect of the frog? Or maybe a side effect of being a squid-pig lying on a rock that has finally become too pointy.

Even before he's taken a step, bullets fly. They pelt against his torso like thrown stones, pushing him backwards. For a worrying moment he almost falls, before leaning his centre of gravity forwards.

"I'll be right with you," he says to the guards, holding a finger up, and moving cautiously down the steps at the front of the portal. "My first time trying stairs in this thing, and with you all shooting me, it's making it considerably harder than it needs to be."

Can they hear him?

Something powerful thwacks into his chest and he nearly goes down. He looks up to see a row of guards with sniper rifles aimed at him. There's an uncomfortable pressure where the bullet hit. A dent he expects. Will the suit hold?

He doesn't wait to find out, leaping high in the air and coming down to land behind the line of soldiers standing before him. He punches and kicks, twirling himself around like a toddler after one too many bowls of ice cream.

It both amazes and frightens him to see the amount of carnage he unleashes in a short amount of time. The remaining guards retreat as he turns the dirt floor in front of the portal red with the blood of their comrades.

The ground around him explodes with more sniper rounds as he sprints for the portal. He skids to a stop behind it.

His heart misses a beat when he realises Terra and Gila are gone. In their place stand two tall, thin figures. A chill runs up his spine as they turn to face him with knives drawn.

He grits his teeth and lunges forward. They take to the air. He reaches up, catches one by the foot, and swings it down into the ground as hard as he can. The other lands on his shoulders and starts a frenzied prying at the edges of his visor with its knife. He can sense the jagged scrape of the blade just above his right eye. Blinks, imagining how badly it would end for him if it slipped through a crack in the suit.

He tries to dislodge the guardian, but the mech's overhead range is limited and he can't quite get to him. The other guardian pushes himself up and, using a radio on it's lapel, calls for back-up.

There's no time for this, so he tries a good old fashioned forwards roll. For a little extra pow he jumps into it, coming down head first smashing both guardians together before finishing the move lying on top of them. The impact rattles him inside the robot, but it doesn't hurt.

He stands. They don't.

"Terra," he shouts.

She and Gila emerge from the tunnel they had used to get here.

"Is that you?" She hesitates.

"Yep."

They look him up and down.

"I'll get you to the power station so you can do your stuff. Just stay behind me."

There's a crack of gunfire and ricochet of bullets as they strike the portal.

"I'll be honest, I didn't think you'd come back." Gila raises the hairless ridges above her eyes. "You think you can get us there?"

"I'm a highly trained operative of His Majesty's Royal Mail. If I can't deliver you to the power station, no one can."

He glances out at the square, knowing full well that he's oversold himself, and that His Majesty has very little to do with the delivering of letters these days.

The nearby guards seem preoccupied with keeping the lacerta back and also deciding whether or not to approach the whirling death machine that just emerged out of a previously inactive portal and splattered all their mates.

"I don't know how much more sniper fire this thing can take."

"Our best route is along the left of the square." Gila motions with a hand. "The buildings that side overhang so we can move beneath the snipers above. Then we cut away into the residential district."

"Sure," Mac tries to give a thumbs up, instead swiping a blade just over Gila's head. "Sorry. Ready?"

They both nod.

"Stay close behind me," he says. Counts to three. Finds he hasn't gone. Counts again. "Go!"

He steps out and is pounded with several sniper rounds. The armour squeezes him a little more with each one, and it hits him with absolute clarity how very dead he would be if he were not wearing it. And also how fragile both Gila and Terra are. He spreads his arms wide, like a mother bird protecting her chicks from the rain with her wings, trying to make himself as much of a shield as possible as they cross the space between the portal and the cover of the buildings on the far side.

He doesn't stop running. Aiming for the buildings Gila had pointed out. Any guard unlucky enough to get in his way is either flattened or clobbered. Most don't bother, deciding to back off and fire upon them from a distance. Most of the guards, however, are doing their best to keep the crowd of panicked lacerta under control.

Mac rips through the fence at the side of the square and follows Gila and Terra out of the rain of bullets and into a narrow alley between two tall housing structures.

A loud crack of electricity causes him to look back. Every lacerta in the square shakes, then falls.

"The Overseer hit the switch," he shouts, then shoots off a jet of fire behind them to push back the pursuing guardsmen.

"Then we have even less time," calls back a panting Gila.

They turn right down a back alley that runs parallel to the square. The ground is flat stone. The buildings are made of a white fibrous material, rather than brick, as if they'd been grown instead of built.

Gila leads them through a maze of abandoned alleys and courtyards between one and two-storey buildings. It reminds him of one of those middle-eastern countries that a spy like James Bond might run through chased by bad guys, leaping over market stalls selling fruit and dishevelling innocent rug salesmen in his bid to get away.

"How much further?" says Terra.

"At the end of this alley is a road that leads up to the factory." Gila slows as they approach.

Mac pokes his head out. To the right, back towards the square, the way is clear. It sounds like chaos.

The other way is the factory. A towering building made from the same material as the houses that surround them. Statues of lacerta holding books and instruments line the front. Ugly looking additional structures, made from concrete and metal, are tacked on here and there.

"It used to be the university," says Gila. "A place where our greatest thinkers could come together to improve our lives with their minds."

A tall barbed wire fence runs around it, connecting at a tall pair of solid metal gates blocking the road.

Across the road from where they stand, a bridge crosses the river. The water goes right under the fence, disappearing beneath the factory complex.

Terra's gaze shifts to him. She scans his chest to his helmet. "How much more punishment do you think this thing can take?"

"It seems to be holding up ok."

The gates in front of the factory float open. Waiting on the other side are roughly twenty armed soldiers. Three hold large black tubes on their shoulders.

"Oh bugger. They've got bazookas."

"We should take the rooftops," says Gila, pointing upward. "Try and sneak past them." She climbs. Terra clambers up after her.

Mac jumps and catches hold of the edge of the building, scrambling up behind them. From up here he can see the lacerta back at the square being pushed and pulled about. Segregated into those with lit up bracelets and those without.

"We don't have much time," he says.

A warning ache has begun to build in his knees. He wonders how it looks down there.

Gila sprints across the rooftops towards the factory, staying low, with Mac and Terra in tow.

When they reach the building nearest the fence, Gila peers over to the ground below.

"The guards are waiting for us," she says. "They'll see you and blast you to bits if you try hacking through the fence. If we can get to it, there's a small hole just up there." She points. "Terra and I should be able to fit."

"What about the river?" says Terra, pointing to the turgid black mass that rolls under the road emerging inside the factory gates. "We could swim it."

"One dip in there is enough to kill anyone. And besides, you'd be swimming under the road for at least a minute, totally blind. It's too risky."

"I could distract them," says Mac. "Draw as many guards away as I can. It'd give you more chance of getting to the power station."

"Makes sense," Gila says. She beckons Terra with a lean of her head. "This way."

Terra waits a moment. "Do you think you can take them?" she asks him.

"Marzle said this thing was bulletproof. Bazooka rockets count as bullets, right?"

She doesn't look so sure.

As if to answer his question he hears a boom followed by a whizz, and a rocket shoots up and over the opposite edge of the building. It hangs in the air a moment like a hummingbird before adjusting its course and heading straight at them.

"Go," he shouts, giving Terra a light shove.

He doesn't look back as he moves to intercept.

Rockets counted as bullets, right?

In Flames

The rocket races towards him and Mac shifts his body with the intention of swinging his right arm to bat it away like a tennis ball.

Not being particularly well versed in the overhead smash technique, he misses completely and the rocket collides with his right shoulder. The detonation throws him onto his back with a wave of searing heat.

He lies there for a moment, his head a blur. Does a quick scan to make sure he's not dead. He's not, but, if it were possible, he feels like he's taken the full impact of a speeding train on the shoulder, and when he tries to lift his right arm, he finds the whole limb too heavy to move.

A diagram of the suit pops up in his vision. It flashes red around the shoulder.

He pushes himself up with his left. His right arm dangles loose by his side. He wheels around, but Terra and Gila are already gone.

Alone again, he sneaks up to the side of the building overlooking the road. The guards have spread out, taking defensive positions behind barriers placed at strategic intervals.

He lifts his good arm and shoots a jet of flame into the road. The guards return fire. Bullets pelt against the building's face. He hears a -chunk- followed by another whistling sound, and the entire front of the building explodes. The roof beneath him cracks and he comes crashing down into darkness surrounded by falling rubble.

He finds himself in what appears to be a living room. Chairs. A sort of sofa. A bookshelf lined with dusty, old tomes he doesn't recognise. Different in so many ways, but so familiar. A thick layer of dust from the collapsed ceiling covers everything. His breath reverberates inside his helmet, condensing on his cheeks.

There's another deafening explosion and the entire front of the house crumbles away, pummelling him with heavy lumps of masonry. Outside, the guards ready themselves for another launch. He lifts his left arm across his face like a shield and ploughs through the front door, not bothering to open it.

Back in the alley they'd used to escape the square, bullets ricochet off his armour. A glance right reveals guards taking cover in doorways hidden in the shadow of the alley.

To the left is the road, and beyond that, the river. Pretty soon he's going to be trapped.

He makes a decision. Right or wrong. Sprints as fast as he can towards the end of the alley, crosses the road while fire and chunks of rock explode around him. Leaps high into the air, splashing down into the thick, black water.

He doesn't immediately drown, which is a good sign, but his right shoulder starts to dampen. Bullets shoot past him as little jets in the water, and another rocket detonates on the surface, temporarily blinding him with silt and air bubbles. He sinks all the way to the bottom. His feet make unsteady contact with the riverbed.

He kicks off, propelling himself with the current, towards the factory.

All light disappears as he swims beneath the road. Something in his helmet's heads up display flashes and all becomes green. Night vision. Nice one, Marzle.

He strides along the riverbed, but the going is slow. He sinks a little more with every step.

It's not long before he sees the first corpse. A skeleton covered in weed, half buried by the buildup of sediment. Then another, slightly fresher, some flesh still hanging from the bones. His mouth goes dry as he spots two more. Are these the prisoners Gila mentioned? What horrors could await on the other side to want to risk this? Or were they just trying to get home to their loved ones? What did their families think had happened to them?

His fingers are getting cold. His arm is soaked to the elbow. A small rivulet trickles down his chest. Splashes tickle around his aching knees. And he can't tell if it's the water outside, or the water inside, but his movements are slowing, like he's moving through treacle. Panic gnaws away at him, but he pushes it down.

He continues on, focussing ahead. A square of light looms before him as the water in his suit laps around his waist, and then his stomach, and then his chest. It's not far. But still perhaps too far.

He takes deeper breaths. That's what divers do, right? Oxygenate the lungs, right? It's hard though. And getting harder to breathe with the weight of the water on him.

More bodies. Tucked under drifts of sand and amongst the hardy weeds that dare to grow in this toxic swill. The Guardians have put the lacerta through hell.

The water tickles his chin - it stinks. He can think of worse ways to die than drowning in turgid water, but not many. He takes a final breath as the water covers his mouth. Looks up at the dim square of light above him, but the splashes of caustic water needle into his eyes. He closes them and tries to jump, but either the suit is too broken or too heavy with water, because he barely breaks the surface. With the water up to his cheekbones, he scrambles to where he believes the side is. The air in his lungs screams to get out. Screams for him to stop messing around and take another breath.

His feet slip on the slime at the river's edge, and he almost falls over completely. He manages to dig his good arm into the river wall - finds it's hard, like brick or concrete. Gouges himself a hand hold. Crunches into it with his feet for purchase.

He throws his arm up and over a lip just above him. Pulls. Pulls. And slowly, he rises, dragged back by the water as if by the hands of dead souls pulling him down to hell.

He opens his eyes. Can see the light. Pulls again. Rises out of the river, but his relief is only momentary. The level of water in the suit doesn't drop to below his nose.

Why isn't it draining? His panic intensifies and he shakes himself frantically from side to side to try and tip the water out.

Why had he not thought to ask Marzle how to open the damn thing? Why hadn't that been his first question? He can't die here, trapped in a water-logged robot.

Completely airtight, Marzle had said.

Completely watertight that meant.

His body reacts and takes a breath of that turgid water. He splutters, coughs, splashing more stinging water into his eyes. What a way to go.

He screams in his thoughts for the suit to open.

And the suit opens.

Easy as that.

The water floods out around him. The gasp of grotesque air he takes makes him cough up that black water from his lungs.

As the air rushes to his legs, he also notices the pain in his knees. A sharp sting as if he's kneeling in shards of broken glass. He gasps again and falls to the ground. He glances down, but the suit covers his legs below the thigh.

He lies there panting, eyes closed, as the putrid river water washes out of the suit, leaving him dripping and stinking and cold.

He's inside, but has his distraction been enough? Will the guards be coming for him instead of Gila and Terra?

When he opens his eyes, he sees several yellow electric bulbs hanging from the low vaulted ceiling. They do little to light the room. He pushes himself to his feet, spitting and clearing his throat. More water pours from the suit.

He stands on a thin stretch of grime encrusted brick next to the river. Steps lead up to a door.

He turns. She surprises him. He did not expect to see such a small face in such a horrid place. A little girl of around four or five watches him from the other side of a set of prison bars. Her cheeks are tear streaked, dirty. Her hair hangs loose about her face. She clutches a glowing doll to her chest. She looks well fed, but that's about all he can say she has going for her.

She steps back as he moves nearer. Three more small children huddle behind her in the prison, pressing themselves against the back wall.

"What are you doing here?" he says, but he thinks he knows and it almost breaks him.

His heart beats hard in his chest. The muscles at the side of his jaw jut as his teeth clamp down. The anger he feels now is unlike anything he's ever experienced. It is a raging bull taunted and stabbed and triggered by matadors.

A tidal wave racing towards a tiny island. The children press themselves against the back wall.

"It's ok. I won't hurt you." He kneels. "My name's Mac. What's your name?"

"Lily."

"Hi, Lily." He realises his purpose. "I'm here to rescue you."

She inches forwards, chin lifted. "Can you rescue Aspid too? And the others?" Her voice is small, wary. "I want to go home. But..." Tears fill her eyes. "I don't think I have one."

He takes a deep breath. "Don't worry, I'll help you find one." He inspects the cell. "Stand back. I'll bend these bars."

The suit closes around him. And he pushes two sets of bars apart with his good arm. "Can you fit?" he says, stepping back.

Each of the children comes forward and climbs through. They all look so small. He wants to hug them. Hold them tight, take away all the pain, all that they've seen in this terrible place. Draw it from them inside himself like a syringe, no matter the consequence. Little eyes should never see such horror. Little hearts should never hold such fear.

But that's not possible. The only way to make it better is to love them through it. Make them feel safe.

Lily points to the other side of the room. "Save Aspid now."

He follows her gaze and sees a female lacerta standing at the bars watching him.

"Why are you here?" she says.

"An army is coming through the portal in the square. We're coming to free Racken."

"Is George with you?"

He skirts around the pool towards her. "He's coming."

Suddenly, the lights in the room go dark. Gila and Terra have done it. The children start to whimper.

"It's ok," he says, trying his best to calm them without facial expressions or hand gestures. "That's my friends. They're going to help us. We'll get you home." Though if the army doesn't pull through, he has no idea how.

He bends the bars so Aspid can escape. "You're the one who helped the other children escape, right?" he says.

"Yes." Aspid squeezes through the gap he's made. "Oh Lily," she says as she rushes across the room. She whisks the little girl into the air hugging her tight to her chest, then rests her on her hip and takes another of the children's hands. "I tried to help them all. There should have been six. Did six make it?"

"I think so."

He makes his way to the door of the prison. It's locked, so he kicks it down with a crumble of powdered rubble. Through the settling dust is an empty corridor with dark, fibrous walls. He guesses anyone usually guarding might be out in the square. Or looking for him. Not that you'd needed to guard small children in a cage. His teeth grind.

He looks to Aspid. "We need to get out of here to meet my friends. Do you know the way?"

"They brought us through a purple door," says Lily, coming forward to point up the corridor. "Like a TV."

Aspid nods. "I can take you to the main hall, but The Overseer and his guards are here somewhere. We have to be careful."

She passes him and leads the way. He follows as closely as he can with the other kids between them.

If Terra's plan is working, the army should be through the portal by now. He wishes he could see it. Wishes he could help.

As they near a door at the end of the corridor, he passes her. "Wait here," he says.

It opens on the back right of a large room with a twin set of curved staircases that head up to the second level. The space seems almost organic. Swirling spirals, like giant ammonites, decorate the pinnacles of smooth archways. The walls blend seamlessly into the floor and ceilings with gentle curves and rib beams. There is a set of double doors on the far side that he expects lead out to the front of the building.

In the centre of the room stand two rake thin, eight foot tall, winged men in black armour. Another, bulkier man, dressed in flowing black robes, marches down one flight of stairs towards them. The Overseer. Mac's fists clench inside the suit.

"What's going on out there?" The Overseer's voice booms, echoing around the great chamber. His robes swish behind him on the steps.

"All hell has broken loose at the portal, Overseer." The two Guardians stand rigid as pencils. "Lacerta and humans are pouring through. They will shortly have taken the square."

"How many are there? How can this be possible?" The Overseer reaches the bottom of the steps and strides towards them. "I find it difficult to believe someone somewhere is sending an army big enough to take the city through the portal."

"Their numbers are few, but they have armour the likes of which we've never seen. Our weapons won't pierce it. They engage the sons in hand to hand combat led by a formidable spear wielding red lacerta and a rather offensive human man whose prime aim seems to be kicking our soldiers in their private areas whilst shouting 'you fuckin' want some?'."

"What about the other fathers? Surely they can't be bested by a few lacerta?" He frowns. "Why aren't the pair of you down there fighting?"

The Guardians look at each other.

"We have just come from a direct assault. They seem to know our weak points," says the first.

"We should have invested in more nut and neck protection," says the other.

"But, but... that's just not fighting fair." The Overseer splutters, unbelieving. "And the portal has been inoperable for years. We salted it. It didn't have any power."

"They fixed it."

"And that's not all, Overseer. The lacerta are waking up. They're fighting back."

"But the spore?"

"They seem to have an antidote."

"If the square is lost, tell the men to fall back here." He prods one in the chest. "You find out what they are using to cure the lacerta and destroy it." Then points to the other. "And you head to the power station. Shut down power to the portal. Both of you gather teams and tell the others to hold the factory perimeter. Order the children brought up from below. Use them as shields. Racken is too important to lose. They won't dare attack with children on the battlefield." He throws his hands in the air and growls. "And if you see anyone that's not supposed to be here, kill on sight, no questions."

Terra, he means.

Mac glances back to Lily and Aspid who peep around the door. Leans his head to one side with a satisfying click from his neck. This has got to stop.

"Oi."

The word pops out of his mouth on its own. An angry shout reminiscent of a lager swilling lout who's just noticed someone checking out his bird. He holds a hand up to Lily and the others, bidding them to stay put and then, although it might not be his best idea, struts further into the room. His legs feel like they are on fire, and he hopes the robot's gait doesn't show how much pain he's in. He's also feeling rather faint. He points his good arm at the three.

"I've had enough of you pricks being pricks."

He has.

"And who might you be?" says The Overseer.

"The thorn in your side. The stone in your shoe. The poorly written address on your envelope." He takes a breath and draws himself up to his full height. "Trent Maca-fuckin'-damia."

The Overseer glances at the two with him.

"Who?"

One Guardian leans in and whispers something into his ear.

The Overseer's whale-like mouth forms into a grin. "I really have been down here too long. They don't keep me abreast of affairs from above." He points. "Kill him."

"Wooooah!" says Mac, holding his good arm up threateningly, but instead of fire, a spattering of black goo pours from the end. He looks at it, disappointed. "Um... you don't want to get any of that on you. It's not just really gross, um... it's super corrosive. It'll melt your face right off."

The Overseer turns to his men. "In fact, carry out my orders. I'll see to this one."

The Guardians nod and leave the room.

The Overseer holds his thick arms out wide and shakes his robes from his shoulders, revealing a pasty, sumo wrestler like torso covered in black etchings. His wings stretch out behind him. Large black sheets of quivering leather. He pulls his arms inwards like a bulldog, straining. Muscles pop on his back and chest and neck... and arms and face and oh my God! Where Mac had previously thought him fat, The Overseer is in fact a human tank.

With a flap of his tremendous wings, The Overseer launches himself like a torpedo across the room. Mac tries again to use the flame thrower at the end of his arm but nothing happens. His right arm, still inoperable and dangling uselessly at his side, spits out a gout flame around his feet charring the ground. Pointing in the wrong direction, it has little affect on The Overseer as his immense bulk collides with Mac knocking him on to his back. The wind is forced from him and red warning signs flash in his display.

Before Mac can muster the energy for a counter attack, The Overseer shoots up into the air above him.

"That is a very nice suit," he says from his position close to the ceiling. "Who made it for you?"

There's a warm, sticky wetness around his legs. He almost can't be bothered to move. His eyelids feel heavy.

"Is that all you've got?" The Overseer sneers.

It might be. And who could blame him? It's been a hell of a week.

The Overseer snorts and leans his head to one side, almost disappointed. Then drops from the air to land beside him. He straddles Mac's waist and, with powerful arms, prises open the front of the suit.

"Oh, you're just a little man." He grins.

He grips Mac by the T-shirt and lifts him out and up into the air. His lip curls when he sees the mess of Mac's legs. "What the hell have you done to yourself?"

Mac steels himself and looks down. Replacing his shins and feet are a mix of human and lacerta legs with hocked joints, made up of white, scar-like strands reminiscent of the mark on George's chest. Purple bruises cover his thighs, and two huge cuts pour blood at the back of his knees, although ultimately, his legs seem whole.

The suit's headband remains secure around his temples and stretches out with him, pulling his neck at an awkward angle. He lets his body relax, hanging from The Overseer's grasp. He has nothing left so allows his eyes to close. Why struggle? He breathes out and awaits the final blow.

The Overseer gives him a shake, clacking his teeth together like castanets.

"Dead? How pathetic."

A little ray of hope, maybe.

The Overseer drops him to the ground. Mac bangs his head hard as his new legs give way beneath him. But he's still alive.

He waits for a moment, then cautiously opens one eye. The Overseer faces away, squatting down to inspect the robot suit.

Mac presses the control headband to his skin. Hopes he's close enough. Raises his left arm and swipes it through the air. The robot's blade arm lifts and sweeps the overseer's legs out from under him. He drops to the ground with a dense thud, cracking the floor tiles. His head catches the blunt metal leg of the robot and blood pours from a fresh wound.

With the last of his strength, Mac pushes himself up to seated and the robot mimics him. He turns his body so that the robot's broken right arm hangs over The Overseer.

"You better get that looked at," Mac says, with a snarl, "wouldn't want it to get... inflamed."

A gout of flame engulfs both the robot and the screaming Overseer.

With a beat of his flaming wings, the burning hulk takes to the air, sweeping almost mindlessly across the hall towards the top of the stairs. But before he can cover half the distance, his wings separate like molten plastic and he falls with a screaming, echoing thud.

"Wouldn't want it to get inflamed?" Mac rolls his eyes. Lucky the only person around to hear that is now a burning pile of muscle. He sighs and lies back, what little blood he has left rushing to his head. He can probably die now.

"I'd have just said 'you're fired'," comes a voice from the front door.

Footsteps hurry towards him, but he can't sit up. Not again. Sitting up is way overrated, anyway. Uncomfortable tiled floors are where it's at.

"Trent, are you ok?" Terra's face comes into view.

"I am not," he coughs.

She kneels next to him and removes something from her pocket. A vial of clear liquid. "Drink this. It'll help."

With a hand on his back she helps him up to seated. He shudders at the pain in his legs. She holds the vial to his lips. His head swims as he drinks. It's buttery and smooth. Warmer than before.

"That's frog juice, isn't it?"

She nods.

"Less unpleasant this time."

The pain in his whole body evaporates, along with his crippling insecurities and overprotective inhibitions.

"I've got some kids over there," he says, proudly waving an arm in whatever direction it'll go. "I saved them." He glances at her. "They're not mine. I'm a single dude, ready to mingle, dude." He bobs his eyebrows meaningfully in a wibbley, frog juice induced way.

She smiles. A lift at the side of her mouth that in his weakened state lights a flame of hope inside him. But it fades as her eyes scan his lower body. Then she turns her head to Gila, who stands behind. "Gila, would you—"

"I'm on it," says Gila, running for the door where Mac had left the children.

"Did you do it?" he says.

"We transferred as much power to the portal as we could. By the sounds of it, and judging by the way the guards outside were retreating, the army came through. We shut down spore distribution, too. The lacerta will be waking from their nightmare."

"Good." He blinks and a few things come back into focus. The last hour seems to have just gone. Time slapped in a blender and whizzed on top speed. A whirlwind of running and fighting. Having experienced it inside the shell of the robot makes it feel almost unreal, like he's just taken part in some sort of ultra-violent video game marathon, and is now just coming out of an energy drink fuelled stupor covered in cheesy tortilla chip crumbs.

The sound of an approaching crowd comes from outside, bringing with it the realisation of what they've done.

"Mac?" Terra puts a hand on his arm.

Those brown eyes, the ones with a white so white you could swear they'd been tippexed, centre him in the moment.

He smiles, and she smiles back.

"Do you think you can stand?"

He looks down at his new legs. The bleeding has slowed. "Do you think you can show me how?"

"I guess that's only fair."

Declaration

With an arm around his waist, she helps him outside. The legs work, but he has to lean on her heavily for support. The cuts behind his knees threaten to split further with every step, and he's not really sure what he's doing with this extra joint he's somehow gained.

Gila and the kids are with them. The girl, Lily, holds hands with the lacerta she'd called Aspid. Her eyes are wide as she takes in the vast open space around them.

The gates at the factory front are gone. A vast crowd of lacerta stands where they once were, bubbling into the grounds like molten rock led by a unit of grey armoured warriors. Agamo and Spoony Phil stand at the head, side-by-side.

The sound is tremendous. Shouts of joy, but anger, too, confusion. The crowd packs the street out of the gate that runs parallel to the river. Every lacerta in the city is there.

Gaspar and Terry rush towards them.

"Are you ok?" Gaspar says as they approach Terra.

"I'm fine. The Overseer is dead. Mac did it."

Gaspar eyes him with an admiring nod. "Any surviving guards from the square back up this way? I guess the cowards have retreated."

"There are tunnels leading from the university," says Agamo, joining them. "We'll send troops to clear them out as soon as the city is secure."

"There might be children down there," says Mac, jabbing a thumb over his shoulder. "We should go."

Agamo looks him up and down. He must look bad because the old red says, "you've done enough." He looks back at the crowd. "Spoony, can you take some of your people down?"

Spoony's whole face, except for his tight white lips, is tomato red. Even his eyes. Mac assumes he's got the bloodlust, and that smashing a bunch more fucknut's heads in is the only thing that'll cure him of it.

"Abso-fuckin'-lutely." Spoony calls out a few names, then leads a detachment of warriors through the university doors.

Woe betide the fucknut who gets between him and those kids.

Agamo looks back at the crowd of lacerta. "Someone ought to address them. The spore will still be in their systems, and they're going to be confused. Three thousand expected to die today, but now they are free."

"It has to be you, Agamo," says Terra.

"I don't know what to say..."

While they discuss, Terry pulls himself up to the top of a short wall that borders a set of steps leading up to the university doors.

He waves a hand at the crowd. Those at the front hiss to quiet the ones behind. The sound ripples backwards through the crowd.

"Alright everyone," he says.

"Welcome," come several staggered replies from the front. "Welcome."

Terry jabs a thumb. "Agamo wants to say something."

With hesitant steps, Agamo climbs up beside him. He glances back down at Mac and the others. Rubs nervous hands together, then lifts his head to the crowd.

"Welcome friends," he says. "The last twenty years have been a struggle for all. Of hardening ourselves to what they have done and putting lacerta progress on hold so that we may survive. But in surviving, we have shown ourselves we can beat whatever threatens to destroy us. We have known hardship, but through that hardship, we have grown resilient. We are a different people now. Things may have been worse for a while, but that doesn't mean they can't get better than they've ever been. Now we are free, we must think of the lacerta way. We must think of improving the futures for those who come next. We must make sure this never happens again."

"How do we do that?" comes a voice from the crowd. Other voices rise.

"The Guardians hold captive lacerta and humans alike in cities and towns all across the world. They bury us beneath politics and division and dogma that they say protects and serves. They tell us we are the cause of our suffering. We tell them they are no longer welcome. We are not quick to anger, but they have angered us. And that is their mistake. It is time we withdrew our hospitality." His eyes scan the crowd. "Brothers and sisters, there is one way to give our children better lives. Brothers and sisters, for all the good creatures of our mother Earth, the lacerta of Racken go to war."

Fish Fingers and Chips

Lily kneels on the soft chair in the main room of Aspid's house, clutching her doll and gazing out of the window. The sound of sizzling comes from the kitchen. Aspid's house is up so high. From here she can almost see the whole city below. Above the gems sparkle. It's all so wonderful. Aspid says it will get better. She wishes she could stay to see it.

"Your go," says Finn, taking a handful of small stones from her side and placing them in a pile next to him.

She jumps down to the floor. It's soft and bouncy. Aspid says it's not carpet. It's like mushrooms. She says the whole house is made of mushrooms.

Aspid hadn't known what a fairy was when Lily had asked if she was one. Still, she was sure that if you lived in a mushroom house then that made you very special.

The few days she's spent with Aspid — since the man in the robot had come and rescued them — have been some of the best days of her life, but today they are taking her and the other children back to the surface.

"How many did you get?"

"Four."

She doesn't want to go. She thinks Finn would like to stay too. There's nothing left for them up there.

She kneels opposite him and empties one of the pots on her side of the board, then proceeds to drop each stone one at a time in the others moving clockwise. The game is easy. She likes it. So does Finn.

The faint smell of fried fish wafts in and Lily looks up to see Aspid in the open doorway holding a plate.

"I'm not sure if this is quite right," she says. Her nose wrinkles.

Aspid moves closer and places the plate next to the board. On it are four curly tentacles, but this time each has a crispy coating.

"Um." Lily's not sure either.

"I added a few of my favourite spices. They should taste nice at least."

Lily picks one up, nervous at the way it wobbles. She crunches into it. Chews a moment. Smiles. It's good. It's really good. She nudges the plate closer to Finn. "You try one."

He does. He let's out an "ooo" of pleasure. "That's the best fish finger I ever had," he says, around his mouthful.

Aspid's face lights up. "Oh good." She puts an arm around him and gives him a squeeze.

Lily has decided that if she had to, she wouldn't mind sharing with Finn.

She finishes her fish finger, and picks up the next.

There's a knock at the door, and her heart sinks.

"Eat up," says Aspid, standing and brushing herself down. "It's time to go."

Her lips press together a moment as she looks from Finn to Lily. Then she moves across the main room and opens the door.

The man at the door has a scar on his cheek. Behind him stand a few other children. He smiles at Aspid and she smiles back.

"The little-uns ready to go?" His voice is gruff but gentle.

"Think so." Aspid holds a hand out to Lily. "Are you ready?"

Lily presses herself to stand. It's now or never. "Um... Am I..." A nervousness stirs in her tummy. "Can I stay here, with you?"

Aspid's mouth opens, but she doesn't say anything for a moment. Lily holds her breath.

"Do you really want to?"

"And Finn?"

"Yes, please," says Finn.

Aspid glances at the man. He shrugs. "Doesn't bother me. I already got this lot to sort out." He leans his head indicating the other children behind him. "Whatever makes them happy."

"I think I'd like that." A wide smile crosses Aspid's face. "I think I'd like that very much."

Butterflies dance in Lily's stomach. Good, excited butterflies.

"I'll let the lads know we've got a couple of kids staying here," says the man. "I'll be down in a few weeks anyway so will come check on them. See if there's anything you need."

"Thank you." Aspid closes the door. She opens her arms and Lily and Finn rush into them.

Lily squeezes her tightly. "Do they have schools down here? And parks?"

"We have school. You'll love it. And soon there'll be lots of things for kids to do."

"Um, and Aspid, have you ever heard of chips?"

"Chips?" Aspid smiles. "Oh yeah, we love chips down here."

"Do you think this can be our forever home?"

"Nothing is forever, but as long as I am here, you'll both have a home with me."

Old Friends

Lacerta across the city work together to tear down Guardian infrastructure, to clean up, to make the city a better place again.

He and Terra walk by the river, heading for the square and the portal there. It's only been a few short days, and the water is already clearing.

It's almost as if the city wants to go back to the way it was.

Above, the purple star stones shine. The colour gives everything a romantic, hazy quality that he thinks might remind him of Paris at night if he'd ever been. He realises he'd never been fond of the brightness of the sun. Maybe one reason why he'd chosen a calling where he could spend nights out and days in.

He likes the way the purple light glows on her skin.

His legs still ache, but he's learning to walk on them with the aid of a stick. Marzle says that he shouldn't need it for long, that he's just waiting for the neural pathways to link up.

High above in the columns, lacerta work to clear away old burnt houses ready for new clean growth. They look like ants in a farm, busily building the hive.

He longs to tell Mum what they've achieved, but instead he's going home to lay her to rest. He knows he will need to explain her passing to Vikram and Amanda. It breaks his heart to think how Vikram must have felt when he'd returned home. The thought has kept him up each night since Racken's reclamation.

His mother's death is the barbed thorn of this beautiful rose, but once he's taken a little time to heal, he'll go on showing The Guardians exactly what he's capable of.

"I've decided I want to come with you," Terra says as they cross the square.

A flicker of that hope in the sadness. "You do? Why?"

Ahead, Agamo and a few others gather near the portal. Today is the day he and a few of his lacerta warriors head out to investigate the off-shore armoury.

"I..." She hesitates. Searches inwards. "I don't know..." She glances at him as they walk.

Over the last few days, he's tried not to look at her properly, hoping his feelings might fade. But he sees something familiar in her. Something he's seen every time he's looked at himself in the mirror. She's as lost and as unsure of herself as he is.

She stops and takes his hand. "I want to make sure you're ok... that you're happy."

"Oh." He rubs the back of his neck. He's not sure how to react. This isn't what happens to him.

A heavy hand grips his shoulder from behind, and he looks to find Agamo having crept up on them. The old lizard glances down at Mac's legs.

"Look at those." He gives them a little tap with an armoured foot. Mac winces, but it doesn't really hurt. "Been a while since the fungus has given a pair to a human. We'll make a lacerta of you yet." He grins and gives Mac's shoulder a friendly shake. "You sure you don't want to come out to the armoury?"

Neither of them say anything.

Agamo's brow drops, and he squints between them. "I interrupted something, didn't I?" A slow, knowing smile crosses his face. "I'll give you a minute." He steps back towards the portal and the others there, then looks back. "Don't be worried. I knew a human girl once. A long time ago. We had been very happy." His eyes search the ground as he remembers a better time. "Very happy." He takes a long breath, blinks, and smiles sadly, then continues back to the portal.

Mac turns back, catching Terra's eye still on him. Her hand remains in his. The sound of everything going on around them fades. He doesn't know how to feel.

"Come on," she says, pulling him after Agamo. "Let's get you home. And then, maybe, sometime soon, we can figure a way for the both of us to be very happy, too."

The portal crackles with purple energy.

"It's all set to take you back," says Agamo. He rubs his hands together, then notices theirs intertwined. "Are you both going?"

Terra nods.

"Good luck." He turns to Pete, who stands with Marzle at the control desk of the portal. "Two for Camden catacombs."

"See ya, Pete," says Mac raising a hand.

Pete skirts around the control desk and gives him a big hug, squashing the air out of him. "Take care of yourself, Mac." He releases. "If you're still keen on staying with us we have another location. It's not as nice as the hotel yet, but we'll get there. I can send you the address."

Mac glances at Terra who nods. "Yeah, but there might be two of us."

Pete laughs out of happiness. "Always the more the merrier."

"Say bye to your bro and Spoony for me."

"Will do." Pete trots back to the control desk. "See ya."

The prickle of being devoured by thousands of tiny mushrooms isn't something he thinks he'll ever get used to, and when he emerges he's not where he expects.

He's also alone.

"Terra?"

Crystals glisten in a corridor just big enough to let him through, almost as if it had been made just for him. He glances back to the door he's just come from. It's unfamiliar, and again, just a little bigger than he is. It doesn't have any sort of lacerta technology or carvings around it, unlike the others he's used. Just dirt and tubes in a plain wall.

"Where am I?"

He waits a moment, but Terra doesn't come through.

The glow in the gems ripples, as if ushering him along the tunnel. He looks to the end and begins walking. Beneath his feet, the ground is loamy and soft. White with millions of hair-like strands. The air smells clean, like fresh earth.

The corridor is short and soon opens out into a cavern roughly the size of a house. Covering the floor and back wall are hundreds and thousands of mushrooms, each glowing and growing in the light of the gems that stretch across the ceiling.

There's a constant crinkling of organic life, much like the cavern adjacent to Racken.

He looks back. Maybe Pete and Marzle accidentally sent him to the wrong place. But Terra should have followed.

"Trent Macadamia." A whispering sound. Not really a voice. More a shot of air through pipes. Two membranes slapping together to make consonants.

"Hello?"

"Don't be afraid. You're exactly where you are supposed to be."

"Where is that?" He stands on tiptoes then leans over to try to see who he's talking to. "Where are you?"

"Everywhere."

No one's there. Nothing but the glistening fungus that covers everything.

"I'm afraid it's not time for you to go back home yet. Your friends need your help."

"Which friends? The lacerta?"

"Nige Davies and his family need you. I don't usually like to interfere, but we don't have much time left. The balance is tipping, and soon we won't be able to stop it."

"I don't understand. Who are you?"

"My children call me Gaia. The All-Mother. Earth."

"Oh, shut up," he says with a long eye-rolling groan. They'd almost got him as well. "Is that Dave or Terry? Did you and Pete think you'd get me with a leaving prank?" He crouches down to inspect beneath the rubbery foliage, but can't see anyone hiding. "It takes more than a load of wet fungus and a whispery little voice to get one over on Trent Macadamia."

"No, seriously, I'm the planet. I've—"

He puts one hand on his hip and wags a finger. "Look, whoever you are, wherever you are, I haven't got time for your shenanigans." He turns, and marches back to the door he came through with an over-exaggerated lift of his knee and swing of his arm to emphasise exactly how little time he has laid out in today's schedule for shenanigans. He's going home to organise his mother's funeral. How insensitive can you be?

"For fucksssake," that whispering voice mumbles as he steps into the portal. "Why does no one ever believe me?"

If he could huff whilst being chewed into nothing, he would.

Once more, he doesn't end up where he's supposed to be. But Terra is there, standing in the dark.

"Trent? I thought you came through before me," she says, clearly confused as to why he's appearing only now.

"Those idiot cultists tried to play a trick on me." He looks around. The cavern they are in appears huge. The walls are out of sight in the darkness thanks to the lack of star stones. "Where are we?"

"I have no idea."

"Who's that?" Comes a dry but low croak from the shadows. He thinks he recognises the voice, but it can't be... A yellow torchlight comes on.

Mac puts up his fists. "Depends. Who's asking?" He lifts his hand to his brow to shield the light from his eyes as the figure approaches. Terra also readies herself.

A sudden and huge clang echoes through the room from the far side, followed by whimpers from other people behind the light. A vibration of the floor shakes his feet. Had that been an explosion?

The portal crackles to life and Agamo and his other lacerta appear.

The person with a torch backs away.

"Mac?" says Agamo, surprised to see him. "Ah, sorry. Marzle must have put in the wrong address for you. This is the offshore armoury location."

"Mac?" says the man from behind the light.

"It's him, Dad," says another. One Mac recognises more easily because he's spoken to them in the last week or so.

The torchlight travels across the lacerta faces. A worried chatter starts from what must be over twenty people hiding there in the darkness.

Then another loud boom, this time from above. Dust crumbles down from the ceiling.

"Lewis?" Mac asks, and he daren't hope, "Nige?"

"Mac," a tall, broad shape steps forward. "Where the bloody hell did you come from?"

"Just through this. It's like a door..."

Nige Davies looks up at the tall circle of stone.

"A door?" He grins at Mac and the lacerta. His bearded face is dirty and bags ring his tired eyes. He looks leaner than Mac remembers. "Am I glad to see you." He gives Mac a hearty pat on the back. "Can you show me how it works? We should get out of here, sharpish."

A third explosion sounds from above. The closest of them all.

"You would not believe the couple of weeks we've had," says Nige.

Mac shakes his head. "Try me..."

Hello!

Thank you for reading! I hope you enjoyed it. I'd be eternally grateful if you could take two minutes to leave an honest review on Amazon or Goodreads. Even if it's just a few words. As an indie author reviews and ratings really help!

As a thanks for buying the book I'm offering all of my mailing list subscribers **a 100% free standalone novel!!**

Sign up to the no-spam mailing list at my website - https://cjpowellauthor.co/amph - and I'll send you an exclusive book for free! I'll also link you to a playlist I listened to while writing the Chrysalis series. I will use the mailing list to update you with new books and offers so it's a win / win!

Please get in touch to let me know if you enjoyed the book - I'd love to hear from you. And feel free to recommend it to some friends!!

You can also find me on Instagram, Facebook, and TikTok by searching C J Powell Author.

Thanks again!!

Chris x

Use your phone camera on this QR code to go straight to my website.

Coming Soon

The Demon Hunter's Wife

Dirk Kilmore is one of The Bureau's top demon hunters. Rumour has it he saved the world from eternal damnation a couple of years ago. But no one talks about that...

And this isn't his story anyway.

When Dirk doesn't come home from work one weekend and strange creatures come for their daughter, his wife, Sadie, is forced to drop the baby off with her demon possessed mother, grab one of his spare wands, and go hunting for him.

Turns out Dirk hasn't been entirely truthful about what he does for a living. Sadie will discover this and more in this darkly funny urban fantasy novel.

Printed in Great Britain
by Amazon

18153495R00169